Lost and Found

A Christine Lane Mystery #3

Dianne Scott

Danforth Press

Cover Design: Lance Buckley

978-1-7776042-7-1 ISBN Print Book
978-1-7776042-6-4 ISBN Ebook
978-1-7776042-8-8 ISBN Large Print Paperback

Danforth Press
diannescottauthor.com

To my husband Michael and my children Claire and Matthew. Thank you for listening to my story ideas, writing challenges and tidbits of cool Toronto history. Your support and encouragement inspire me to continue.

Books in the Christine Lane Mystery Series

Final Look: A Christine Lane Mystery Book 1
Missing: A Christine Lane Mystery Book 2
Lost and Found: A Christine Lane Mystery Book 3

These books are standalone mysteries and can be read independently or in order.

Praise for *Final Look*

"I've just devoured *Final Look*. I especially enjoyed the historical and political insights, the nostalgic trip back to Toronto's hippie-dippy days, Scott's loving, detailed description of the Toronto Islands and the chase scene!" *-Pearle Gemyndig*

"Original and entrancing." *-Maureen Jennings*, author of the *Murdoch Mysteries*

"Dianne's writing pulled me in from the very beginning. The characters and setting were well-developed and kept me page-turning. I can't wait to read book No. 2 when it comes out!" *-Martina K*

"This was one of the best 'whodunnits' I have read in a while. This was an exciting page-turner. Keeps you guessing all the way. I was so enthralled that I read this book straight through. Highly recommended by this bookworm." *-Roseanne Doiron*

"Take a boat trip out to the Toronto Islands, circa the 1960s, when skirt-wearing cop Christine Lane takes on bad guys and the male local constabulary in Scott's debut novel. A fun romp!" *-Robert Rotenberg*, best-selling author of *City Hall*

Chapter 1

April 1969

The ax flew through the air. Its blade hit the wooden target sideways, clattering to the ground in front of the willow tree.

"Too much force," said Police Constable Geoffrey Fillingham. "Try a lighter touch,"

Policewoman Christine Lane gave her partner a baleful look before retrieving the ax from the ground. "I can't help it if I'm strong." She brushed mud off the ax and handed it to Fillingham.

The officers were ax-throwing on their break, warmed by the fire pit in the Centre Island police station's backyard.

"Hercules," he said, "throw another log on the fire while I demonstrate that ax-throwing, like life, is about finesse."

Her partner lined up his shot. He was in uniform but coatless and hatless on this April afternoon. His short blond hair was long on top—he'd have to get it cut soon. With a year-round tan from sailing and skiing, he had the pearly smile of a toothpaste ad.

Christine tromped over to the logs stacked against the building's brick wall. The backyard was in that muddy state of early spring, the snow receding to the lawn edges, baring twigs, dead leaves and detritus. In the next month, the grass would green, crocus and snowdrops would push through the soil and snow shovels and long johns would be stored away.

She placed a log on the pyramid of burning wood in the stone fire pit and turned to see Fillingham throw the ax with a flick of his wrist. The blade stuck in the blue ring circling the red bull's-eye. Three points.

"Ha!" he said. "That's fifteen points to your eleven, Lane." He pulled the ax out of the target and handed it to her. "You got one throw left before victory is mine."

His maniacal laugh made her smile. Her partner was a combination of silly, fun-loving and energetic, which made their patrol entertaining. Even during the winter months, when few visitors ventured to Toronto Island and the officers' duties were minimal, he found them a challenge: snowball toss, sit-ups or a floor-mopping contest.

Christine stared at the red bull's-eye ringed with a circle of blue and an outer circle of black, reminding herself to point at her target when she released the handle. She pictured the ax moving through the air and embedding in the red circle so she could smugly watch her partner wash and dry all the dishes. After a few practice swings of her arm, she threw the ax with a grunt. The ax rotated, handle over head, until it bit deeply into the center of the red bull's-eye. There was a loud crack, and the target split in two. One half of the wooden circle fell to the ground.

Christine's hands rose in victory.

"You wrecked it!" he exclaimed.

"I won," she said. "Five points for a bull's-eye."

"The bull's eye is gone, Lane. Not sure if we can count this last end."

"I won fair and square!" she protested. "It doesn't matter that the target broke."

"The Olympic track runner gets the gold, even if he sets the stadium on fire?" he asked.

"Not the same thing," she said.

They approached the tree and regarded the broken circle.

He tugged the ax out of the trunk. "We're going to have to find another log slice for the target."

A telephone rang from inside the station. It was the local line Islanders used to call police directly. Fillingham motioned for her to get the call. "I'll manage the fire," he said.

They always smothered the fire before returning inside, even if there was a blizzard that would quash the flames. She was vigilant about this rule, maybe because her mom and her stepdad had been smokers, and she had spent her childhood worrying that a forgotten cigarette might burn down their apartment. Even now, with her stepdad long gone, she did a final tour before bed, checking that her mom had placed her ashtrays in the sink.

Christine hustled up the porch steps of the station and ran across the waiting room, leaving muddy boot prints she would have to mop later. Grabbing the receiver off the wall, she answered, "Centre Island Police station. Toronto Police. PW Lane speaking."

"PW Lane, it's Samuel Fairmont from Clergy House."

"Mr. Fairmont. What can I do for you?" Fairmont was the owner of Clergy House, an upscale restaurant by the boardwalk that edged the south side of the Island. He didn't often call the station. She recalled a request to help with a belligerent customer who refused to pay his hefty alcohol bill. And theft of a cast-iron patio table. But that was it. And in the winter, the restaurant's hours were limited, with locals dining midweek and mainlanders boating in for a weekend dinner. The summer tourist season kept the business alive.

"PW Lane, can you come to the restaurant? Someone wants to speak with you."

"Okay," she said. "What is the concern?"

"I think it's private."

For some crime victims, the need for privacy was paramount. "No problem," she said. "PC Fillingham and I will be there in a few minutes."

"Can you come alone? The person asked for you."

"Certainly." When a caller requested a policewoman, it often meant the complainant was a woman in distress. Possibly an assault case. "I'm on my way."

After checking in with her partner, she headed to the garage attached to the bungalow station. Grabbing her bike, a comical thing covered in plastic flowers given to her by her favorite Islander, Mrs. Polotov, she rolled it down the driveway. She glanced at the garden in front of the station, covered in dead leaves and the skeletons of old plants. Last fall, Mrs. Polotov had arrived with a burlap bag of daffodil, tulip and crocus bulbs, and they had planted them on either side of the front door. Gardening was foreign to Christine, since she had lived in apartments all her life, but she had gamely tilled the soil and buried the bulbs deep in the earth. She'd have to ask Mrs. Polotov when the buds would push through, if the squirrels hadn't gotten them first.

Christine's bike bumped onto the concrete path that wound eastward toward Ward's Island. The three main islands that made up Toronto Island—Ward's, Centre and Hanlan's Point—were connected by concrete, stone or dirt pathways for pedestrians and bikers. Thank goodness she didn't have to look out for cars. Only emergency services and parks and recreation staff were permitted vehicles on the Island.

Not too cold, Christine thought as she pressed hard on the bike pedals. She'd switch back to her skirt uniform when the spring warmth was more consistent. The heavy wool of her pants already felt heavy and scratchy now that the sun was peeking out from behind a cloud.

She passed the white Tudor church that welcomed Islanders for Sunday worship and glanced at her watch as she passed the fire station: 5:20. In the winter months, it was dark by dinner and the afternoon shift seemed to last forever. It was refreshing to be back on bike patrol when the daylight extended later into the evening.

Turning off Lakeshore Avenue, she pumped her legs twice and coasted into the gravel parking lot in front of Clergy House. She hadn't been to the restaurant since Christmas time, when the Island Residents Association invited the police to a community gathering. Fillingham sometimes ordered takeout dinners from Clergy House, but there was a reason he was nicknamed Richie Rich. The food was delicious but out of her price range. Her dinner of a sandwich, apple and milk was stored in the station's fridge in a calico cotton bag her mother had sewn.

Pushing the restaurant door open, she spotted Samuel Fairmont behind the bar. He was a tall, friendly bear of a man with a mustache and goatee. He had bought the Clergy House several years ago, bringing quality food to the Island when the only options were the hamburgers and hot dogs from the amusement park.

Fairmont smiled. "PW Lane. Nice to see you. Your table is over here."

Before she had a chance to ask about the complainant, Fairmont headed into the dining room.

Christine followed, then stopped dead when she caught sight of the man in an elegant suit sitting at a back table.

Deputy Darlow. There was no mistaking the dark hair streaked heavily with gray, the ramrod posture, the cool brown stare.

She made herself continue walking, her breath quickening as she scrambled to figure out why one of the force's top brass wanted to meet with her. On Toronto Island. On her patrol.

Deputy Darlow rose from his chair. When Christine arrived at the table, she stood at attention, saluting.

"At ease, Constable," Darlow said.

Fairmont pulled out a chair for her. Mutely, she sat down, eyes wide with alarm.

Fairmont said, "Our dinner sitting isn't until six thirty, so you'll have privacy until then."

Forcing herself not to tuck in a loose strand of hair or adjust her uniform jacket, she sat silently across from the deputy. Why would he call her over to Clergy House? He was five rungs above her sergeant's rank. And when she had met with Darlow in the past, he had upbraided her, warning her to stop her investigations and follow protocol. And querying why she got injured on the job so frequently.

But she had done nothing wayward lately—there had been no cases to investigate. A few domestic calls, illegal fires on the beach, a person falling through the ice, but that was the extent of station calls during the winter. The six hundred residents weren't up to much except hustling home from the ferry after their day jobs on the mainland.

"PW Lane," the deputy said. "Thank you for coming."

Should she say *you're welcome* when she hadn't known he was the complainant? She wished Fairmont had warned her. And she was curious why Darlow hadn't met her at the Centre Island station or called her in to headquarters.

Had something happened to her family? Alarm stabbed through her. "Is it my mother, sir?" she asked. "Or my siblings?" Donna and Wayne were in elementary school.

"They're fine. This is not about them," he answered quickly.

Christine exhaled. If her family was safe, this couldn't be that bad.

"I'm sure this meeting is a surprise," Darlow continued. "The subterfuge was necessary." He gave a small smile.

Christine regarded him. His dark gray business suit, the typical attire of a deputy chief working out of headquarters, looked custom-made. He was distinguished-looking with his side hair part, square jawline and penetrating brown eyes. Back straight, feet planted on the ground, he looked taller than his height of six foot two.

"I want to discuss an opportunity," he said.

Her brows rose in surprise.

"We've had a few interactions over your career," he said. "I know your skills and deficits."

Interactions? Was that what he called the reprimands and threats to can her?

"There is a growing movement by local politicians and prominent businesses to clean up Toronto," he said, "starting with Yorkville Village."

Yorkville, also called the Village, was a downtown Toronto neighborhood known for its folk music, cafés and swarms of youth that inundated the area. Two years ago, hippie activists had organized a sit-in to shut down Yorkville Street to car traffic. Police hauled away hundreds of protesters. It was all over the news.

"There's been complaints about the Villagers," Deputy Darlow said. "Landlords can't get them to pay rent, businesses want them off their doorstep as they deter paying clients. Drugs are more potent. There are overdoses. Cases of hepatitis. City Hall has had enough. They want the flotsam and jetsam cleared out to allow room for legitimate businesses and customers.

"Okay," Christine said. What did this have to do with her?

"Police have a regular presence in Yorkville, but the relationship with the residents and visiting youth is strained. Young people don't trust police, government or any institution. So there's conflict. More protests."

She nodded.

"We are starting an undercover police operation in Yorkville called Operation Niagara." His hands opened. "It's referencing Niagara Falls. They want to flush out the drug dealers, criminals, addicts and loiterers." He paused. "I've requested you for the operation."

She sat back in her chair in surprise. Why would he pick her? She wasn't in the Morality Squad, whose mandate focused on alcohol, drugs, prostitution and gambling. And she'd only completed a few short-term undercover assignments. Usually for one day. Maybe two.

Samuel Fairmont came over with a carafe. "Coffee?"

Christine nodded, happy to have a few moments to digest the deputy's request. They waited in silence as the restaurant owner filled their ceramic cups and placed the cream and sugar on the table.

Christine looked out the window at the treed landscape. She was going undercover as a groupie to a Village band? A hippie? At six feet, Christine didn't fade into the background. And, according to her Women's Bureau friends, she wasn't groovy. Julie accused her of being a stick-in-the mud. Prim and proper. Christine didn't fit with the anti-establishment, free-spirited flock that hung around the Village.

Deputy Darlow sipped his coffee, eyes on her.

Christine placed her cup down on the saucer with a rattle. "Sir, I'm not sure I've had enough experience in this area."

He dismissed her comment with a wave of his hand. "Sergeant Buckman from Morality is leading Operation Niagara. He'll find roles for you and PC Fillingham."

"PC Fillingham has the assignment, too?" she asked, alarmed. He wouldn't like that. Her partner had picked Toronto Island patrol, despite its reputation as a place where officers were sent to pasture, to be near his Island sailing club. She was pretty sure he didn't want a mainland gig.

The deputy nodded. "Sergeant Buckman wants a specific crew for Operation Niagara, as it's a volatile and politically sensitive situation. He also believes that policewomen undercover are more believable and less identifiable as officers. He'll be requesting PW Julie Spark, PW Gail Hilton and PW Sarah Keefe."

Christine's mouth opened, then closed. She tried again. "Sir, but sir. These are my friends. I've worked with them at the Women's Bureau. And known them since police college."

A waitress set the table next to them with cutlery and dinnerware. They waited in silence until she moved to the far corner of the dining room.

He nodded. "Yes. That's intentional. It's a complex and possibly dangerous operation. Yorkville Village is overrun by bikers, gangs and thugs. There are assaults and thefts. Missing persons. Operation Niagara requires a tight crew. There's no time to develop that. The mayor calls the chief regularly regarding his concerns about Yorkville. We must move now—with people we can trust and who can trust each other."

Christine blinked several times, trying to absorb the new information. She was going undercover with her partner and friends. That wasn't how operations were staffed. The Morality Squad used their own officers. As did the Youth Bureau and Hold-up.

She couldn't imagine being out of uniform for months, working on a sting. Her stomach gave an upset roll. When she put on her navy wool uniform, pinned her hat to her hair and strapped her police-issue purse over her shoulder, she felt competent, able to talk with people, manage situations, be directive and problem-solve. But in her civilian clothes—her miniskirt and gingham shirt—how would she be effective? Charm them? That was more like Julie and Fillingham.

The deputy regarded her. "PW Lane, you've demonstrated solid investigative skills and a singular drive for justice." He took another sip of coffee and placed the cup down. "You don't always follow the rules."

She had gotten in a lot of trouble for not following protocol, from the deputy, her sergeant and the investigators.

"And, of course," he added, "there will be overtime."

He must have looked at her pay stubs, which showed the shifts she picked up at community dances and public events to earn extra money, since finances were tight at home. What else did he know about her?

"After Operation Niagara is completed, you will have your pick of stations in the next round of transfers. If that's what you want."

He knew about her career aspirations, her need to get more experience and more leadership roles so she could sit for the sergeant's exam.

He checked his watch as if ready to finish up.

So this was it. She had a new assignment. She reached for her purse from the chair beside her.

"There's one more thing," he said.

She placed her purse down.

His hands steepled on the table, his eyes cast downward. A full ten seconds went by. "I believe my daughter is in Yorkville."

He looked up at Christine, his expression pained. "Kelly is sixteen. Two years ago, she started going down to the Village. At first it was on the weekends, to hear a fiddler, to meet up with girlfriends for a coffee. Then she went more often, a couple of times a week, staying out late, sleeping in, missing school. She was dozy, not herself, dressing differently. Talking back. One night when she came home, I could tell she was on something. Drugs. We grounded her, took away her allowance. She laughed. Said we couldn't stop her. That she had friends to stay with. If we didn't give her money, she'd find a way to make cash."

Many runaways got into drug dealing or theft to fund their lifestyle. Some ended up as prostitutes. Christine guessed the deputy knew this.

He exhaled a long breath. "She contacts my wife occasionally if she needs money. But we haven't heard from her all winter. I'm worried she is in a desperate situation. I need you to find her and bring her home."

Christine remembered how fearful she had been when her brother's life was in jeopardy. "I'm sure the Operation Niagara team will make your daughter's search a priority."

He shook his head. "We'd like to keep the situation with our daughter private. My wife is uncomfortable with publicity. Also, if locals find out she's a cop's kid or that people are looking for her, I worry about the consequences, given the company she keeps. Kelly doesn't use her real name. She goes by Alice Dodgson."

"The probability of finding her is much higher if the whole team searches for her, not just me. They would be careful about their queries."

He shook his head. "She's skittish. And quick. If she discovers people are asking about her, she'll leave Yorkville. I'm afraid she'll disappear forever."

"Are you sure I am the right officer for the assignment? I appreciate your confidence in me, but I lack experience undercover. You should have the best searching for her."

"In some ways, you *are* the best, PW Lane. Young, female, attractive. You can chat with the locals without arousing suspicion. You won't give up on her. You will search and dig until you find out where she is. And then I can bring my daughter home."

"Everything okay here?"

Darlow and Christine turned to Fairmont standing beside them.

"Can I get you some starters?" Fairmont asked. "Soup or a shrimp appetizer? On the house."

Deputy Darlow shook his head as he stood up. "No, thank you, Mr. Fairmont. I've taken enough of PW Lane's time. I'm grateful for the loan of the table. And thank you for the coffee." He extracted a ten-dollar bill from his wallet and placed it on the table.

Ten dollars. For two coffees.

Darlow shook Fairmont's hand and walked toward the exit.

Christine stood up. What just happened?

Fairmont accompanied Darlow to the door, and Christine heard the owner offering to drive him to the ferry terminal.

In the parking lot, Christine watched the deputy step into the golf cart local businesses used to get around. The pair drove away.

Christine wheeled her bike onto the pathway, shaking her head, trying to clear her thoughts. She was no longer on Toronto Island patrol. She'd spend the next couple of months with Fillingham and her friends undercover in Yorkville—the musical, psychedelic, drug-using center of Canada. And she was on a separate mission for her deputy. Double subterfuge.

Christine headed west toward the police station, her mind churning. Aside from the shock, a small part of her felt flattered. Darlow chose her for the mission because she persevered on a case until justice was served. But having to report to the deputy chief made her stomach flip. What if she couldn't find the girl or was terrible at undercover? Failure might mean the end of her policing career. Certainly, she would never make sergeant.

The fire captain waved at her as she biked by his station, and she absentmindedly waved back. She breathed in and out slowly as she rode, trying to tamp down her rising alarm. Undercover work required lying, deceit and bluffing. Fillingham and Julie would be naturals, able to charm and persuade. But without her uniform,

Christine didn't have any power, like Samson without his hair. Sure, she was comfortable with her friends, but with other young men and women she was inept. She'd been that same awkward girl since high school.

A bicyclist emerged around the corner and rang her bell three times.

"Mrs. Polotov!" Christine waved. The septuagenarian was one of Christine's favorite Islanders, regularly offering Christine tea, cookies and conversation about the locals and Island events.

They stopped beside each other on the pathway.

Mrs. Polotov's short, round body was clothed in a red winter coat, woolen leggings and heavy boots. "Where's young Fillingham?" she asked.

"He's back at the station," Christine replied.

"You doing all the work?"

"As usual," Christine said, laughing. Christine knew Mrs. Polotov was charmed by her partner, as were most Islanders. "Hopefully, he's making coffee."

Mrs. Polotov chuckled. "Let's hope so. I'm just heading back from a Women's League meeting."

Christine nodded. The Islanders were a close-knit group, often meeting for choir or crafts at the community center or a tennis match on the nearby courts.

"We could hear banging from Centreville," Mrs. Polotov said. "They must be getting it ready for the season."

The Centreville Amusement Park was the major tourist draw to Toronto Island, attracting thousands of summer visitors to its Ferris wheel, antique cars and roller coasters.

"I got a call from Hawk the other day," Mrs. Polotov said.

Christine could feel the smile leave her face. Hawk Johnson. Her old love. The man she had a secret affair with last summer, hidden because he was from the Anishinaabe tribe and she was a white woman, and there was no way people would leave that alone. Christine couldn't bear the persecution of her work peers, family or friends if they found out. Tired of the furtiveness, Hawk had ended it.

She thought of his muscular arms around her, how big and solid he felt. And the way he had made her feel beautiful. And smart. And funny. And how Christine had been replaced a couple of months later by a new woman, an old friend he had met again on his reserve.

Mrs. Polotov was one of the few people who knew about Christine and Hawk's relationship. Hawk and Mrs. Polotov had been neighbors and friends. Since the breakup, Mrs. Polotov had mentioned him a few times and updated Christine on his life.

"Hawk signed on again at Centreville," Mrs. Polotov said.

Christine nodded. Last year Hawk had worked as a ride mechanic and rented a house on Ward's Island from May until October. Otherwise, he lived on the Whitefish reservation near Sudbury.

"He's not here yet," Mrs. Polotov said. "He's delayed because his girlfriend is having difficulties.

Christine gritted her teeth. Did she really need to hear this?

"She has a problem with alcohol, dear," Mrs. Polotov said. "Hawk is trying to help her. Help the woman's daughter."

It would be like Hawk to do that, stick by someone in need. He often helped Mrs. Polotov and other seniors on the Island with tasks like changing light bulbs and trimming tree branches. In return, he was given cups of tea and thick slices of banana bread.

"Children's Aid is involved," the older woman added. "He's staying in Whitefish to help Remi sort things out."

Remi. Christine had seen her once, a petite, dark-haired woman with a heart-shaped face and eyes only for Hawk.

After a few ticks of silence, Christine said, "I better head back. See if my partner is up to mischief."

The women said their goodbyes and continued on the trail in opposite directions. Christine passed the St. Andrew by the Sea church, which had hosted the Women's League meeting, its Tudor walls glowing a soft white in the low sun.

Being undercover in Yorkville Village meant she wouldn't have to see Hawk this summer. She wouldn't spy him tinkering with an engine in Centreville or riding his bike along the boardwalk. When she patrolled Ward's Island, she wouldn't have to avoid his rental house on Second Street. And she'd have a break from the tourists, illegal beach fires and lost wallet calls that inundated the Centre Island station.

As she turned down the pathway, the blue neon police sign came into view. She had found the silver lining to the Yorkville assignment. Now all she had to do was brace herself for the thunder of Fillingham's response.

Chapter 2

"You won't believe this!" Fillingham called out to Christine as she entered the police station.

She lifted the hinged counter and walked into the office. "What's up?"

"The Morality Squad called!"

"Really?" She entered the small kitchenette that doubled as a locker room. Crossing the linoleum, she paused at the stovetop to pour herself a coffee from the metal pot.

"Lane!" He strode over to stand beside her. "They want us to go undercover! In Yorkville!"

"What!" she exclaimed, forcing herself to sound shocked, which wasn't hard, since she was still grappling with the new assignment.

"Sit down!" he urged. "Listen to this!"

He sounded more consternated than excited. What if Fillingham didn't want to go? Officers were given their work assignments from headquarters, from their first placement out of police college. Sure, there were some specific jobs candidates applied for, but most jobs were allocated. But Fillingham was the one officer who might refuse an untenable assignment, because he didn't need employment. Richie Rich came from old Toronto money. Would he quit the Toronto Police Force to avoid going undercover?

No, he couldn't do that, Christine thought. He had to go to Yorkville with her. She wouldn't let him refuse. After working with him for a year, solving two fatality cases, risking their lives for each other, she couldn't envision policing without him.

She sat across from her partner at the square kitchen table, hands clasped around her mug, staring at him apprehensively.

Fillingham gestured to Christine. "Everything okay at Clergy House?"

Christine nodded. "No problem. A minor issue with a customer."

"Anything I need to know about?" During the off-season, Clergy House customers were almost exclusively Island residents. It was helpful to know if there was local discontent.

She shook her head.

"As soon as you left for the restaurant," he said, eyes wide, "I got a call from Sergeant Buckman from Morality. Our names were put forward for an undercover assignment."

"Really?"

"We were hand-picked by the brass for a sting called Operation Niagara."

"Operation Niagara?" she repeated.

"In Yorkville."

"Julie and I went there two years ago to have dinner and listen to live music. It was crowded but fun," she said.

He nodded. "Yeah. I've been to the Purple Onion and the Penny Farthing. The Toucan, too. Fantastic headliners. I was there when Neil Young blew the roof off."

"So, what are we doing there?" she asked.

"Cleaning it up. Getting rid of the criminals so they can usher in high-end restaurants, couture shops and upscale apartments."

"Is the focus drugs?" she asked.

He nodded. "We arrest the pushers and clear out the users. Find out if the supply is coming from Montreal, Windsor or Niagara Falls. Morality wants us to look high up the food chain. The Holy Grail is to nab the source."

No mention of looking for the missing teen, Kelly Darlow.

"Sounds exciting," she said, "which is up your alley." *Please, take the bait.*

He leaned back, shaking his head, his light blue eyes looking translucent, like the sky above Lake Ontario on a summer day. She often forgot her partner was good-looking, unless someone else commented. His fair looks, friendliness and banter attracted women. To Christine, he felt like a brother—someone to joke around with but who had your back when the chips were down.

"I'm happy here in our Centre Island station." His arm swept around the room, from the yellow curtained window to the row of metal lockers, bathroom, office and waiting room beyond.

"Why not try something new?" she urged. "It's just for a couple of months over the spring and summer."

He shook his head. "And miss the sailing season?"

Her partner was a member of the Royal Canadian Yacht Club on Toronto Island. His family had belonged to the RCYC for three generations. Fillingham sailed competitively and often took his racing scull out before or after work, training for the next race.

"You can still sail," she said. "The ferry dock is a five-minute drive from Yorkville."

"It's not the same."

She raised her eyebrows at him. "It might be fun. As I recall, you like fun."

"I've already planned my training schedule." He looked around. "This," he gestured to the office, "fits my agenda perfectly."

"I can't believe *I'm* trying to convince *you* to be adventurous," Christine said.

The phone shrilled. Fillingham hopped out of his chair, as if eager to end their conversation. He picked up the receiver on the office wall.

"Julie, hi," he said, his tone surprised.

Julie Spark was Christine's policewoman friend and had been Fillingham's girlfriend for the last eight months. Christine had introduced the two last summer and wasn't pleased when they became an item, in case it went south. Both were fickle in the romance department. But to everyone's surprise, the bubbly blonde pair had endured over the winter and seemed genuinely fond of each other.

Did Julie know about Operation Niagara?

Christine got up and turned the kitchen faucet on full, clattering dishes in the sink as she filled it with soapy water, trying to give her partner privacy.

"You did too!" Fillingham's voice was loud.

Her hands paused in the sink water.

"Lane!"

She looked toward the office, where her partner had stretched the phone cord until he was standing on the kitchen linoleum. "Julie, Gail and Sarah have been assigned to Operation Niagara! Can you believe it? It's like they hand-picked your friends!"

Operation Niagara was really happening.

Fillingham listened for a few seconds on the phone, then addressed Christine. "We meet next week at 51 Division to get the details. Constable Malo will brief us alongside Sergeant Buckman."

He walked back into the office, receiver in hand. Christine heard him say to Julie, "I don't like it. I'm happy on Island patrol."

Christine rinsed the dishes and placed them on the drying rack. Her stomach gurgled uneasily. What was going on? This was not a normal assignment. Sure, officers could be reassigned at a moment's notice, but this felt like a machination, and the puppeteer moving their strings was Deputy Darlow.

Chapter 3

Christine sat across the table from her two uniformed friends and leaned back into the blue leather booth. They were at Fran's Diner on College Street. The restaurant was bustling with families, tourists and shoppers eager for a good meal on a budget. Christine wore casual clothes because it was her day off; Sarah and Gail had come from work and were still in uniform.

Fillingham and Julie hadn't arrived yet, but the latter was notoriously late, sometimes even for work, which didn't go over well with the sergeant.

"How's Ken?" Christine asked Sarah.

Sarah was the only married policewoman in their group. She had been a social worker when she met her husband, a police cadet. Soon after, she joined the force.

"He's good." Sarah smiled, her hazel eyes and freckles making her seem approachable and younger than her twenty-nine years. "We are on opposite shifts. I'm on days, he's on nights, so I haven't seen him much."

"How's work?" Christine addressed Gail.

Gail grimaced. "Some guy tried to stop me ticketing his car."

"I bet that didn't go well," Christine said, raising her eyebrows at Sarah. Gail had been a nurse in the Canadian navy prior to policing and had received rudimentary combat training. Christine had only seen her use her skills a few times, but she was highly effective.

"Hello, everyone!"

The three women turned at the familiar voice. Julie waved as she made her way down the aisle toward them, Fillingham in tow. Julie's berry lipstick matched the dress under her cream wool jacket.

"Ladies," Fillingham said, acknowledging the seated women. He wore dark dress pants and a white dress shirt but no tie. Odds were they were heading out somewhere after the dinner get-together—a bar or music club.

Julie sat beside Christine and pressed against her to get her to scooch over so Fillingham could sit on her other side.

"So," Fillingham rubbed his hands together, "we're the new members of the Morality Squad. An undercover team. Hand-picked for who-knows-what reason. Is it me, or is this whole arrangement peculiar?"

Julie shrugged. "I think it sounds fun. Hanging out in Yorkville, sipping coffee on a patio while Joni Mitchell plays guitar. It beats the Cattle Crossing."

Policewomen were assigned crossing guard duty at busy downtown intersections, including the Queen Street "Cattle Crossing" where officers dodged elbows from open streetcar windows while keeping the jaywalkers in line.

"What do you think, Sarah?" he asked.

"Yorkville needs to turn around," Sarah said. "A regular police presence hasn't decreased crime rates. Maybe Operation Niagara is a different approach." She sighed. "Ken is not keen. He thinks the Village is too violent now. And there was that hepatitis scare."

"That was a hoax," Gail said.

"It got citizens and police officers lining up for vaccinations," Sarah responded.

Gail said, "Yorkville is not a great place if you're female. Women come for the music and end up aimless groupies or addicts pimped by their boyfriends."

Julie raised both her hands in the air. "Let's save these young women, kick out the gangs, clear out the drugs and have some fun!" She smiled. "C'mon, guys! When are we ever going to have another opportunity to work together? The five of us. As a team. *Undercover.*" She looked at each of them. "I'll tell you. Never!"

Sarah smiled. "It would be like police college all over again. We studied hard, but we had fun. And became friends."

Julie wrapped an arm around Fillingham. "And we have the bonus of Geoffrey!"

"I'm not keen," he said.

"Why not?" Julie scolded, shaking him by the shoulders. "How could you resist being with the Fabulous Four?"

His hands gestured open in front of him. "I like Island patrol. Friendly community. Easy-going shift. It's close to RCYC."

"Sail, sail, sail," Julie said mockingly, her head bobbing left and right with each repetition. "That's all you think about."

He leaned his shoulder into hers. "I think about you, morning and night."

"Great!" Julie clapped. "Then you'll want to join me on this job!"

Christine wondered if Fillingham wanted to see his girlfriend daily and if undercover work with her was a good idea. But if having Julie nearby enticed him to accept the assignment, then Christine applauded the strategy.

The waiter came over, and they ordered their meals of meatloaf and chicken pies.

After he left, Fillingham said, "Lane, you on board?"

"You're acting like we have a choice." She added, "I heard there was overtime, which would be good."

Her partner shrugged.

"Truth be told, partner," Christine said, "I'm not sure we can handle Operation Niagara without you."

His eyebrows rose.

Christine continued. "Who's going to keep Julie out of trouble?"

"Yes!" Julie said. "You know how flighty I can be." She winked at Christine. "Musicians, free-loving hippies and muscular bikers. So tempting."

Fillingham addressed Julie. "You do get yourself into trouble."

Gail said, "As a male, you might get access to information that we can't."

Sarah added, "Ken would feel better if he knew you were part of the operation."

"I need you there, Fillingham," Christine said. This was true. What would her life be without her sunny and quirky sidekick?

"You're ganging up on me!" Fillingham flung his arms in the air in defeat.

Chapter 4

Christine, Gail, Julie, Sarah and Fillingham filed into a conference room in 52 Division with its mug-stained wooden tables, scratched paint and worn office chairs. Battered metal filing cabinets anchored one end of the windowless room. A skinny man in jeans with thin long hair and a handlebar mustache leaned against the wall beside a tall, big-boned man in a dark suit and tie. The latter motioned for the five of them to sit around the two front tables. Julie and Fillingham sat at one table while the three remaining women sat at the adjacent table.

The five officers looked expectantly at the standing men like students waiting for the professor to start the lecture.

The mustached man gestured toward the front tables. "Who the fuck are these guys?"

Christine met the wide-eyed glances of Sarah and Gail.

The suited man tilted his head. "The officers we've been expecting."

The mustached man responded, "What am I supposed to do with *them*?"

The suited man sighed and turned to the seated officers. "Good morning. I'm Sergeant Buckman. This is PC Malo. Morality Squad. Thank you for coming."

The man spouting profanities was a police officer? Christine was shocked. He looked more like an informant, twitchy with the need for his next hit.

Fillingham scraped his chair back, walked over and extended his hand to Sergeant Buckman. "PC Fillingham, Toronto Island Patrol." He offered his hand to PC Malo.

Malo waved him away with a quiet "Fuck off."

Fillingham's eyebrows rose, but he returned silently to his seat. The policewomen introduced themselves to the sergeant, stealing glances at Malo, who leaned against the wall, ignoring them.

Sergeant Buckman began. "You've been assigned to Operation Niagara. The objective is to plug the funnel of drugs into Yorkville permanently. Get the addicts, vagrants and transients out. Kids back home with their parents." He turned to the other officer. "Malo, want to take it from here?"

Malo slowly pushed himself off the wall, walked over and stood in front of Julie, staring at her. A flush darkened her cheeks, but she kept her gaze level, her red lips unsmiling. Julie was used to men looking at her.

Up close, you could see the pockmarks on Malo's cheeks; he looked sallow, almost yellow, dark circles under his brown eyes as if he didn't sleep well. He could be twenty-five or forty-five.

"How the fuck is Miss Toronto supposed to look like an addict who hasn't eaten in a week and will blow you for the next hit?"

Sergeant Buckhorn regarded Malo, nonplussed.

Julie's eyes fluttered at the crassness of his comment. Malo stepped back so that he was standing between their tables. He pointed to Christine. "Milkmaid here looks like she could wrestle a steer. What'd they feed you on the farm?"

"I grew up in Parkdale," Christine replied, referencing her urban neighborhood.

"She's a goddamn giant," Malo said, addressing the sergeant. "She could bench-press me."

"That wouldn't be hard," Fillingham said.

Christine frowned at her partner, warning him not to egg on the constable.

"Ah, Sailor Boy." Malo turned to Fillingham. "What the hell do you offer other than your daddy's bank account and your ability to tack and jibe? And," he turned to Gail, "are you even a woman?"

"Fuck you," Gail said.

Christine never had a work meeting like this, laden with hostility and profanities.

Malo turned to Sergeant Buckhorn. "Send the next group in."

Sergeant Buckhorn sighed, crossing his arms. "Malo, you know there's no other group. This is it. Top-down request."

"Fuckin' brass," Malo spat out. "They don't know their arseholes from their dicks." He sighed heavily. "Sailor Boy, you're a skinny fuck, so you have potential. Don't shave or cut your hair or wash."

Julie looked at Fillingham in alarm.

"Hilton," Malo said, fluttering his fingers at Gail. "The man/woman thing you have going might work. Half the fuckin' hippies look androgynous, unless you find their tits."

Julie said, "I think you're underestimating our talents." Her voice was quiet but firm.

He placed his knuckles on the table in front of her, leaning close, his lank, dark hair hanging forward. "Yeah, doll, I'd love to hear about your talents."

Julie didn't flinch. "I'm friendly." She looked at him with her large brown eyes lined with kohl eyeliner. "I talk to everyone. I notice things."

Malo addressed the sergeant. "We could use her as a prostitute." He turned back to Julie. "How far you willing to go, doll, to get the job done?"

Fillingham stood up. "That's enough."

Sergeant Buckman waved a hand at Malo. "Tone it down, PC Malo. We could use her as a waitress in a café or music club. Any of those places have go-go girls still?"

Malo pressed himself up off the table and stepped back. Fillingham slowly sat down.

"Fine," Malo said. "Let's get her in as a server at the Toucan or the Boathouse. See what's being piped through the clubs."

His two fingers pointed at Julie, then Fillingham, and back again. "I hear you two are cozy. You need to shut that down during the operation. A flirty waitress will get more info if she doesn't have her boyfriend sniffing around."

"We're not going to break up," Fillingham protested.

"I don't give two shits about the hot stuff you get up to in your own apartments. In Yorkville, you're not an item."

Malo regarded Gail on the other side of Christine. "You're the nurse." It was a statement, not a question. He had obviously studied her file.

"Royal Canadian Navy," Gail answered.

Christine had to give it to Gail. She was not ruffled by Malo's antics. Her gray-brown eyes watched him levelly, her expression un-intimidated. She must have been hardened to this type of language and behavior during her military stint.

"She'd be good for the Trailer Project," Sergeant Buckhorn said. "They got funding for another year."

Malo said, "That's good news. Lots of addicts and riffraff go through there. Solid sources of info." He nodded. "It gives us more options."

"What's the Trailer Project?" Gail asked.

"It's a forty-foot mobile home they hauled to a parking lot on Avenue Road last summer," Sergeant Buckhorn said. "It was sponsored by a community agency—I can't remember which one. Inside was a medical clinic with a doctor from Women's College. Social workers to help with housing and counseling, lawyers to help Villagers with vagrancy charges. That kind of stuff."

Malo pulled on one end of his handlebar mustache with fingers yellowed from nicotine. He nodded his chin at Fillingham. "You're an educated prick, right, as well as having a silver spoon up your ass?

Fillingham did not look pleased but nodded.

Malo said, "Every take a law course at Western?"

Malo knew which university Fillingham had attended. For all Malo's rage and opposition, he knew a lot about them.

Fillingham nodded again. "A few. I was pre-law." He sounded like he was talking through gritted teeth.

Sergeant Buckhorn said, "He could work with the lawyers in the Trailer Project. They have rotating volunteers, so he could fit in easily."

Malo said, "Throw in the social worker," he pointed to Sarah, "and we have a team inside the Trailer Project. Not as good as having someone embedded with the hippies, greasers or motorcycle gangs, but it's the best we can do with this lot."

Buckhorn said, "That would work."

"Okay," Malo said, addressing the group, "you can get the fuck out now."

Christine stood up. "What about me? Where do I go?" She had to go on Operation Niagara. She had Deputy Darlow breathing down her neck.

Malo grimaced. "Thing is, Milkmaid, I can't see a role for you." He looked at Christine's friends. "Everyone else has skills to offer the operation." He shrugged. "And reaching the highest shelf in the kitchen isn't one of them."

Gail said, "She's solid. Has integrity."

Malo snorted. "No room for integrity in undercover work."

Fillingham said, "She comes, or we don't."

Malo laughed. "What are you going to do, Jack? Quit because you don't have Godzilla with you?"

He nodded.

Malo threw his hands in the air. "You gotta be fuckin' kidding me!" He glared wild-eyed at Buckhorn and then stomped out of the room.

Chapter 5

"Math is stupid!" Christine's stepbrother, Wayne, threw his pencil down on his workbook.

Christine hung the tea towel on the oven door from dish drying and sat down beside him at the kitchen table.

"Which question are you working on?" she asked. Wayne was in grade five and had little patience for homework. He was easily frustrated, which worried Christine, and he gave up too quickly. In life, you needed more stick-to-it-iveness.

He pointed to a question at the bottom of the page.

"Why don't you take a break," she said, "while I review the examples, and then we can work on the assignment together?"

Thirty minutes later, Wayne had been fed peanut butter crackers and had finished his math homework. She had gone back in his workbook and reviewed the questions he had completed on time differences and had him apply his knowledge to the current problem.

"Can I see if Tommy is around?" he asked.

She glanced out the living room window of their apartment. It was a sunny April day, suddenly warm, as if spring was truly here and the shivering winds of winter were gone for good. Christine's mom Phyllis was having a nap, as she often did in the late afternoon. Phyllis did shift work at the Toronto Police Records department, so she was always trying to catch up on her sleep. And Christine's stepsister, Donna, was playing with a friend across the hall.

"Sure. Be back for dinner." The boys would grab their baseball gloves and find a patch of yellow-green grass in front of their apartment or in the schoolyard to practice their throws. Christine and her mom usually let Wayne roam the neighborhood during daylight hours. Parkdale was busy then with families shopping, women hustling home from their office jobs and children coming home from school. Things sometimes got rougher at night with drunken arguments outside bars and released patients from the nearby mental health institution wandering the sidewalks.

After Wayne left with his baseball equipment, the place was quiet. Christine swept the apartment: the hallway, kitchen, living room and bedroom she shared with her sister. Since her siblings were out, she filled a bucket with soapy water to wash the kitchen floor. One tile was peeling up. She'd have to remind her landlord to fix it or pick up glue from the hardware store herself.

Closet hangers rattled in Phyllis's room, and Christine quickly put the kettle on. The kitchen floor could wait. She needed to talk to her mom about Operation Niagara.

"Tea, Mom?" Christine asked as her mom passed her on the way to the washroom.

"Yes, thank you," Phyllis said.

Ten minutes later, they were settled on the couch with their teas. A line ran down Phyllis's left cheek from sleeping. She was tall, like Christine, but thin; her arms as she lifted the mug to her mouth seemed half the diameter of Christine's. She had dark circles under her eyes and long wavy brown hair threaded with equal amounts of gray.

"I have a new assignment," Christine began.

Phyllis's eyes were pinned to Christine's.

"Fillingham, Julie, Sarah and I are going to work undercover in Yorkville Village."

Phyllis frowned. "What would you do there?"

"We'll help with the runaway kids, drug users and transients."

Phyllis's frown deepened. "That sounds dangerous."

Christine sighed. Ever since Christine switched from working at Records to policing five years ago, her mom had been apprehensive. Even though policing meant higher wages, Phyllis still viewed it as a man's job.

"Why do they need policewomen for the assignment?" Phyllis reached across the table for her package of filtered cigarettes.

"The Morality Squad often uses women for undercover. It's less obvious. In Yorkville, Julie can be a waitress, Sarah a social worker. Gail and I will work in the community program helping people."

Phyllis lit her cigarette and took a long drag, then exhaled. "I don't like it. Look what happened to you on Toronto Island."

Christine had been hospitalized twice in the last year. But her injuries were minor. And she and Fillingham had solved two homicide cases.

"We are gathering information, Mom. It's not dangerous. We'll be talking to the Villagers, visitors, drug users, tourists and business owners to get an idea of where the drugs are coming from. We send the information along to the Morality Squad. They take it from there and perform the arrests."

Phyllis puffed away on her cigarette.

Christine took a sip of her tea. "It'll mean more money because the shifts are longer. We could increase the payment to Fillingham." Much to Christine's chagrin, her partner had paid Phyllis's gambling debt to a loan shark. Christine repaid her partner every paycheck, something she found both humiliating and life-saving.

Phyllis said nothing.

"Or I could put a few dollars aside each paycheck to save for a bigger place." Their apartment hardly fit the four of them. Donna and Christine had the one bedroom with twin beds so close to each other, the sisters could hold hands when lying on their respective mattresses. Wayne didn't have a room; he slept on the sofa and kept his clothes in a side hutch in the living room. Phyllis's room was a closet converted to a bedroom furnished with a cot, clothing rod and shelf.

Christine used to dream of moving somewhere more suburban, where fewer people pushed their possessions in grocery carts and the sidewalks weren't crowded. But when she had patrolled pockets of Scarborough and North York when working at the Women's Bureau, the neighborhoods seemed sterile, as if no one lived there. Parkdale had energy and a sense of community. Christine's goal was to save enough money to rent the main floor of a three-bedroom neighborhood house.

"We'll have to pay close attention to our schedules," she told her mom. "And your bingo nights."

"Why?"

"The shifts at the Trailer Project start at three in the afternoon and go to three in the morning. That means I'm not around after school, for dinner or bedtimes most days."

"That's a terrible shift," Phyllis said.

"I know, Mom. It's like permanent afternoons. And it's weekends. But it's just for a couple of months." Christine didn't know how long it was going to last. Two months? Maybe three?

Christine continued, "So you can't stay late at bingo on Saturdays."

Phyllis looked annoyed. Christine was sympathetic to her mom. Phyllis loved the game. Her group of friends smoked and chatted while they managed five to ten bingo cards each, vying for the grand prize of a mix master or set of frying pans. Sure, Phyllis probably lost more money than she won, and the prizes weren't exciting, but her mom had fun, and it was better than her drinking and gambling days.

Phyllis shook her head as she exhaled. "I can't do it by myself. It's too much. Donna. Wayne. Shift work. Meals. Cleaning. Laundry." Her voice sounded overwrought.

Christine put a hand on her mother's thin forearm. "Mom, I'll still be around to do all that stuff. Just not in the evenings. I can make sure Donna and Wayne get off to school, pack their lunches. Do laundry and keep the apartment tidy. If they need help with their homework, I can do it at breakfast. Plus, my days off are Monday and Tuesday. You can go to bingo then. Or if you want to go out on the weekend, just come home earlier. Wayne can babysit Donna for a few hours. He's old enough."

"Can't you say no?" Phyllis tapped her cigarette against the clay ashtray Donna had made last year at summer camp.

Christine shifted on the worn couch cushion. "It's an assignment. You do what you're told. The brass asked for us. I can't say no."

"What brass?" Phyllis squinted at Christine through the gray cigarette smoke. Since she worked at headquarters, she knew most of the senior officers by sight.

"Deputy Darlow." Christine wasn't going to talk about Darlow's missing daughter, but she saw no harm in mentioning his name.

Phyllis's eyes widened. "You keep putting yourself in danger. You had a concussion. Stitches. Black eyes. Burns."

"I'll be talking to the clients of the Trailer Project. Gathering information. That's it."

"You're going undercover because a deputy asked you? You don't owe him anything. Let someone else take the job."

"Mom, you know that's not the way it works in the police force. When someone taps you, you step up. This will look great in my file. Help me get a job as sergeant, where I'll make more money."

Phyllis gently mashed out the cigarette. Maybe she was calming down.

"I love policing. I'm good at it. And Fillingham's with me. And my Women's Bureau friends. We're a team. We'll help each other out. Look out for each other." Phyllis loved Fillingham, mesmerized by his good looks, money and sweet talk.

"I'd like to talk to Geoffrey," Phyllis said as she reached for another cigarette.

Great. Just what Christine needed. Her partner involved in more of her family life. Wasn't it enough that he had paid off her mom's gambling debt and helped clear her brother's name when a classmate had drowned?

"Sure," Christine said. "I'll ask him to call you."

Knowing Fillingham, he would charm her mom, like he did most women. Christine would have to bake him something to say thank you or take his turn waxing the station's wooden floor.

Chapter 6

Julie held up a multicolored cotton skirt. "Christine, you'd look good in something long and flowing." She handed the garment to Christine, who was standing beside Sarah and Gail in the clothing store.

"Can I go now?" Fillingham asked, his thumb pointing to the shop door. "The Portuguese bakery down the street makes fantastic custard tarts. My treat." The five officers were shopping in Kensington Market with money from Sergeant Buckhorn to outfit themselves for Operation Niagara.

"No," Julie said. "I saw a leather vest in a perfect shade of tan. Let me dig it out."

Fillingham raised his eyebrows, and the rest of the women shrugged. Julie was a force to be reckoned with, especially in her role as fashion maven.

While Julie searched for Fillingham's wardrobe, Christine disinterestedly shuffled hangers along a rack. She wasn't an enthusiastic shopper. When you were a tall, muscular woman with wide shoulders, a chest, hips and powerful thighs, few items hung well. Shopping meant grabbing whatever fit, regardless of style or color.

She looked at the skirt on her arm that Julie had chosen, its hues of brown and turquoise. Pretty. And she wouldn't have to worry about its length, as she did with minidresses that often came just below her bottom because she was tall. Maybe she could find a blouse or tank to match. She felt a spurt of interest. The friends already looked different since their meeting with Buckhorn and Malo a week ago. Fillingham was growing a goatee and mustache, his hair already floppy on top. Julie had asked the women over to her apartment this morning and had teased their hair in different styles and applied makeup on Christine and Sarah. Gail had waved Julie away, saying she was fine as she was.

Christine's brown hair had been back-combed so that it rose above her head and spilled down her shoulders. Her peach lipstick was subdued below the dramatic black eyeliner swept across her eyelids, which gave her a feline look. She felt like an actress. She *was* an actress, she reminded herself, in her undercover role in Operation Niagara.

Julie stood in front of Christine with an armful of clothes. "Here. Try the tie-up top with the flared jeans and the white shirt with the buckskin skirt. There's a purple sleeveless top that goes with the peasant skirt." She dumped the pile into Christine's arms and then pushed the middle of Christine's back with her hand. "Off you go. Get dressed and come out to show us."

Christine walked between racks of clothes to the back, passing the shopkeeper behind the counter, who nodded at her. The owner was smartly letting Julie have full rein over the shop. It was a Friday morning, and they were the only customers.

As Christine unzipped her pants, she could hear Gail protesting. "I can find my own clothes, Miss Spark. I know what medical staff wear."

"How about a bit of jewelry," said Julie, "to pick up the hazel in your eyes? Change your look. Take a break from the khaki and vests with a hundred pockets."

"Yah, grab the diamond necklace," Gail responded.

Christine was in her bra, zipping up the flared jeans, when the curtain on her changing stall rattled open.

Julie stood there, appraising her, fist clutching a handful of necklaces.

Christine crossed her arms over her chest.

"Jeans fit well," Julie observed. "You'll need new bras. This one looks like it's on its last legs. I'll pick some up for you at Eaton's. What are you: 36 C? D?"

"Shhh," Christine said, finger over her lips. Everyone in the shop could hear Julie, including Fillingham.

"Put that one on," Julie said, pointing to a shirt on the hook.

Christine slid her arms into the long, flowing sleeves, adorned with loopy flowers in turquoise and red and green, and tied it under her breasts, her stomach showing above her jeans.

Julie threw two necklaces over Christine's head and stood there, nodding. "Not bad. Let's get a second opinion."

Before Christine could protest, Julie pulled her by the elbow into the shop.

"This works, right?" Julie said to Fillingham, Sarah and Gail. Gail glanced at Christine in pity, but Sarah nodded enthusiastically.

"Geoffrey?" Julie asked.

"Her stomach looks flatter than mine," he commented.

Julie smacked the flesh of Christine's stomach with a loud thwack. "I know, right?"

"Ow!" Christine said.

"This is a good style on you," Julie said, her finger flicking up and down. "The shorter top, the wide sleeves. Very feminine. And the jeans show off your curves. It's better than a minidress, which looks like a sack on you." She looked over at the store owner. "Can we have more of this style? The tie shirt and pants."

The shopkeeper nodded and headed for a clothing rack.

"Try the buckskin skirt next," Julie said to Christine. "It'll work if we pair it with a turtleneck."

For the next hour, Christine tried on clothes. She seemed to be Julie's pet project, as Gail resolutely found her own clothes, mostly plain long-sleeved shirts and jeans. Fillingham agreed to try on several wildly patterned shirts and a few vests and then snuck out on a bakery run. Julie bought a few things for herself: a minidress, two miniskirts and a pair of go-go boots,

"I'm more of a mod than a hippie," Julie announced. "A bit more Twiggy, less Janis Joplin."

Sarah bought a dress for herself and a shirt for her husband, saying she had lots of social worker clothes from her previous employment, and the group exited onto Augusta Avenue.

Julie insisted everyone wear their new clothes out of the store; the more they acted like their undercover characters, the easier it would be when they arrived in the Village. Christine wore her jeans and tie-up blouse beside Julie in her boots and Fillingham in a tie-dye t-shirt. The five friends walked along the sidewalk, arms linked as they passed fruit stands and record stores, the new bangles on Christine's wrists clattering musically. She felt like they were in a scene from *The Mod Squad.*

"You look different," Fillingham said, addressing Christine.

"I know," Christine said.

"Nice. I mean, not just nice but—"

"What about me?" Julie interjected.

He turned to his girlfriend. "Miss Toronto, your gorgeousness goes without saying."

"Hold hands!" Julie commanded. "Raise them high!" All arms went up in the air as they walked. Julie shouted, "Operation Niagara, here we come!"

"Do you think we're done with the winter coats, Mom?" Christine asked Phyllis as she stood beside their front door closet.

"Let's hope so," Phyllis responded from the kitchen.

April weather in Toronto could be tricky, from sun showers to balmy weather to snow squalls.

Christine walked down to the kitchen with coats hanging over her arm. Her mom sat at the table with her cup of tea, smoking a cigarette while paging through a romance magazine.

"I'll wash our coats," Christine said. "Which reminds me, I'll check if Donna's spring jacket still fits her. She's gotten taller."

Christine grabbed a basket and went downstairs to the basement laundry to put in a load. She had three days off before Operation Niagara started, and she had a list of chores to complete. As she searched for coins for a second load, the butterflies in her stomach fluttered as she pondered undercover work. Policewoman on the Morality Squad must feel this same anxiety—never knowing if their next role was a woman in distress, a prostitute, a door-to-door magazine salesperson or the pretend girlfriend of a fellow officer while on a stakeout. Christine had completed a few short undercover jobs. Morality often looked for small, pretty policewomen for assignments. One look at Christine's height and girth and their glances moved on to Julie or Sarah.

Fillingham had tried to get her to relax about Operation Niagara now that they had accepted the assignment. Yesterday, they had sat down for their dinner break at the Centre Island station, Christine with her cheese sandwich and Fillingham with takeout from the Clergy House.

"What if I'm terrible?" she asked.

"At what?" he said, his voice muffled as he chewed a bite of steak.

"At undercover. What do I know about acting? Being convincing as another person?"

"As Christina?" he asked. They had chosen their undercover names. Malo had said to make it close to their Christian names but to alter their surnames. Christine was Christina. Geoffrey was Geoff. Julie was Jewels. Sarah was Sarah-Jane and Gail, for some reason, remained Gail.

Christine nodded. "I know how to be a good police officer. But that's because the badge gives me authority. People have to stop and talk to me or risk arrest."

He took a gulp of milk and wiped the mustache off his upper lip. "How many times do you do that? Muscle citizens around? You're good at reasoning with people. Checking how you can help them. That's exactly what you'll do at the Trailer Project."

"I'm not chatty, like Julie. Or warm, like Sarah."

"You're more approachable than Gail."

"I'm worried I can't pull it off."

He waved her concern away with one hand. "You're not going to jabber with every Tom, Dick and Harry or be the life of the party, but you're calm and reliable. People will sense that. You're caring too. You have friends. A family. Stop acting like you're a social outcast who can't function outside her job."

Christine smiled. Maybe she will be okay. She took a bite of her sandwich.

Fillingham pointed at her with his fork. "Your main deficit is your taste in men."

Christine stopped chewing. He must be referring to Hawk Johnson. Fillingham had warned her it wouldn't end well. And it hadn't.

"Lane," he continued. "I've spoiled you. Working all day with someone as dynamic, athletic and charming as me. No man measures up."

"You mean someone as egotistical and self-delusional?" she said.

"Look at those fancy ten-dollar words."

"I'll add snob to the list." She took another bite of her sandwich.

Christine took the clean coats out of the washer, trying to shake off her concerns about Operation Niagara. Really, Fillingham had been right. She was competent in her patrol job. Why wouldn't she be in her new assignment? And they were a team. Her partner had likened them to the Fantastic Five, after Marvel's Fantastic Four. With Fillingham in the Village to back her up, the reliable Gail and the empathetic Sarah, Operation Niagara would be an opportunity to experience an extended undercover assignment. And it would be an excellent experience to have on her file.

Christine returned from the basement laundry room and hung up the damp coats on the shower rod to dry. In her bedroom, she pulled out the flared buckskin skirt, beaded belt and cream turtleneck. Julie had told her to wear it tonight when the gang went down to Yorkville to have a bite and listen to live music. Like Julie, Christine had purchased a pair of knee-high boots to go with the outfit, except Christine's were tan and Julie's were white. Tonight would be their initiation into Yorkville, a celebration of working together.

She stood in front of the mirror, staring at herself in her new garb. Along with the beaded belt, she had a large pendant necklace and long beaded earrings. She'd never buy this outfit for herself in a hundred years—too much jewelry and too flashy. But she was Christina now, and the sooner she started thinking, dressing and acting like her alter ego, the smoother Operation Niagara was going to go.

Chapter 7

"Follow me," Fillingham said to the four policewomen as he descended the stairs into the Boathouse Café.

"Have you been here before?" Christine asked Gail. The nautical-themed venue had porthole windows, brass poles and brass door handles.

Gail nodded.

The group stopped beside a young woman in a floral dress who was collecting the cover charge.

"I got it," Fillingham said, waving Gail off as she reached for her wallet.

"Richie Rich," Julie said, smiling.

"It's Geoff," Gail reminded her. They were using their alternative names tonight.

"It's busy," Christine said as the staff made change for Fillingham.

Gail said, "In the summer, the Village is shoulder-to-shoulder people. Lineups to get into the music venues. Cars bumper-to-bumper on Avenue Road, Cumberland and Yorkville Avenue."

"I see a table," Julie yelled, immediately grabbing Christine and marching the group toward the middle of the room.

Christine followed Julie's short little steps in her white go-go boots and matching white minidress. Julie, like the rest of them, was dressed in new clothes.

"Walk confidently, Christina," Gail said from behind, jabbing two knuckles into Christine's back.

Christine forced her shoulders back, restraining herself from covering her chest or checking the shortness of her suede skirt. Adding a little saunter to her step in her thigh-high boots, she felt several eyes on her as she settled into the booth opposite Julie. Gail slid in beside her, momentarily hip-checking her.

"Ow!" Christine said. "You're like a brick wall."

"Hockey," Gail replied. Gail played defense for a winter league.

On the other side of the booth, Fillingham slid in beside Julie, then Sarah followed.

"Sorry, lovebirds," Sarah said, "I'm squishing you together."

Julie leaned into Fillingham. "He doesn't mind!"

"Cool it," Gail said.

Julie scowled, her pink lips pouting, a shade that matched the hairband around her white-blond bob.

Gail scanned the group, her hazel eyes serious. "We're in the Village. We're undercover, starting now. So whatever people see today is what they should see when we officially start our assignment. So, *Jewels*, like Malo said, you and Geoff are not a thing in the Village."

Julie straightened away from Fillingham. "Lucky for you, Gail, you get to keep the same name and the same dull personality."

Sarah said, "Enough!" She often acted as Mother Hen and group mediator.

Gail said, "We should check out the clientele, the staff, the entertainment," she pointed her chin toward the stage, "for potential leads."

Christine said, "I noticed a few people wandering around the Boathouse entrance. Men and women. They were young and very thin, talking to people in line. Maybe panhandling?"

Christine didn't add that she had checked every face for Deputy Darlow's daughter—the long brown hair, the big doe eyes—from the school photo he had given her. She would sneak back later and ask the woman collecting the cover charge if she knew an Alice Dodgson.

Gail said, "They could be asking patrons in line for a joint or where they could find the next hit."

Julie scanned the room. "This audience looks well-fed. Shiny hair. Clean clothes. They can afford the cover. And food and drink."

Gail said, "They're mostly visitors, weekenders they're called, who come from the suburbs to hang out in the Village. Or are attending university nearby. They don't live in Yorkville. They may smoke weed while they're here, buy off hippies or greasers, but they're not heavy drug users. I don't think they'll lead us to big-time suppliers."

The waitress came over, and they ordered coffee.

Fillingham looked up from the menu. "What do you recommend for a snack? The pie? A croissant?"

"You want something sweet?" the waitress asked. She looked like she was only eighteen, with long blond hair, freckles and gray eyes.

Fillingham pressed a hand against his chest. "I'm sweet enough. It's my friends here that need a bit of sugar."

"Is that so?" the waitress said, smiling.

The four women watched Fillingham flirt with the staff. Christine felt sorry for Julie. It was what Fillingham was supposed to do, get to know staff in the Village, but it was grating to watch.

As Fillingham informed the waitress he was both sweet and addictive, Gail interrupted. "We'll all have the strudel."

The waitress sashayed away in her minidress and pumps.

Christine had ordered a cappuccino after Sarah explained it was coffee with steamed milk, even though it was double the price of a regular coffee. Fillingham had paid for the cover, and Christine hardly went out. And maybe Morality would foot the bill.

Five minutes later, Christine sat, coffee in hand, listening to her friends' chatter. It was nice to be out, eating together, talking. She didn't do this often enough. Julie was regaling them with the time she went undercover as a little old woman to catch a purse-snatcher.

The place was filling up, the hubbub louder as people took their seats. Even though the Boathouse was underground and window-less, it felt cozy, maybe because the air smelled like coffee and cinna-mon. Or the wood paneling and brass rails made patrons feel they were on a ship. The sign by the stage advertised that a folk-singing legend was headlining tonight. Big names played at Yorkville venues: Gordon Lightfoot, Murray McLaughlin, Joni Mitchell and Buffy Sainte-Marie. It would be fun to hear someone famous, someone she had read about in the newspaper's entertainment section.

Sarah addressed Gail. "When do you two start at the Trailer Pro-ject?"

"Tuesday," Gail answered.

"We're opening the trailer, prepping it for the season," Christine said. "Are you there as well?"

Sarah shook her head. "The social work days are Thursdays and Fridays. I'll see you then."

"Part-time?" Christine asked.

Sarah nodded. "That works out better for me. I'll spend the other half of my time at the Women's Bureau." She turned to Julie. "When do you start?"

"Monday," Julie said. "And guess what? I get to be a dancer and a waitress!" She clapped her hands as if applauding herself.

"That sounds fun," Sarah said. "Are you in the front window?"

Gail interrupted, "Are your clothes on?"

Both Fillingham and Julie said, "What?"

"Haven't you seen the signs in the Toucan window? *Topless waitresses. Bottomless bartenders.*"

"No! I–I..." Julie stuttered.

"Morality wouldn't have you work topless," Fillingham said.

"Malo would," Gail said, looking at Julie, whose eyes were wide, mouth agape.

"I'm sure that's not the case," Sarah said, shaking her head.

Gail met Christine's glance and winked. Of course, Gail was jerking Julie's chain.

Gail said, "On another topic, I spoke with the doctor who supervises the Trailer Project. Last year, the chief complaints were housing, mental health, malnutrition, drug overdose, venereal disease and skin rashes."

"Gross," Julie said.

"After the music set," Fillingham said, "let's mingle in front of the venues; I'll ask people if they know where I can get weed. Get a sense of the suppliers. See if visitors buy off the same seller when they come to the Village."

"I saw a few groups openly smoking up," Gail said. "We can ask them too."

"Let's split up. It will look less suspicious," Christine said. And she could check if anyone knew Kelly Darlow.

They were interrupted by the manager of the Boathouse introducing the evening's entertainment. A thirty-year-old man with glossy brown hair and mustache strode onto the small stage with his guitar. He flashed the audience a warm smile and began a song titled "Maverick" as he picked expertly on the guitar strings. Christine smiled; she felt like a maverick herself, cutting loose, being adventurous, going undercover. The singer caught her smiling and smiled back. Christine, or should she say Christina, held his glance.

Maybe she was going to enjoy working in Yorkville after all.

Chapter 8

Dr. Sandra Reid unlocked the door of the mobile home with Gail, Fillingham, Christine and two hospital candy-stripers in tow. The doctor wore her hospital lab coat over an olive sweater and khaki corduroys. Christine guessed her age to be about forty-five or fifty, with short brown hair streaked with gray, high cheekbones and a no-nonsense but friendly manner. The group trailed down the wooden stairs behind the doctor, arms filled with cleaning equipment: garbage bags, rags, detergents, pails, sponges and mops. Dr. Reid opened the metal door with its faded entrance sign and propped it open. A waft of putrid air washed over them.

"Ew!"

"Yuck!"

The group covered their noses and mouths.

"Those buggers!" Dr. Reid said. "They didn't clean the trailer before they stored it!"

Six of them had gathered in the Avenue Road parking lot that morning to prep the forty-foot caravan for the season. On the exterior, it looked like a mobile home: a rectangular box with curtained windows and wooden steps up to the entrance and exit doors located fifteen feet apart.

The trailer had white aluminum siding, darkened by dirt, with rusted metal edges and a faded sign beside the entrance: *No narcotics or money kept on the premises.* Another sign posted the Trailer Project hours: 3:00 p.m.–3:00 a.m., Wednesday–Sunday.

The caravan looked huge to Christine, taking up the entire length of the parking lot. A sliver of snow topped the flat roof. No one had used it since last fall; it had been stored in an open field north of Toronto. During the colder months, the Trailer Project staff had moved inside to Rochdale College on Bloor Street, where hippies and university students were creating an alternative learning experience.

The crew stepped inside as Dr. Reid continued to castigate last year's Trailer Project staff. The smell of rot overwhelmed them.

At first Christine was worried that her head might bang the roof, but the ceilings were eight feet tall to accommodate storage cupboards.

"Did something die in here?" Fillingham beelined toward the window above a couch by the kitchen. After a few grunts, the pane slid open. He continued down the aisle, opening windows as he went.

"We have to find the source of the smell," Gail said. She yanked open the kitchen cupboards, revealing water glasses, plates, coffee machine, popcorn maker, canned food, paper plates, bandages, gauze, blood pressure cuff and a scale.

"Girls," Dr. Reid said, addressing the two teenagers, "the medical area is at the far end." She pointed south. "You can help me with inventory. Geoff," she said as he returned to the kitchen, "when you've finished ventilating the place, check the law and social work office at the other end. Likely, it's a dump."

"You two," she pointed at Gail and Christine, "are on garbage patrol. Find whatever the heck stinks and get it out!"

The teenagers snaked behind Dr. Reid as she headed down the aisle.

Gail opened the mustard-yellow cupboard doors under the sink to reveal a bin of overflowing garbage with rotting food in shades of gray and fuzzy green.

Gail squatted down, hand over her mouth and nose. "I see a dead mouse. Grab the garbage bags, and let's clear that out first."

Christine and Gail pulled on rubber gloves and got to work, double-bagging the rotting garbage and triple-wrapping the dried-out mouse carcass before taking the detritus outside. Then they emptied the kitchen cupboard contents onto the coffee table and couches, tossing out open boxes of cocoa and pasta and expired food. They spent the next hour scrubbing the shelves and countertop with bleach and baking soda.

They wiped down the vinyl couches, coffee table and counter surfaces. Together they walked down the middle aisle, tossing newspapers, magazines, application forms, used gauze, dried husks of food, empty food containers, a pair of worn sandals and a smelly pile of clothes into green garbage bags.

Around noon, the group gathered in the middle kitchen area. With the doors and windows wide open and the smell of vinegar and detergent in the air, the interior was getting more endurable.

Fillingham arrived with cappuccinos and croissants, and the six of them sprawled on the two terracotta orange couches.

"Ah, Yorkville," Fillingham said, toasting his coffee cup to the group. "Strumming guitars, poetry readings and pastries."

Gail lifted her cup. "And dead vermin, old bandages and rancid food."

Dr. Reid shook her head. "Those damn volunteers from last year, Edith and George. The Villagers loved them, but they were disorganized as heck. I must have told them five times when the trailer was going to be picked up, and they promised a big cleanout."

Fillingham said, "The offices aren't too bad. Once I removed a couple of boxes of old paperwork and garbage, it just needed a wipe-down. It's pretty bare. A desk, a couple of chairs, a filing cabinet. The other two spaces are just chairs, a table and storage cupboards."

"We've done quite a bit in a short time," Dr. Reid said. "The girls," she smiled at the candy-stripers, "did inventory and cleaned the medical area, so I know what to order to restock for things like bandages, syringes, gauze and medical tape. I'll bring equipment like stethoscopes and blood pressure cuffs from the hospital. Medications never stay here, or else we'd get ransacked daily. Either I or a resident will bring them to the Trailer Project at the beginning of a shift and return them to the hospital at the end."

The doctor took a sip of her cappuccino and put it down on the coffee table. "The water tank has been drained and refilled. They'll hook up electricity this afternoon, fingers crossed. We can get most of the cleaning completed this week, and we'll be good to go for the weekend."

"Do you think we'll be busy?" Gail asked.

Dr. Reid held up a hand and tilted it back and forth. "So-so. It will be a slow start, but once we have a few sunny days in a row, and the snow is gone for good, the weekenders will come down. And the out-of-towners. The Villagers will come out of the woodwork. Last year, the Trailer Project served over twenty-five hundred clients. That's why they funded it again. Young people come here for help, more than a hospital, shelter or community agency. And as long as we are welcoming and nonjudgmental, we'll get the numbers again this year." She brushed crumbs off her lap and stood up.

"Our union break over?" Fillingham kidded.

Dr. Reid smiled. "You guys may work out after all. I may pop back to the hospital to pick up equipment and supplies. Geoff, you said you had a car? Can you grab the garbage, and we'll drop it in the large hospital bins. Then I can pack both our vehicles with equipment and supplies for the return trip. The rest of you, continue what you're doing, and we'll meet again in two hours."

After Dr. Reid and Fillingham had left, Christine and Gail wandered through the motor caravan to check the layout. At the medical end was a door leading to a private office with a desk, examination table and small sink with cupboards above and below.

"If the doctor has someone in her office, it looks like you can also treat people here." Christine pointed to the examination beds on either side of the aisle with a curtain on rails for privacy.

Gail looked at the smaller treatment offices. "Not very private. People can hear every word, but it will do."

As they wandered to the far end of the mobile home to check the other offices, Christine smiled to herself. It would be good to work with Gail. Christine had worked with her for a short time at the Women's Bureau and in a few assignments for the Youth Bureau but never consistently on the same shift. Gail didn't talk a lot. Not like Julie, who was chatty and social, full of news about celebrities, trendy hairstyles and police gossip. Gail spoke if she had something to say, which was fine by Christine.

As Fillingham had said, the legal and social work space was minimally furnished. The end office had a door and a similar footprint to Dr. Reid's office at the other end. It had a desk with a rolling office chair and two uncomfortable-looking wooden chairs for clients. There had been a beanbag chair, but Fillingham said it was torn and tossed it out. Two bankers' boxes held empty file folders and had been used for client files. A two-shelf bookcase below the window held worn versions of local and provincial laws and legal reference books. Brown adhesive marks on the walls showed where posters or signs had been taped.

A buzzing sounded, and the lights flickered on.

Christine and Gail looked at each other and smiled. They went through the caravan, testing the light switches, turning the office lights off and keeping the kitchen and aisle lights on. Before returning to cleaning, Christine retrieved a radio from the law office and plugged it into the kitchen outlet, then dialed it to CHUM FM. The sound of The Doors' "Hello, I Love You" filled the trailer.

When Dr. Reid and Fillingham returned, minus the candy-stripers, who had finished their shifts, Christine and Gail were spraying the inside windows with vinegar water. Dr. Reid looked up at the lights and gave a thumbs-up. Christine went to turn off the music, but Dr. Reid waved her away.

"The radio is always turned on at the Trailer Project," Dr. Reid said. "And the coffee pot has fresh brew. There's food for clients, even if it's just a milk shake or banana. Trailer Project rules," she added with a smile.

Fillingham said, "Any other credos we need to live by?"

"No judgment," Dr. Reid said. "Whatever the client's complaint: an STD, lice, drug overdose, gang fight, vandalism charge, delusions. No judgment, just treatment or service."

They nodded.

"Okay," Dr. Reid said, "I'll be stocking the medical offices. I've got supplies in my car. You ladies, continue cleaning."

Fillingham addressed the doctor. "Do you want me to help you?"

"Now that we have water," Dr. Reid said, "I'll get you to give the exterior a wash. The hose is stored in a bin by the back tires. The water tank is underneath us here." She stomped her right foot on the kitchen floor. "There's a hookup for the hose beside it."

"Yes, ma'am," he said, saluting.

Dr. Reid smiled. "We may just get along, Geoff."

As Christine wiped down a door with a soapy rag, she jumped when a spray of water splattered the outside metal. Gail turned up the radio so they could hear the music above the sound of Fillingham hosing down the siding.

A few minutes later, he stepped into the trailer. "Christina!"

She still had to get used to that name, her new identity as this easy-going, caring, social work student joining the Trailer Project for clinical experience.

Fillingham pointed to the spray bottle on the kitchen counter. "Can you grab the vinegar and come outside to clean the windows? They're caked in dirt."

"You good here?" Christine asked Gail.

Gail nodded and waved Christine outside.

Sprayer in one hand and newspaper in the other, Christine descended the wooden stairs and scanned the parking lot. Where had Fillingham gone? She would need a stepladder to wipe the top half of the windows. He must have used one to scrub the siding.

"Geoff? Aaaah!"

A spray of water hit her in the back. Christine turned, dropping the vinegar water. Fillingham stood grinning with the garden hose nozzle pointed at her. A blast of water hit her in the chest.

"Aaaah!" she yelled again. Her shirt was soaked, rivulets wetting the front of her capris. Sure, they were her old clothes for cleaning, but still.

"Gotcha!" he said.

The trailer door opened, and Dr. Reid and Gail peeked out. "What's going on?"

He turned to them. "Somebody walked into my water spray. You should look where you're going, Christina."

"Liar!" Christine said, hands on hips as water dripped into her shoes.

"I see we have two eight-year-olds working for us," Dr. Reid commented.

Gail shook her head. "They're fine. Leave them to duke it out." The door closed with a firm click.

Christine ran toward Fillingham and stepped on the hose with one foot. She grabbed his hands and tried to pry his fingers from the nozzle. She changed tactics and put him in a headlock. He squeezed the nozzle handle, and a blast of water hit them both in the face. Gasping, Christina threw him over her hip and pressed him flat on the pavement, her knee and fist in his back. With one hand, she tossed the hose away. She was dripping, her hair flattened from its teased crown, her carefully applied eyeliner probably running down her face.

"Hey," a man's voice said.

Christine and Fillingham looked up. Two women and a young, bearded man stood beside them.

"You cool?" the bearded man asked, looking at Fillingham, who was resting his head on one elbow as he lay on the ground.

Fillingham nodded.

"Looks like she got one up on ya," the man said.

"She weighs a ton," Fillingham said. "An unfair advantage. I can't get up."

Christine pushed her knee harder into his back, causing him to gasp.

"What word am I looking for?" she asked, just as she did during their wrestling matches on the Island.

"Heavyweight?" he said.

She leaned harder.

"Goliath? Sasquatch? Okay! Okay! *Uncle.*"

Christine eased back on her heels and let Fillingham up.

"What's all this?" the man said, pointing to the mobile home. Christine could hear Steppenwolf on the radio inside singing about a magic carpet ride.

Christine stood up, pushing the wet hair off her face. "It's the Trailer Project." She gestured to the caravan. "If you've got a problem, feeling sick or sad, rent issues or can't pay a loitering charge, there's somebody here to help." She was impressed with the way she rattled off the services, as though she had been working at the Trailer Project for months.

Fillingham brushed small stones and dust from his jeans and smiled at the two women. His beard and mustache had grown in a darker blonde, and his hair had lost that shaved officer look, even though it was still short. He had a plaid shirt on, plastered wetly against his chest.

"You work at the Trailer Project?" one young woman asked Fillingham. She wore a black minidress with matching hairband. The trio must be here to lunch or sip coffee at a Yorkville café. They had the affluent sheen of weekenders and didn't look like they needed Trailer Project services.

"I do," Fillingham said enthusiastically. He stepped in front of the two women. "Geoff at your service." He made an elaborate bow. The minidress woman giggled and introduced herself as Carla and her red-haired friend as Wendy.

"What's going on with you two?" Carla asked, pointing at their damp clothes.

"Christina hadn't showered this morning, so I thought I would do her a favor."

"Okay, you lagabouts," a voice called. Dr. Reid leaned on the open trailer door. "I have a job for you."

Fillingham and Christine said goodbye to the group.

Walking backward, Fillingham yelled to the two women who had crossed the street, "I'll be here Wednesday to Sunday, from three to three. Come visit. Or else I'll be lonely."

Christine coughed. "Like you are ever lonely." He had Julie, after all.

Dr. Reid must have heard their conversation because when they got to the base of the stairs, she said, "Lots of blarney I'm hearing."

"Exactly," Christine said.

Fillingham pretended to look hurt.

Ignoring Fillingham, the doctor asked, "You two have a change of clothes?"

They shook their heads.

"Keep a change at the trailer. In case someone throws up, or bleeds on you or has crabs." She looked them up and down. "Or sprays you with a hose."

"That was not my—"

Dr. Reid waved away Christine's protest. "Head into the Village and pass out these Trailer Project postcards. Let people know we're opening soon." She held out her hand, and Fillingham ran up the steps to take the cards from her. "If you need to, buy a change of clothes at the vintage store. You can get a shirt for a couple of bucks."

Christine scanned a postcard. *Coming down from a bad high? Got a rash? Need birth control? Is your landlord threatening to kick you out? Friendless and alone? Money problems? We can help at the Trailer Project. 70 Avenue Road. Come by for your medical, social and legal needs. No questions asked!*

"Head into the cafés, music venues and businesses," Dr. Reid continued. "Introduce yourselves to owners and staff. Most of them will remember the Trailer Project from last year. They'll let you keep a stack of postcards at the counters, bulletin boards and on café tables. Then hand some more out to customers, people walking on the sidewalk and sitting at the patio tables."

"No problem," Fillingham said. His hand waved back and forth between Christine and himself. "Mr. and Mrs. Charming, at your service, letting everyone know the Trailer Project has what you need, be it legal, housing or—"

"Birth control," Dr. Reid added.

"I'll lead with that." He gestured to Christine. "After you, my lady."

"Don't get the postcards wet," Dr. Reid remonstrated before closing the door.

"My loafers are squelching," Christine complained as they walked across the parking lot.

"Take 'em off," Fillingham suggested.

She stopped. "And do what? Walk barefoot around the Village?"

He pointed a finger at her. "Exactly. You got it. That's what any chill, easygoing, free-loving Villager would do."

"And get my feet sliced by a broken Coca-Cola bottle or stabbed by a discarded syringe?"

He waved away her concerns. "It'll be five minutes. We'll get a pair of canvas loafers at Ernest's when we buy the t-shirts."

As she contemplated, he grabbed her by the wrist.

"What are you doing?" she said. She let him drag her toward the wooden table.

"Take them off," he instructed.

She toed her shoes off. He grabbed the pair and placed them on top of the picnic table in the sun.

She wiggled her toes, which looked blindingly white. "It's April," she said.

"A gorgeous day! At least seventy degrees. And you are easygoing, shoeless Christina. Embrace your bohemian self."

"Fine." She took a few tentative steps, a small stone crunching in one arch. "You are the most annoying person I've ever met."

"Head toward the sidewalk. It's smoother than the asphalt."

They jaywalked across Avenue Road and turned south toward Yorkville Street.

"Shoes first," Christine demanded, "postcards second."

She picked the cheapest shoes she could find at the store, a pair of blue sneakers and a moss-green sweater because she was freezing. Fillingham paid, saying Malo would pay him pack. His shirt was almost dry, so he didn't need a change of clothes. They chatted with the shopkeeper, who seemed nonplussed by her bare feet, and handed him a pile of postcards for the front counter.

As they left the store, Fillingham said, "Race you to Record World!" and took off before the sentence was complete.

He was faster, but she grabbed him by the back of his shirt as he was opening the shop door, elbowed him out of the way and stumbled in ahead.

"Not fair!" he yelled as he followed her in.

The man with the long beard at the cash glanced up at the noise and went back to reading his RCA newsletter.

Fillingham went over and chatted him up, asking him what was hot this week and if they had the latest Rolling Stones album. Christine eventually interrupted, taking a handful of postcards from her partner and presenting them to the store clerk. They told him about the Trailer Project and asked if they could leave the cards near the register for customers.

The clerk nodded. "Last year I had some guy seizure in the store—he was on some whacked-out stuff. Scared the shit out of me. Doc Reid came over, did CPR until the ambulance came."

"Do people come into your store high?" Fillingham asked.

The clerk shrugged. "Sometimes."

"Do they need help?" Fillingham said.

Again, the clerk shrugged. "They're spacy, giggly. Anybody on anything harder is not out shopping."

Christine and Fillingham exchanged glances. They could ask the clerk about dealers another time. For now, it was important to introduce themselves and get familiar with Village staff.

"I'm glad you know about the Trailer Project. Our number's there." Fillingham pointed to the bottom of the postcard. "If someone is in distress. Or doesn't have a place to sleep. Landlord issues. Or are stealing because they're hungry. Call us. Open three to three."

Fillingham promised to come back to buy the Stones' *Beggars Banquet* album on his way home, and the two officers continued down the block. It was quiet, mostly people having coffee or wine in the late afternoon sun on the café patios. Live music or theater acts didn't start until eight or later. Christine and Fillingham popped in and spoke to several club owners and managers and introduced themselves to the waitstaff. Three proprietors said they'd waive the cover charge if Christina and Geoff dropped by for a set. They should just let the ticket taker know they worked at the Trailer Project.

"Want a pop?" Fillingham asked as they stood in front of the Grab Bag on Yorkville Avenue. "My treat." He flashed his white, straight teeth. "You can wait here. Take a load off."

It wasn't quite an apology for soaking her and forcing her to go barefoot, but it was good enough.

As the door closed behind him, she stood up and headed back to the record store.

"Forgot something?" the clerk said as she approached the counter.

"Actually, I did. Have you seen this girl anywhere in the Village?" She showed him the photo of Kelly from her tony private school. She seemed tall and elegant in her white blouse. Her caramel brown hair rippled with shiny highlights. She had wide brown eyes, a straight nose and a warm smile. Her skin looked unblemished, as if all she drank was milk.

He leaned over to look then grimaced. "That's her."

"Who?"

"I don't know her name."

"Was it Alice?"

He shrugged. "Maybe. All I know is that she was stealing. I literally caught her twice. She'd stick the record under her baggy shirt. I told her if it happened again, I'd call the police, and she went nuts. Started throwing records around, kicked my plant over, ripped the posters off the wall. She left when she heard me on the phone calling the police. I haven't seen her since, thank God."

"When was this?" she asked.

He looked up. "September? October?"

"Was she high when she lost it?" Christine asked.

He shook his head. "I don't think so. She wasn't tripped out. She was twitchy. Like she needed to score."

"Are you sure it's the same girl as the one in the picture?"

"Not a hundred percent. She looks different now. But the eyes look the same." He shook his head. "I tried to be nice. The first time she stole, I told her I'd buy her a coffee and muffin if she was hungry. She told me to go fuck myself."

Christine said her goodbye and rushed out of the store, walking behind a group of university students.

"There you are!" Fillingham said as he stood holding two bottles of ginger ale in front of the variety store. "Where have you been?"

"I was handing out postcards and ended up chatting."

He retrieved a chocolate bar out of his pocket and handed her half. They settled on the stairs in front of the store with their drinks and chocolate.

"Should we get one of those for the Trailer Project?" He tilted his head toward an inflated chair in a store window. "Invite people to hang around outside."

She regarded the neon-colored furniture in the blow-up shop. "One strong wind and it's careering down Avenue Road straight into the lake," she said.

"Maybe there's a tab and I can anchor it to the asphalt."

"A stab of a needle or pen and it's finished," she said.

"True." He drank a mouthful of pop. "You know what would work? Some boat benches."

"What do you mean?"

"Outdoor furniture. Made for the hulls of boats. Or for docks and outdoor patios. The cushions are made of waterproof material."

"We have the one picnic table."

He shook his head firmly. "Not enough. We need to create an ambiance. A place where youth will hang out, even if they don't need the services of the Trailer Project that day."

"Dr. Reid said that people hung out on the couches inside the caravan, drinking coffee."

"That's good for when it's raining, but we want an outdoor vibe." He gestured to the cafés and restaurants along Yorkville Avenue. "Just like them."

"What are you going to do? Put in some plant boxes, candles and outdoor lights?" Her tone was teasing.

"Great idea!" he said, standing up. He reached out his hands and pulled her to her feet. "Time to move on. Converse with the gents and the ladies on the street." They had decided their goal today was to get to know people in the Village, start a connection, especially with staff and the youth who seemed to be regulars.

They made their way along Yorkville Street and then down Cumberland Avenue, calling in at each shop, chatting and joking with staff and customers. They kept an eye out for those who looked like true Villagers. Malo said the rougher a youth looked, the more likely that they were an addict, impoverished or crashing at someone's place, and a potential informant.

"Can't really see anyone who looks like a Villager," Christine said as they headed toward the Toucan, where Julie had started waitressing. Julie had said that the owner was more concerned about her bra cup size and her ability to dance in the window than any restaurant experience.

"Well," Fillingham replied, "Villagers are hibernating. Visitors won't ramp up until the summer. Maybe we'll see a few university students hanging out before the term ends. It looks like nobody's migrated from Rochdale."

Rochdale was the new university around the corner at Bloor and Avenue. Malo said students hung around doping while discussing social theorists they had never read.

"Julie better have her clothes on," Fillingham said as they stopped in front of the Toucan.

It was unlike Fillingham to be jealous. He must be anxious that she was undercover alone. Everyone else was working for the Trailer Project.

She said, "Why don't you save a patio table for us outside and hand out postcards to passersby? I'll head inside with some postcards and see if we can get Jewels to wait on us."

She headed up the stairs of the club. The Toucan was one of the wildest entertainment venues in Yorkville, featuring nude movies, topless waitstaff and body-painting parties. Malo thought it possible that drugs flowed through the premises as well.

It was quiet inside, just a handful of customers. Yorkville businesses made the bulk of their income on weekends and in the warmer months. The local artists, students and drug users who lived in the

Village were relatively impoverished and usually did not have funds for eating out.

Julie was at the back in a miniskirt and white vinyl boots, laughing with a table of three businessmen, her fire-engine-red lipstick matching her red top. She looked up and spied Christine. Tapping a man lightly on the shoulder, she said she'd be back with their drinks and headed toward her.

Christine introduced herself, gave her the spiel about the Trailer Project and asked if Jewels could serve them outside.

"Sure, honey." Julie gave her a wink. "Put your postcard on the community board, and I'll be outside in a minute with menus."

Five minutes later, Julie came over to their patio table with menus. Standing beside Fillingham, she tapped his shoulder. "What can I get you, sailor?" She smiled at him, her cake makeup creasing into lines around her mouth and eyes.

He leaned back in his seat, arms crossed, as he regarded her heavily made-up face and bright outfit. Clearly, he was having difficulty with Julie's undercover assignment. She had confessed they had argued about it, with Julie asserting she could take care of herself and him having no faith in her skills.

"Not ready to order yet, sir?" Julie quipped. "How about you, Christina?"

Christine glared at Fillingham, but he didn't make eye contact. Turning to Julie, she said, "Can we have two cappuccinos to start?"

"Absolutely," Julie said. Fillingham watched her walk away and her cute little wiggle in her boots.

"Get over it," Christine warned.

"What?"

She continued, "You are making it harder for her to do her job. Is that what you want? To add more pressure when she is undercover by herself at the café?"

"No," he said reluctantly, unfolding his arms.

"Then get over it. Be a good boyfriend and officer. Support her and make her feel we have her back."

"Fine," he grumbled.

Julie returned with frothing coffee mugs in hand, which she placed in front of them.

"Miss," Fillingham said, holding the menu, "what would you suggest for two hungry workers? You look like you have good taste in food."

Julie smiled at Fillingham, looking relieved. "I have good taste in everything."

"I'm not surprised," he said, smiling back.

As they chatted, Christine inwardly sighed with relief. Good. They were making up. She just had to suffer through their flirting, and Operation Niagara would chug forward.

"If you're hungry, the hamburger is good." Julie stepped beside Fillingham to point it out on the menu, her right thigh brushing his arm.

"I got a sweet tooth," he said.

"How about an ice cream sundae?"

That seemed excessive to Christine, but Operation Niagara was paying, so she agreed. They had a stipend for food and other expenditures.

Julie returned with the three-scoop dessert featuring a banana layered in caramel and chocolate sauce, topped by a maraschino cherry.

"I haven't had one of these since I was eight," Christine said. Actually, it was the only time she'd had one, when her mother treated her for her birthday. Before her stepfather, Eddie, had come on the scene.

"You haven't lived, Christina," he said.

"So people tell me." In a quiet voice, Christine asked, "How's it going?"

Leaning close to Christine to pass her a spoon and napkin, Julie whispered, "The owner, Sal, locks himself in his office with different salesmen, not sure what any of them are selling or if there's something going on there. Malo wants me to look at some photos to see if I can identify any. Otherwise, it's fine. Some wise-ass customers, but the girls look out for each other."

Julie stepped away and said in a louder voice, "The kitchen's featuring chocolate-covered crickets this weekend, if you're interested."

"Any topless dancing?" Fillingham asked.

Christine kicked him under the table.

Julie's smile fell for a second. "No, sir. That's not my bag. I'll dance in a window, but my top stays on."

"Thanks for the sundaes," Christine said.

"My pleasure," Julie responded.

Fillingham handed Julie a wad of money and told her to keep the change.

Julie smiled at the big tip. "Anytime you need something," she said, looking at Fillingham, "give me a call. My name is Jewels."

"You can count on it, Jewels," Fillingham said as Julie sauntered away.

Chapter 9

"You're juggling oranges?" Christine asked Fillingham as she stood beside Gail.

It was midnight, and the trio had spent the last two hours stringing lights on the mobile home's exterior. Fillingham had placed spotlights on the perimeter of the lot, but they needed longer extension cords to link them to the electrical outlet behind the trailer. Over the last two weeks, the parking lot had been transformed into an outdoor living room with chairs and couches covered in waterproof material that Fillingham had bought or nabbed from his yacht club. He added an outdoor rug and a wooden coffee table. All they needed were lamps, and they'd be all set, Christine thought.

Dr. Reid had asked the city to provide another picnic bench. The two tables were lined up beside the outdoor furniture so that twelve people could sit together. On top of the tables were bowls of food—oranges, apples and muffins. Plus a bowl of condoms. Sometimes they received donations from a bakery. If food supplies were low, Dr. Reid gave them cash from the Trailer Project budget and sent them shopping.

Fillingham had rigged a canopy over the picnic tables to protect them from rain so staff and clients could hang outdoors regardless of the weather.

Cradling three large oranges, Fillingham said, "Watch me. I'm pretty good."

"This I gotta see," Gail said. Christine and Gail sat down on either end of the outdoor couch with bottles of pop.

"How old is he again?" Gail asked as an orange hit him on the head and the other oranges spilled onto the ground.

"Twenty-six, going on twelve," Christine answered.

"Look! Look! I'm doing it!" he yelled as he juggled the three oranges in wide ovals. He sidestepped to catch an errant orange. "I need music. Where's the music?" he shouted. A table of café patrons across the street cheered as he juggled.

Christine walked over to the portable stereo unit and clicked it on. "Born to Be Wild" blasted from the radio station.

"Hand me another orange, Christina," Fillingham gasped, his eyes glued to the oranges as he juggled.

"You can juggle four?" she asked.

"My audience demands more!" he said as whistles and applause sounded from the patios and bars across the street.

Christine grabbed an orange from a bowl and walked over to Fillingham.

"One, two, three," she said and tossed the orange at him.

"Ahh!" The orange hit him on the side of the face. He ducked belatedly, and the fruit tumbled down.

Boos and applause could be heard from across the street. Fillingham turned toward Avenue Road and bowed.

"What was that!" He turned back to Christine. "You pitched it at my head."

"How else was I supposed to do it?"

"If you had waited for my instruction, you would know to hold it in your outstretched hand, and I would pick it up when I was ready."

A door banged. Dr. Reid stood at the exit in a white lab coat over a dark gray minidress, one hand propping open the aluminum door.

"Okay, Ringling Brothers, it's midnight and we don't have clients. Go into the Village and spread the word. Bring the backpack and shoulder bag. They're filled with transit tickets, a first-aid kit, food coupons, skin cream and info cards for support services. And don't forget, we're not just looking for drug addicts. We treat venereal disease, birth control needs, depression and anxiety. Check if people are going to school or have jobs. If they have family or friends around."

Gail said, "I'll stay with Dr. Reid." She turned to Christine. "Don't forget to check on women who look vulnerable, doped-out or drunk. Make sure they can get home safely."

Christine nodded. She was always on the lookout for young women in distress, since she was constantly searching the crowd for Kelly Darlow. Quite a few times already she had introduced herself to thin young women with sunken eyes in the Village. None of them were Kelly, and no one knew "Alice Dodgson" or anyone who looked like her.

Fillingham grabbed the knapsack from the doctor, and Christine grabbed the bag. To each bag they added oranges, a handful of condoms and Trailer Project business cards.

"Can we grab a bite to eat after our rounds?" Fillingham asked the doctor.

"Sure," she said, "Take a break, and we'll see you back at one thirty."

When your shift started at three in the afternoon, then six o'clock was "lunch" and midnight was "dinner."

"I'm not feeling so good," a male voice said. They turned to see a young man crossing the street, half-crouched, propped up by a woman with long, dirty-blonde hair. When he reached the sidewalk, the man kneeled and threw up.

"We got this," Dr. Reid said, waving Christine and Fillingham away.

The two jaywalked across Avenue Road. It was Saturday night. Popular venues like Boris's and the Purple Onion had lineups. Dr. Reid said it was nothing compared to the summer, when the masses spilled into the Village streets and people in cars gawked at the outlandishly dressed weekenders, greasers, motorcycle gangs and hippies.

Christine and Fillingham strolled along. The night felt cool but windless, and there was enough of a crowd to make the area feel energized. They greeted people as they walked along, asking where they were going, handing out cards. People were coming from live music sets or were heading out for a bite to eat or late-night coffee with friends. A few groups looked like they were mildly drunk but amiable. Youth sat on the stairs in front of the galleries and stores, smoking or toking, leaning back against the brick walls, looking half asleep. They were clearly buzzed, but they didn't seem in harm's way. Fillingham asked them about their dealers, saying he wanted to pick up something after work. One man said his dealer was in North York, while the others said they didn't ask for the guy's name or couldn't remember it. He had just met him that evening.

Christine targeted the young women, pulling them aside as Fillingham talked to the guys. Some girls were barely sixteen, and a few were fourteen. Christine asked if they were feeling okay and how they were getting home. Most of them laughed her questions off, happy to be in the company of a guy or friends. For a few, Christine tucked a postcard and taxi chit in their purses, telling them they could get home on their own if they needed. For two girls who looked drunk, one already sweating and turning green, they hailed a taxi and sent them home.

Christine and Fillingham completed their circuit of the Village, Yorkville Avenue to Bay Street, back along Cumberland Avenue and up Avenue Road.

Fillingham went into a café to pick up Hungarian cabbage rolls, advertised to be the best east of Bloor West Village. Christine sat down in front of the adjacent art gallery to wait. It felt good to get off her feet and be quiet after talking nonstop for the last hour, checking every young female with long chestnut hair to see if she was Kelly Darlow.

Christine had called the deputy right away with the story about the girl who had trashed the record store. The incident had happened last July, almost ten months ago. The deputy was keen to see if his daughter had been in the Village more recently than last summer. In the past two weeks, Christine had checked with most of the businesses in the Village. Only one person, a waitress at the Penny Farthing, thought she recognized the girl in the photo.

"That looks like Alice," the waitress had said.

"You know her?" Christine said as they stood on the patio together. "Alice Dodgson?"

"I don't know her last name. She was here on and off last summer. She was bothering customers on the patio. Begging for money."

"What happened?"

"My manager would come and tell her to move on. At first, she did. Then she started sitting down at the tables with customers, refusing to leave." The waitress tucked a strand of dark hair behind her ear. "People were trying to be nice. Offered to buy her a meal. She looked like she could use one. But she didn't want food, just cash."

"For drugs?" Christina asked.

The waitress bent to pick up the dirty plates on a nearby table. "Who knows? She had the look."

"When did she stop coming?"

The waitress straightened. "By the end of the summer, my manager had had enough. She was swearing at people when they ignored her. Going from table to table. She threw someone's dinner plate on the ground."

"Did he call the police?"

She gave a short laugh. "Better than that. He told her every time she was here, he was going to take a picture. He has one of those Polaroid cameras. Then he was going to date it, show it to every Village business and make a copy for the police. And that was it. She never came back."

Kelly was probably worried her dad would find her.

Christine had told the deputy that Alice might have been spotted in August or September at the café. He hadn't seemed shocked at her belligerent behavior, just quiet. He urged Christine to find places Kelly might have stayed over the winter.

Christine spotted Fillingham walking toward her with coffee and cabbage rolls. For the moment, she would push aside thoughts of Kelly and enjoy dinner.

She took the coffee from him. "Just in time. I was ready for a nap. I'm still not used to these late hours."

"Had to elbow my way through the line of greasers. They know good food. Let's head to the park," he said. "Or do you want to sit out here?"

"Quiet would be good. I need a break from people." The park was the grassy area of a schoolyard that featured a soccer field, playground and a few benches. She and Fillingham had gone there on their lunch break.

"Look what I brought!" he said, pulling a Frisbee out of his jacket. Since they were no longer ax-throwing or wrestling, her partner's newest activity for them was Frisbee. They played in the trailer's parking lot.

"In the dark?" she asked. He already complained she had clumsy hands.

"You need the extra training," he said.

"I didn't spend my youth throwing Frisbees on the yacht club lawn while drinking Champagne with my fraternity brothers."

He pressed his hand to his heart, as if hurt. "It was gin and tonics."

She shook her head as they turned up Hazelton Avenue. Her partner cut a bohemian figure in his puffy-sleeved white shirt and jeans; he looked like an art gallery curator. She sported red flared pants, a peasant blouse and big silver hoop earrings—all chosen by Julie.

Two minutes later, they reached the school and headed for a picnic bench beside the playground.

"Looks creepy at night," she said. Two lights on either end of the school partially lit up the yard. The trees behind the playground were dark blobs, swaying slightly in the breeze. Most of the soccer field was cast in dark velvet shadow.

As they sat down on the bench, he asked, "Wonder if anyone parties here or meets here for a brawl?"

"I hope not," she said. "There would be elementary students here in the day." She unwrapped her cabbage rolls. "Do you think anyone would sell drugs to school kids? Should we check that angle?"

He shrugged. "I wouldn't put it past the down-and-out hippies. They sell in order to make money for their own drug use. And greasers will push pills to anyone. They pimp their girlfriends out. And the motorcycle gangs? Not sure if they draw a line at—"

"Did you hear something?" she interrupted.

They sat in silence.

"Was it from this direction?" His chin pointed toward the fence line that separated the school from the adjacent businesses.

"I think so," she said hesitantly.

"Was it a yell?" he asked.

"More like an animal sound."

"Let's check it out," he said. Leaving their half-eaten rolls on the table, they headed for the treed fence.

"Careful," he said, "it might be a raccoon. Their claws are razor-sharp."

She pulled a small flashlight out of her bag, and they followed the tunnel of light until they reached the fence and began walking north.

They stopped when they heard a sound, waiting to see if it was repeated. She walked faster, moving into a jog, Fillingham beside her. Was that a person lying on the ground? Were they sleeping or passed out?

She covered her mouth and nose with one hand.

"Vomit," Fillingham said. "It's probably a teenager who couldn't hold his liquor and crashed here for the night."

They had reached the shape. In the ribbon of light, they saw a man on his stomach, arms stretched out, wearing a dark, knee-length trench coat ripped under the armpit.

Kneeling, Fillingham said, "Sir, are you okay?" When the man didn't respond, Fillingham shook his shoulder. "Sir, can you answer me? My name is Geoff. I'm from the Trailer Project. What's your name?"

Christine kneeled on the other side of the prone man. "Let's turn him over."

"On the count of three," Fillingham directed. The man was a dead weight, but thin, and they turned him onto his back.

He had sunken cheekbones, eyes slightly open in slits and mouth agape. The smell of vomit was strong. He had thrown up down the front of his shirt.

She pressed her fingers against the man's neck. "I feel a pulse. It's shallow."

"Gloves?" he asked.

She handed Fillingham a pair of rubber gloves from her bag and put on one herself.

Fillingham pressed on the man's sternum and yelled, "Sir, can you hear me?"

He pressed harder. Pushing on the chest bone was a test to see if a client could feel pain. The man gave a low groan. Pushing his thumb against the man's eyelid, Fillingham pried it open. "He's so high, the whites of his eyes are crimson."

"Overdose?" she asked.

Fillingham pulled up the man's coat sleeve to reveal needle track marks.

"We need to get him to the hospital," she said. "He's going blue around the mouth." Dr. Reid had given the staff training regarding the most common medical conditions of Trailer Project clients, including overdoses and their treatment.

"Stay with him," he said. "I'll find an open restaurant and call an ambulance and call Dr. Reid to come."

He took off across the park at a brisk run.

She looked down at her charge. His breath was so shallow, she could hardly tell his chest was rising. Dr. Reid had said you couldn't always determine what drug someone took, but the key concern was their breathing. Keeping a hand on his chest, Christine guessed the man had overdosed on heroin. Or maybe speed.

Malo had told them marijuana and hash used to be the drugs of choice in Yorkville for weekenders and Villagers alike. Very few overdoses. But in the last two years, the drugs had become harder. The psychedelic and intravenous drugs were deadlier than their predecessors. And the users were sicker.

She flashed a light on her watch, trying to time the man's breath to give the paramedics his vitals. He certainly wasn't breathing at a normal rate of fifteen breaths a minute. She looked up, scanning the shadowy playground. Where was Fillingham? Dr. Reid? The ambulance? She was afraid the man was going to die on her.

"Hey," she said, shaking his shoulder, "my name is Christina. I'm here to help. What's your name?"

She leaned in to see if he was saying anything, but he seemed to be deeply unconscious. His face was angular, with sparse remnants of a beard and mustache, dark eyebrows against the putty color of his skin. His hair lay in oily strands down to his shoulders.

He was probably in his twenties, maybe hitchhiking from Sudbury or the East Coast to the Village in search of the rumored hippie lifestyle of drugs, music, free love and freedom. But that Yorkville was fading fast. It was still there for the weekenders who came down from the suburbs to listen to live music, smoke a few joints and head back to their jobs or university classes. But for others, like this man, Yorkville had turned poisonous.

With gloved hands, she searched inside the pockets of his overcoat for identification or a clue about the ingested drug. A dirty tissue. Loose tobacco from a broken cigarette. She felt around his shirt and pants pocket, monitoring his chest to ensure he was still breathing. She found a stretchy cord, probably used to tie off his arm to find a vein. Gosh, he was thin. Her hands slid over his bony hip. There was something in his front pocket. She pulled it out. It was a box of matches, black with silver lettering. *Kalinka.* It must be the name of a bar or restaurant.

Christine checked her watch and measured his breathing: four breaths a minute. She kneeled over him, both hands on his chest, prepared to do CPR, thinking how Operation Niagara would shut down Yorkville's drug business so she would never have to be in this park again at one in the morning, trying to keep a man alive.

Chapter 10

A week after Christine and Fillingham found the overdosed man in the schoolyard, Malo called the four of them to a meeting in a Kensington neighborhood park before work. Fillingham had driven Julie and Christine, and Gail arrived on her motorcycle.

It was a sunny May day, cool due to an easterly breeze. Windbreaker weather. Malo was sitting at a picnic table with a large piece of paper in front of him, pencil nub in one hand. He wore a jean jacket over a Harley-Davidson t-shirt.

"We going back to school?" Fillingham inquired as Gail sat beside Malo and the rest settled on the other side of the table. They were partially hidden by a line of cedars.

"Isn't that up your alley, frat boy?" Malo said, a lit cigarette hanging on his lower lip.

The four officers looked down at the paper. The page had been blocked into sections. Each section had a label in block letters: hippies, out-of-towners, weekenders, tourists, greasers, bikers and Americans. Beside each label were names. Christine recognized the names of two Villagers who sold weed to finance their addiction.

"Here's the network of drug suppliers in the Village as we know it," Malo said. "Each of these groups," he jabbed at the paper with his nicotine-stained finger, "has a finger in the pie. But who has the largest slice, or should we say, the most profitable slice, is the question."

Gail said, "I see names provided by our Trailer Project clients. Antonio Russo," she pointed to the greaser label, "and Frederick Stanley." She pointed to the word *American*.

Malo took a deep drag on his cigarette, then whooshed the smoke out. "I want to give you the big picture so you can focus on areas of interest. See here," he pointed to the hippies, "pretty sure the hippies and weekenders are low-level businesses. The hippies get dumped with a small supply of weed, maybe from a university student or an American draft dodger who picked up a couple of pounds in Buffalo. It's small quantities, small profits. And out-of-towners from Kingston or London are just here for a fun weekend in the Village and to make pocket change from unloading marijuana or hash."

"Are greasers bigger players?" Julie asked. There were four names by the greaser label, surnames either Portuguese or Italian.

Malo wagged his head. "Yes and no."

Greasers were not regular clients of the Trailer Project. They seemed suspicious of the program or of getting help. Dr. Reid had treated a greaser with a septic leg burn from his motorcycle muffler. Gail had a client named Carla with herpes, whose boyfriend was a greaser and pimped her out. Two greasers had dropped by to see if the lawyers could help with their car theft and reckless driving charges. But that was it.

Malo continued, "Greasers sell higher-price products, amphetamines, LSD pills. Barbiturates. So the average seller makes more money. But it's not a full-time job for most. Unlike hippies, and wannabe hippies, most greasers work in trucking, auto mechanics, construction."

Gail asked, "Is their product clean?"

Malo shrugged. "Mostly. Users still OD or walk off buildings when they're hallucinating on LSD. People don't like that. So getting rid of the greasers' business is one focus."

Fillingham said, "That leaves the heavy-duty stuff, the injectables like heroin and speed, sold by the bikers?" He pointed to the label on the page, which listed four motorcycle gangs but no specific people.

"Ding, ding, ding! We have a winner!" Malo said. He held up his hand. "But again, yes and no. There's been word that bikers have moved into the drug business to diversify from loan sharking, prostitution and theft. This is a more recent development. But we have another contender."

"Who's that?" Christine asked.

Malo looked at her. "You provided the informant's name, Christina."

"Who?" she asked.

"Dean Hillside."

Christine shook her head. "I don't know who that is."

Malo reached into his jacket pocket and pulled out a black matchbox with *Kalinka* written in gold script. It was the same box she had found in the pocket of the man who overdosed in the park.

Gail said, "Kalinka is Russian. The name of a tree. Or a flower."

"I like you the more I get to know you, Hilton," Malo said. "Yes, it's Russian, which means one thing."

"What's that?" Christine asked.

"That we have a new player in town." He drew a hammer and a sickle with a star above. In big capital letters, Malo wrote the word *Russians* in the upper corner of the page.

Chapter 11

"Can I take these?" Gail asked Dr. Reid, holding up a box of condoms. "They're expired."

Dr. Reid was sitting on the couch, reviewing the budget from last year, while Christine washed dishes in the trailer's kitchen sink.

"Don't use old condoms," Dr. Reid replied. "Take some from the bowl on the picnic table."

"Hot date?" Christine asked Gail. She had known Gail since police college, but she knew little about her friend's personal life. Gail didn't talk about men or dating. Christine didn't either, but it was because she usually had little to say.

Christine had wondered if Gail liked women, as some Women's Bureau officers did, but chastised herself for the thought. Policewomen were often stereotyped as either mannish lesbians or party girls out to hook a policeman. If a constable asked a policewoman out, and she refused, the rebuttal was that she mustn't like men.

"You caught me!" Gail said, hands in the air. "Me and Andrew got a thing going."

Christine and Dr. Reid smiled. Andrew was a Villager who sometimes worked at the variety store. He had shown up at the clinic for sores on his penis, an obvious case of gonorrhea. Dr. Reid knew him from last year, when she had treated him twice for the same issue.

"We have to stop meeting like this," Dr. Reid had told Andrew as she examined his genitals behind a curtain, causing all within earshot to laugh.

"You and Andrew and about thirty other women, I'm guessing," Dr. Reid said to Gail.

"Actually, Christina, these are for you," Gail said, holding up the condom box.

Christine paused, coffee cup in hand.

"For Geoff," Gail said.

Christine frowned. What was Gail getting at? Sure, she and Fillingham joked around on the job, causing Dr. Reid to raise her eyebrows as if they were two frisky pets, but that was all in character. She was Christina—friendly, easygoing, helpful. Was Gail intimating that she and Fillingham were lovers? In character? In real life?

"Look at you all flustered," Gail said. As Christine glared at her, Gail added, "I'm kidding. It's payback time."

"What do you mean?" Christine asked.

"Didn't Geoff get you with the hose when we opened up shop?"

"Yes."

"That type of aggressive, masculine behavior needs a response."

"Been reading *Ms.* magazine?" the doctor asked Gail.

"I'm listening," Christine said and sat beside Gail on the couch.

Gail plucked a packaged condom from the box. "Let's fill these babies with water, tie 'em up and bombard Geoff with water balloons when he returns."

It was eleven o'clock, and Fillingham was picking up dinner in the Village.

"Outside," Dr. Reid said, "I'm assuming."

"Of course," Gail said, smiling up at the doctor. "We'll fill them from the water tank and wait for him behind the trailer."

"If we have any clients," Dr. Reid said, "Operation Water Balloon is canceled."

"Postponed," Gail said.

"Fine," Dr. Reid responded. "I hope you have a change of clothes. You're not getting off early if you're soaking wet. And I'm locking the door. No hiding in here when Geoff counterattacks."

"Fair terms," Gail said. She turned to Christine. "Start opening the condoms, and I'll find a box for the filled balloons."

"Okay," said Christine. She hesitantly tore the square packet and pulled out a condom. She'd seen them before, of course, once or twice, but that had been in the dark, and she hadn't handled it. They were rubbery, the smell immediately transferring to her fingers.

She shook her head as she grabbed another handful to open. It was good to have a bit of fun. The midweek nights could be slow, although they had been picking up as the days got longer and warmer. Last weekend was the May long weekend holiday, and on Saturday it was bonkers. Clients with alcohol poisoning, a broken ankle from jumping off a table. Someone had run through a glass door.

"All done?" Gail had returned with a cardboard box. Dr. Reid had gone into her office to work.

"Almost," Christine said.

"We have to hurry before Geoff—"

"There you are!" a male voice said.

The women turned. A man with dark braids stood inside the door, his shoulders taking up the width of the aisle, smiling at Christine.

Hawk!

Christine could feel Gail looking at her, but she could only stare at Hawk Johnson, her old lover. Had he come back for her? Was he finished with his girlfriend?

Then another panicked thought. Was he going to break her cover?

Before Christine could speak, the door opened and Fillingham stepped inside, almost running into Hawk, a brown paper bag in hand. "I got some croissants—"

Hawk turned around, and Fillingham and Hawk met glances.

"What's going on?" Gail said. When no one answered, Gail addressed Hawk. "Sir, how can we help you?"

Fillingham placed the paper bag down on the side arm of the couch. "He's got the wrong place. He's just leaving." He moved to give Hawk a clear path to the door.

Hawk addressed Christine. "I need to talk to you."

Christine looked at him, alarmed. Would Gail figure out what was going on?

Fillingham stepped closer to Hawk, blocking Hawk's view of Christine. "You need to leave."

"This has nothing to do with you." Hawk went to step around Fillingham.

Fillingham pushed Hawk's chest. Hawk staggered back several steps.

"Don't touch me," Hawk said.

The two men stood by the door, glaring at each other.

"Time to go," Fillingham said as he reached past Hawk for the door handle.

Hawk grabbed Fillingham's wrist, an elbow came down on the lever handle, and the two men tumbled out the door.

Christine could hear them crashing down the wooden stairs.

Heck. Christine ran toward the door, hoping that the two didn't kill each other and that Hawk didn't blurt out that they were police officers. She could hear Gail following behind her.

Fillingham and Hawk faced each other by the picnic tables, three feet apart, oranges spotting the ground where they had been dislodged from their bowls.

Christine ran over between them. "I'm not sure what's going on here, Geoff, but we need to remember where we are. Clear heads." Her eyes were wide with warning. *Don't blow Operation Niagara. I haven't found Kelly Darlow yet.*

She stepped close to Hawk and whispered, "I'm Christina. We're undercover. You need to—"

"Leave now," Fillingham interjected, loudly.

Hawk stared at Fillingham for a full five seconds. "Make me."

Fillingham launched himself at Hawk. The two men grappled with each other and crashed down on an outdoor couch, pushing over a wicker chair.

"Stop!" Christine yelled. "Geoff! What are you doing? Stop!"

The two men pushed themselves upright and stared at each other across the upended coffee table, shifting sideways back and forth, preparing for the next tackle.

Christine tried to get each man's attention, calling his name, asking him to look at her, but neither of them would break eye contact.

"You need help?" a male voice said. Christine turned. It was a waiter from the café across the street. He and two men and a woman stood watching Fillingham and Hawk circle each other.

"Isn't that Geoff?" the waiter asked Christine. Some businesses knew Trailer Project staff by name.

"It's fine," Christine said. "Just a misunderstanding."

Fillingham bent and ran into Hawk's midsection, wrapping his arms around his torso. Christine could see him trying to get Hawk to trip over his foot to wrestle him down.

Hawk bent over, grabbed Fillingham's waist and lifted him into the air and threw him into the loveseat, cushions tumbling off.

The waiter jumped onto Hawk's back, one arm under his neck in a choke hold, and the two other men ran at Hawk.

"No!" Christine said, grabbing one man by the arm. "Leave him!"

Hawk turned in circles, the waiter on his back, slipping, until the man lost his grip and slithered to the ground and Hawk fell to one knee.

The two men jumped on Hawk.

Christine heard a commotion. A string of young men was running across Avenue Road toward them, yelling. They wore narrow black pants, dress shirts and had short, slicked-back hair. Greasers.

Christine waved them back with both arms. "Stop. It's okay. We don't need help."

She turned and ran over to Hawk.

"Get off!" She grabbed one man who had Hawk in a headlock and pulled him off. Before she could get to the other man, she was pulled away by the waist.

"Let go of me!" she said as she struggled to regain her foothold.

"Christine!" Hawk said, standing up.

Fillingham and another man launched themselves at Hawk. On-lookers pushed the furniture aside, grabbing at the men who were fighting. One man stood up and punched the assaulter in the stomach. Another greaser joined the melee and punched the assaulter in the back.

There were now twelve or fourteen people pushing and shoving each other, some yelling in glee, others laughing as they tackled one another.

"Christina!"

Christine turned. It was Gail at the open door of the caravan.

Christine yelled, "Get inside. Lock the door. Keep Dr. Reid safe!"

Gail slammed the door shut.

Christine pulled herself up and got shoved aside. There was a central knot of people surrounded by overturned furniture and another small group off to the side. Was Hawk under all the people? She ran toward the shoving mass and grabbed the man on top, pulling him to the ground and pinning him there with her knee.

Suddenly, the parking lot was flooded with red and white light. A police car skidded to a stop ten feet from the dominant group, and two officers jumped out, billies raised. A second police vehicle unloaded two more officers.

"Toronto Police!" yelled the officer in the lead as the four men approached.

Christine froze, unsure what to do next. Would any of the officers recognize her? Should she go inside the caravan? Or hide? Where the heck was Fillingham?

Two of the greasers crouched low behind the group of men and disappeared behind the trailer. Several men stood up, squinting in the car headlights, while a core group in the middle continued fighting, oblivious to the police.

One officer raised a bullhorn to his lips. "Hands in the air! Toronto Police!"

Everyone froze, kneeling on the ground, sitting, standing up, all of them turned toward the police, the tableau basking in alternating white and red light.

On the sidewalk a crowd was gathering, faces shadowed, voices murmuring, asking what had happened.

The officer with the bullhorn must have heard them, too. He was a sergeant; Christine could tell from the badges on his epaulet. He faced Avenue Road. "Back off, everyone. Back to where you came from. The show's over." Another officer approached the group with open arms, pressuring them back to the curb.

"Fucking pigs!" someone shouted.

"Everyone move along," the officer yelled. "Nothing to see here."

"What did they do?" a woman asked. "It's the Trailer Project. They help people!"

A vehicle pulled into the parking lot, forcing the crowd to separate. It was a paddy wagon used to haul away protesters like police did two years ago when youth sat on Yorkville Avenue to protest car traffic.

A female voice near Christine yelled, "What the hell is going on here?"

Christine turned. Dr. Reid stood in the open door of the trailer in her white lab coat, hands on hips, shaking her head as she gazed at the scene: police officers getting the men to stand in a line, the paddy wagon back door swinging open, another officer searching the group.

"Dr. Reid," Christine began, "it was a mis—"

Ignoring Christine, Dr. Reid approached the sergeant. Christine could hear her identifying herself, pointing back to the mobile home, telling them she did not know what happened or why the brawl took place in their lot.

"We got a call that the Trailer Project was under attack," the sergeant said.

Christine walked over. "It wasn't that way."

"Stay where you are, Miss." The sergeant held his hand up in front of Christine.

Dr. Reid said, "Christina is one of my staff. So is Geoff." Dr. Reid gestured to Fillingham, lined up by the paddy wagon.

"Right now," the sergeant said, "they're part of the mix." He addressed an officer standing at the back of the paddy wagon. "Cuff 'em. Get everybody in. We'll get the story at the station."

"Officers," Dr. Reid protested, "Christina and Geoff work with me at the Trailer Project. They are not part of this brawl."

"I don't care if they're the pope, ma'am. We can't sort it out here." He glanced at the sidewalk, where the group had swelled to thirty on-lookers who were booing the cops, calling out "Shame" and "Peace, not war." More youth were jaywalking toward them across Avenue Road.

Dr. Reid said, "I am lodging a complaint, Sergeant—" there was a pause as she leaned closer to check his name tag, "—Brady, with your chief."

Sergeant Brady had his eye on the swelling group of spectators. "Everyone in the wagon. Now!"

"Ma'am," he acknowledged the doctor and hastened to the other officers.

An officer came over to Christine and another man and hand-cuffed them. The rest of the brawlers were getting handcuffed and led to the paddy wagon or the back seat of a police car.

Fillingham was standing by the wagon. When he got handcuffed, a chorus of boos rose from the onlookers.

"Geoff, what's going on?" a female voice said.

Fillingham turned toward the spectators, raising his shackled wrists in the air.

"He's a volunteer!" someone yelled out. "He helps people!" Another person yelled, "Fascist pigs!"

Fillingham said, "The Trailer Project is open from 3:00 p.m. to 3:00 a.m. If you're on a terrible trip, have landlord problems, got a rash in a place you don't want to itch or have been unfairly arrested by the local constabulary, come on down. We got food and coffee—hey!"

A police officer grabbed Fillingham by the shirt collar and dragged him toward the back of the wagon. Fillingham staggered as he tried to keep his balance.

"Don't hurt him!" a female voice pleaded.

The officer pushed Fillingham's head down and shoved him into the vehicle.

Outside, people began singing, "We shall overcome."

"Get in," a police officer said to Christine. He held her elbow as she stepped up into the cab and sat beside Fillingham. In the corner across from her sat Hawk, his dark eyes on her. She shook her head, gesturing for him to be silent, and turned away, praying he wouldn't say anything in front of the other men.

"Fancy meeting you here," Fillingham said, elbowing her.

She turned her body away from her partner. This was Fillingham's fault. If he hadn't launched himself at Hawk, none of this would have happened. Anger made her hands shake, and she clenched them inside her shackles. She was going to kill her partner. He just might have wrecked Operation Niagara.

Greeted by her silence, Fillingham turned to the other men who were joking with each other, excited, jocular friends now that the punching and pushing were over, the ride down to the police station another part of their adventurous night in Yorkville. Three of them were greasers. One man had an eye that was puffing closed while a second had a bleeding nose.

The overhead light illuminated their faces a sallow yellow as the vehicle moved. They all leaned to one side as the wagon turned right. They must be heading to 42 Division, Christine thought.

She kept her eyes down, not wanting to make eye contact with the bantering passengers. The cabin smelled like cologne and male sweat. She wanted to punch the wall in frustration, throw herself against the metal sides. Better yet, throw Hawk, Fillingham and these brawling weekenders and greasers out the paddy wagon door. She had enough of men with their posturing and fighting and egos. Everything was in jeopardy, including her search for a missing sixteen-year-old girl.

When they filed into the police station, Christine orchestrated being the last one out of the paddy wagon. A policewoman was waiting to search her, as was protocol with a female prisoner. It was

Stella Arlin; Christine had worked with her at the Women's Bureau. Stella motioned for Christine to step to the side. Their glances met.

"What the heaven!" Stella said.

Christine shook her head at Stella, warning her with her eyes. The line of men, including Hawk and Fillingham, shuffled off to be searched.

Stella stepped close to Christine, grabbing her by the arm. "What's going on?" she whispered.

Christine looked down. "I'm undercover," she whispered back. "Another officer, Fillingham, is here too. We are working at a community agency in Yorkville. Spring us first, saying we were the victims of the fight. Or pretend we got bail. Some men were onlookers, trying to help us. A waiter named Ben. Also, a man named Hawk Johnson. Let them go too."

"All right," Stella said. In a louder voice she said, "Miss, this way," and led her into a small interview room with a table and two chairs facing each other. The door clicked behind them.

Stella let go of her arm. "Anything else I need to know, Christine?"

"Have the sergeant call PC Malo from Morality." Malo was going to blow his stack if Operation Niagara was jeopardized. A lot of money and manpower were going into the assignment. But he had to know. And who knew if Hawk had said anything to the other prisoners? Not likely, but it was possible.

"All right," Stella said. "I got the story. I'll leave you here to keep you separate from the men. Handcuffs still on, okay?" She left.

Christine sat in the hard wooden chair, arms on the table with her handcuffed wrists. She still had to look like a prisoner. Banging her fists lightly on the table, she tried to tamp down her anger at Fillingham, at Hawk and the hooligans downstairs behind bars.

An hour later, Stella returned. "Met up with a friend of ours—Gail Hilton."

"Gail is here?" Christine asked.

Stella nodded. "She's acting on behalf of the Trailer Project to bail you out." Stella smiled, shaking her head. "What are you mixed up in, Christine? I thought you were strolling Toronto Island, getting a tan while talking to the seagulls."

Christine laughed. Her Toronto Island patrol seemed a million miles away. "Normally, I am. And that assignment looks pretty appealing right now."

An hour later, she was released. Gail had already gone home. Fillingham, Hawk and Ben would be let go shortly.

Stella walked Christine outside. "That Malo guy seems quite the character."

Malo's response to their arrest had been: "Bravo! Good job fitting in. Didn't think you had it in you."

Christine had shaken her head when she heard this. At least Malo didn't think their cover was blown.

"Are you sure you don't want me to call you a cab from here?" Stella asked, scanning the sidewalk. It was four in the morning, the twinkle of streetlights illuminating the empty road.

Christine shook her head. She would walk down to the main street and hail a cab from there; buses didn't start for another two hours.

"Before I go," Christine said, "have you seen this girl? Maybe searched her? She goes by the name Alice Dodgson."

Stella leaned to see the small black-and-white photo of Kelly Darlow that Christine had pulled from her pocket. Christine had made several copies and tried to keep one tucked somewhere on her person, since she never knew when she would have an opportunity to show the photo.

Stella said, "I don't think so. How old is she? Fifteen?"

"In the picture, she's fourteen. She's turned sixteen now and may look rougher."

"Sorry, she doesn't ring a bell. Maybe the Youth Bureau could help."

After exchanging goodbyes, Christine headed toward Yonge Street. She couldn't wait to get home. The officers had been rough, cuffing some of them if they didn't get out of the wagon fast enough, calling them hippies and potheads. Sitting for hours in handcuffs wasn't something she would forget. Jail made you feel dirty and alone.

Not that she wanted company, Christine thought as she walked down the street. She'd had enough of Fillingham and Hawk. All she wanted was a shower and to fall into bed.

Chapter 12

The next morning, Christine made her way along Bloor Street, her legs leaden and her eyes blinking sleepily. She had woken up at ten this morning after four hours of sleep so she could head into work early to clean up last night's mess. Dr. Reid shouldn't have to right the furniture, sweep up the broken lamp pieces and put up the lights and canopy that had been hauled down during the brawl. The doctor had closed up shop right after the melee and taken the medications and some of the equipment to the hospital for safe storage.

Christine turned up Avenue Road, pulling her jacket tighter against the light wind sweeping down the street.

A man stepped out of a side alley.

"Ah!" Christine said, holding out her hands so she wouldn't run into him.

Hawk!

"Can we talk?" he asked.

She stared at her old lover, her tired mind trying to choose a response as people edged by them on the sidewalk. "Not here."

He tilted his head toward the laneway behind the Park Plaza hotel, where valets parked patrons' cars. They passed the back entrance of the hotel and found a bench in the corner of the lot, hidden by the profiles of parked cars.

They sat down on either end of the rough wooden seat. She allowed herself to look at Hawk, really look at him. He was tanned, as if he'd been outdoors, and he looked animated, as if the dust-up and sleepless night hadn't affected him.

He was so handsome, his warm brown eyes looking at her. She melted a bit, sitting there so close to him. She wanted to lean in closer and smell him again.

Hawk broke the silence. "Thank you for getting me out."

She nodded. "How did you know it was me?"

He shrugged. "An Indian doesn't get the benefit of the doubt."

She leaned forward. "You didn't say anything, did you? That you knew Fillingham or me? That we were police officers?"

He shook his head.

"How did you know where to find me?" she asked.

"Mrs. P said you were on summer patrol in the Village."

Christine had mentioned her new assignment to Mrs. Polotov but hadn't revealed that they were working for the Morality Squad. "We're undercover in Yorkville at the Trailer Project, trying to gather information about local crime."

"How's that going?" he asked.

"Good. Until yesterday."

"I didn't come to fight. I came to talk to you."

"What about?"

"You sound suspicious," he said, raising his hands in surrender.

He was wearing a gold ring on the fourth finger of his left hand.

"You're, you're married?" She stood up.

"Wait!" he said, holding one hand up. "Let me explain!"

"What's there to explain?"

"It's not what it seems."

She shook her head. "Your marriage has nothing to do with me."

"Christine, I had to get married."

She turned and walked through the parking lot.

"They were going to take Remi's daughter," he said.

Christine stopped walking but didn't turn around.

His voice was behind her when he added, "Remi, the woman you saw me with, has a drinking problem. She has since she came back from school. The nuns messed her up—made her feel bad about being an Indian. They cut her hair, told her she couldn't speak Anishinabe, that she was a savage."

Christine turned around to face Hawk. She had heard that native children in rural areas were sent to religious schools to give them a good education.

He stepped closer. "Remi is a good person. I've known her all my life. But she's sick. Three months ago, she drove her truck into a tree. When the RCMP saw that she was drunk and Layla was in the car with her, they called Children's Aid, who already had a file on the family. They took Layla away from Remi. Forever, this time."

"How about Layla's father?"

He shook his head. "He's long gone. Disappeared after Layla was born."

Hawk rubbed his face with his hands and then let them drop. "It's my fault too. Remi and I had a fight. That's why she took off in the truck. I told her she had to get a hold of herself, stop the drinking, or I was out of there."

"But you married her," Christine said.

He nodded. "When Remi came home after the accident, after her time in the hospital, and Layla was gone, she went out of her mind. I didn't know what she would do. I thought if Remi and I were married, they would give Layla back."

She followed him back to the bench. She felt nauseous. About the sad tale of alcoholism. The daughter being taken away. That Hawk was married.

Sitting down, she turned to him. "Why did you come to see me?"

He reached for her hand, placing his large one on hers. She let herself be warmed by his palm for a moment, then slid her hand away.

"I wanted you to know the truth about me and Remi."

She nodded. He must love her if he came all the way down from his reserve to tell her this.

"And," he continued, his brown eyes looking into hers. "I have a favor to ask."

Christine pressed her back against the bench. Of course, Hawk had an ulterior motive, like every man she had ever met.

"I've tried to get Layla back," he said. "I went to the courthouse. Showed the judge my marriage license. Talked to the social worker from Children's Aid. Let them know I was Layla's dad now. That there would be another adult in the house, another parent for Layla. That I could help Remi. I was sober and hardworking. I could provide for the three of us, make things work."

"They didn't go for it?" she said.

He shook his head. "All they see is another Indian in a house where there's too much booze. The lawyer I talked to said the marriage was too late. They had already taken Layla away, so I didn't have any legal rights as a parent. He said that maybe Layla would be better off with a foster family or an adopted family, where she would have food, new clothes and an education."

"That doesn't sound so bad." Christine had attended a few calls where children were taken away from parents who were violent, addicts or neglectful. Where the children had licked the mustard jar dry because there was no other food in the fridge and the baby's skin had blistered because she had sat in sodden diapers for three days. And the furniture had been sold for drugs.

He shook his head. "No!" His glance was fierce. "Layla is not better off in a stranger's home. They don't speak Anishinabe; they know nothing of beading or powwows or ceremonies. They will make her feel bad about being Indian, make her want to forget it, just like they did to Remi at school. And look how that turned out."

Christine clasped her hands in her lap. "I don't know what you want from me. Layla's case is decided in court. It has nothing to do with the police. The judge accepted the Children's Aid recommendations of removal and adoption. The only option is to appeal."

"Remi has no money for lawyers. Even if she did, there'll be too many delays. Another family we know went through this. The children were seventeen by the time the courts returned custody, and the kids wanted nothing to do with the parents."

"Hawk, I see you care for Remi. For Layla. But there's nothing I can do." She looked at her watch, then stood up. "I have to go to work."

"I didn't tell you the favor yet," he said, standing up close to her. She caught the scent of sweetgrass that used to stay on her pillow after he left.

"What is it?"

"I want you to find Layla. See if she is in a foster home. Or got adopted."

Christine crossed her arms. "I don't have access to that information. The court transcript in adoption cases will be sealed."

"Can you try?" he asked pleadingly.

"What would be the point?" she asked.

"Because I'm going to get her back."

Christine shook her head after she left Hawk and continued north along Avenue Road. Was Hawk going to kidnap the girl from her foster or adopted home? He would be on the run for the rest of his life. There was no way she would help with that. It wasn't possible to find the girl in a closed adoption.

Why would Hawk ask her this? He knew her job was the most important thing to her, aside from her family. And that there were many challenges to being a female officer.

She slowed her steps to calm herself. Of course, he was upset. He cared about Layla. And he felt somewhat responsible for the accident that led to the girl's removal from the home. But it was a done deal now. And there was nothing either of them could do.

As Christine neared Cumberland Avenue, she spotted the string of lights on the trailer and the canopy. Someone had put them back up.

Fillingham. His name started a simmering in her gut. She was so mad at him. For his petty animosity toward Hawk. For putting the entire undercover operation in jeopardy. For risking the Trailer Project. For potentially shutting down Christine's search for Kelly Darlow.

He was a child. A rich, spoiled, twenty-six-year-old child.

As she approached the trailer, she spotted her partner moving around the lot. He set a cardboard box on the coffee table. Boxes and paper were strewn around his feet. She looked for Gail's yellow motorcycle, but it wasn't there.

He spotted her. "Christina, look what I got for the patio!" He pulled a lava lamp out of the box, globs of red moving in the transparent liquid. "I got it in blue and green as well."

The ceramic lamps must have broken in the melee. Scanning the parking lot, she saw that the furniture had been set right, the two couches aligned at right angles. The canopy over the picnic tables had been set back up. The debris of broken glass, bowls, fruit and food had been swept up and discarded. Two new beanbag chairs in bright yellow and orange were arranged beside the couches. The broken wicker chair had been removed.

He continued to unpack the lava lamps, placing two on the milk-crate end tables and one on the picnic table and connecting them to extension cords. He mustn't have slept after being released from jail. Probably just showered and then went shopping. His penance for starting the brawl. Trying to buy his way back into the good graces of Dr. Reid and Christine.

"Are those groceries?" she asked, pointing at two paper bags.

He nodded.

Christine grabbed the food and went inside the recreational vehicle. She needed to stay as far away from her partner as she could today, or she'd throttle him. And then they'd have another brouhaha. Placing the groceries on the kitchen counter, she looked around. At least the inside of the trailer was undisturbed. Gail had been smart enough to lock everything up and stay inside with Dr. Reid as soon as she saw people running in off the street to join the ruckus.

Christine got busy unpacking the groceries, washing the dishes, making coffee, to keep her mind off last night. What if Dr. Reid came today and fired Fillingham and Christine for being involved in the fight? Right when Operation Niagara was gaining momentum. They continued to add names to Malo's list of drug dealers in the Village as weekenders and clients chatted about their suppliers. And Christine was following Kelly Darlow's trail, even if it was eight months old. It was a start.

And for Fillingham to mess it all up now. Christine shook her head as she placed the apples and bananas in bowls and took them outside.

Fillingham smiled at her as she placed the bowls on the picnic table; he gestured at the lit lava lights on the end tables and the one on the picnic table.

Christine nodded but didn't smile. She returned with more food.

Fillingham came over. "Not talking to me?"

She ignored him, unpacking a tray of muffins, licorice sticks and a box of saltines.

"I got something for you." He handed her a white paper bag.

She didn't want to take it. It was obviously a bribe—the rich kid buying forgiveness.

As she took it, she wondered if she should throw it in the garbage.

"Smell," he urged.

She opened the bag and took a breath. Chocolate. Sugar. And something else.

"It's chocolate, with pecan and caramel." He smiled, eyebrows raised in encouragement.

Darn. He knew she loved anything with a butterscotch flavor.

She crumpled the bag closed.

"Not even tempted?" he asked. He showed her his thumb and index finger squeezed close together. "Not even a little?"

She held the bag up. "This doesn't fix anything."

"I know. You have the right to be mad at me. I'm sorry. I was out of line."

"Out of line! *That's* what you're calling it?" She lowered her voice. "Operation Niagara is in jeopardy. Our employment at the Trailer Project is now questionable, and I'm not even thinking about what would happen if this incident is noted in our file."

"It was a mistake."

"Your first mistake was not letting me handle it. Hawk Johnson was coming to talk to me. I don't need you as a bodyguard. *I* will decide who I speak with. Not you. And if you thought Hawk might blow our cover, then there are options aside from throwing him through a door. From Dr. Reid's perspective, you attacked a client coming to the Trailer Project for help. And started a brawl that shut down our services and got a bunch of young people jailed."

"Well, I wasn't in control of that. They just joined."

She glared at him.

He placed one hand over his heart. "I get it. I messed up. I was concerned about you. And I thought he might blow our cover."

Christine crossed her arms.

"I know, I know," he said. "It's not an excuse for my behavior. But I want you to know that I'm really, really sorry." He took her hand and bent on one knee. "Can you forgive me?"

"I see you made up," a female voice said.

They turned to see Dr. Reid.

Christine quickly pulled her hand away, and Fillingham stood up.

"You cleaned up," Dr. Reid added, looking around the lot.

"Dr. Reid, I'm so sorry," Fillingham said, placing his palms together. "My sincerest apologies for my behavior."

Dr. Reid stood in a short trench coat over brown chinos. Her hair looked uncombed, the circles under her eyes darker. Her usual good-humored expression was missing.

"I bought you this!" Fillingham hustled over to a large box and held it up to show the picture of a coffee urn on the side. "It's the best they have. It can make twenty-five cups at a shot."

The doctor had been complaining about the eight-cup coffeepot in the kitchen and how they had to fill it up four or five times a shift.

"Mmm," she said.

"I'll rinse it out and set it up on the picnic table." He held up a grocery bag. "Bought more coffee, too. A dark roast. Peruvian." Again, another of the doctor's favorites.

"I can't decide whether to fire you, Geoff," Dr. Reid said.

Christine said, "I think—"

"Don't say anything." Her finger pointed at Christine. "You're no innocent. I saw you throwing people around."

"I was—" She thought better of it and closed her mouth.

Christine and Fillingham waited, hands clasped like two penitents.

"I'm not sure what the deal is between the two of you," Dr. Reid gestured at them, "but it can't interfere with the operation of the Trailer Project. We serve Villagers and all visitors to Yorkville."

Christine and Fillingham listened silently.

"When a prospective client walks through our door, we help them. End of story. Understood?"

The two officers nodded.

Thank goodness, Christine thought. Dr. Reid was not going to fire them. Operation Niagara could continue. Christine could find Kelly Darlow.

"And when you're finished out here," Dr. Reid said, "the two of you can come inside and clean the latrine." She climbed the four steps to the trailer door. "And I'll take my coffee with two creams."

Chapter 13

"Hi everyone. Nice to see you again." Julie smiled at the three under-cover officers sitting around the table inside the Toucan. The group had seated themselves in Julie's serving area. Another waitress with long ash-blonde hair was taking orders from a group at the back of the restaurant.

Julie passed each of them a paper menu.

Christine skimmed the offerings. Coffee, wine, beer. Sandwiches. Desserts. Chili. Hamburgers and hot dogs.

"Chocolate ants?" Gail pointed to the bottom of the menu.

"Fourteen dollars!" Christine exclaimed.

Julie waved them off. Her nails were painted neon pink. "Only on weekends, when the naked chef is working."

"Remind me not to come here on weekends," Gail said.

Julie said, "Can I get you guys drinks before I take your dinner order?"

"I'll have a beer," Gail said. Malo had told them they should drink a bit when they were out in the Village to fit in, get to know people, start conversations. That was how they'd find nuggets of informa-tion. When they'd asked Dr. Reid if they could grab a drink while on their breaks as they listened to music or sat on a patio, she conceded to one drink. If they returned tipsy or drunk, they'd be cut off.

Christine wasn't a big drinker, but after last night, she felt like one. She needed something to get through the shift. "Red wine, please."

"A beer for me, my lady." Fillingham smiled up at Julie, their eyes meeting.

A few minutes later, Julie returned with a tray of drinks. "Here you go," she said, placing the beverages in front of the three friends.

"I'm treating," Fillingham said.

"That's awfully nice of you." Julie batted her false eyelashes at him.

"He's buying his penance," Gail said.

Julie put her hands on her hips. "Have you been a bad boy?"

"More like an idiot," Gail said. Christine gave a snort of agreement.

Julie ignored Gail's comment. "Were you protecting the Trailer Project from the wicked men trying to get inside? Who was it? Bikers? Greasers? An addict?"

"Hah!" Gail protested. "That's not how it went down."

"No?" queried Julie. "Lance from the Purple Onion said Geoff threw someone out of the trailer—someone getting out of hand. And you," she looked at Fillingham, "showed him who was boss."

Fillingham smiled, then met Christine's glare. "It was...it was just a guy in the wrong place at the wrong time."

"Geoff," Gail said, "he took one step into the caravan, and you pushed him out the door."

Julie wagged her finger at him. "What a troublemaker."

"A troublemaker who almost got us fired," Christine said, "who started the melee of twenty people jumping on top of each other, breaking furniture and tearing down the lights."

"Wow," Julie said in mock horror.

Gail said, "We had to shut down the program for the night. Get the doctor safely back to the hospital. And I spent the rest of the night at 42 Division sorting things out."

"A brief ride in the paddy wagon," Fillingham said. "Got to know a few greasers. Bonded with the café staff. None the worse for wear, right, Christina?"

Christine glared at him.

"The Trailer Project staff is having all the fun," Julie said.

"It seems exciting around here." Christine pointed to a poster on the wall advertising the Saturday night body-painting extravaganza.

Julie looked over at the poster. "I'm doing that!" she squealed.

"What do you mean?" Fillingham asked.

"We've been practicing," Julie responded. She showed them her calf, where a chain of daisies had been painted up the back.

"How far up does it go?" he asked.

Julie smiled back. "Stick around, and maybe I'll show you."

"Tone it down," Gail said.

Julie stuck her tongue out at Gail. "Anyway," Julie continued, "Marie and I," she gestured at the other waitress, "are going to paint each other's bodies. Peace signs, flowers. I've been practicing a dove."

"What part of your body?" Fillingham asked.

"We're not naked, silly," Julie said, swiping at his shoulder with one hand. "We have bathing suits on."

"What's the point?" Gail asked.

"Entertainment!" Julie said. "Art appreciation! I don't even have to wait on tables that night. Just go around and chat, see if anyone wants to add another rose or peace sign. Sal says I have fabulous social skills."

"Or something," Gail muttered under her breath, then took a sip of beer.

"What's your problem, Gail?" Julie asked, frowning.

Gail shrugged. "Not my scene."

"What *is* your scene?" Julie asked. "The Nile Room?"

The Nile Room was frequented by lesbians and featured performances by men in women's clothing.

Gail met Julie's glance steadily. "I'm more of a homebody."

After a few seconds, Julie said, "Let me check if your sandwiches are ready."

Gail, Christine and Fillingham sat in uncomfortable silence. Julie could be nasty, honing in on a person's Achilles, pressing until she got a reaction.

In a few minutes, Julie was back with their orders. "Enjoy!" she said, giving them her best waitress smile. "And don't forget to tip big!"

"If the service is good," Fillingham teased.

She leaned over and whispered, loud enough for the rest of them to hear, "How about I meet you later for a quality check."

Chapter 14

"Crouch down lower," Christine said as she faced Gail on the outdoor mat.

Gail knew Christine was a wrestler and had sparred with Fillingham on Toronto Island during their breaks. Gail was keen to learn new tackling techniques, so today she had pushed aside the outdoor furniture and placed a large mat on the rug. Dr. Reid said wrestling was okay as long as no one misconstrued it as fighting, provoking another street rumble. When it was slow, the doctor encouraged them to hang outside so people would know they were open.

"Feet farther apart," Christine advised. Both Gail and Christine were in jeans—not the perfect outfit for wrestling, but better than the policewoman's uniform of jacket and skirt. It was midnight, and despite the three lava lamps and hanging lights, it was shadowy and hard to see Gail's hands. But officers took down suspects day and night, so this was good practice.

"You're strong, Gail," Christine said, "and your base is solid. Be ready to move your feet so I don't push you over."

Gail bent her knees. They both reached out, arms extended, grappling to find a hold on each other.

A roar sounded from the street and grew deafening as an unmuffled motorcycle turned into their parking lot. Christine and Gail let go of each other, standing up to watch the motorcyclist.

He was a gang member, Christine could tell. She had seen bikers around the Village with their motorcycles parked in front of the café tables. The man's dark, curly hair, almost in ringlets, reached his shoulders. He had no helmet. Engine off, he dismounted. On the back of his black leather jacket was the word *GRIZZLIES* in white and red lettering and underneath a large patch of a grizzly bear with bared teeth.

The Grizzlies were one of the four biker gangs Malo said frequented the Village and were possibly dipping their toes into the drug trade.

Christine and Gail put on their shoes. Show time.

"Hi there!" Christine said. "Welcome to the Trailer Project. I'm Christina, this is Gail." She pointed to her peer. "How can we help you?"

"What were you doing?" he motioned to the mat. "Fighting?"

Christine laughed, waving away his guess. "No, just wrestling. Had a quiet moment, so we were practicing holds."

"Show me," he said. It was a command.

Christine said, "We were just horsing around."

He crossed his arms.

Christine looked at Gail, who gave a nod. Malo would want them to engage with the biker.

"I'm teaching Gail a few moves," Christine said as she slid her shoes off. "I used to be on the wrestling team."

"Really?" he said.

"I know! A girl! Shocking!" She flashed her best Christina smile.

Back on the mat, Christine and Gail grappled. As their heads lowered near each other, Gail whispered, "Give him a show."

With a quick swipe of her leg, Christine knocked Gail off her feet onto all fours, then pressed on top of her. They broke again, and Christine weaved in and out, gauging for the moment where Gail would be off-balance. She forced Gail to stumble to the ground. The next time she let Gail get her down and then reversed out of the hold, twisting and rolling so Gail was under her. Gail smacked the carpet with her hand in surrender.

Christine helped her friend up. "We better get back to work," she exclaimed. "Break time's over." She wiped her brow with the back of her hand.

The biker approached. "Impressive."

Gail replied, "Comes in handy when a client gets out of hand."

He laughed, hands in the air. "I've been warned."

Christine waved Gail off. "Ignore her. Why don't you come inside, and we can tell you about our services." She climbed the stairs and opened the door. The interior light shone on his face as he stood at the base of the stairs. He had dark eyebrows, a trim beard and mustache, and a few lines around his blue eyes. He looked twenty-eight, maybe thirty years old.

Christine wondered what he saw as he looked up at her. A tall woman with long, straight brown hair past her shoulders. Natural-looking, with a bit of makeup. Warm and welcoming and open.

He climbed the stairs, pausing in front of her, their bodies close together. They were exactly the same height. He smelled like leather and cigarettes and motorcycle oil. And he was mesmerizing close up. The glossy curls. The deep blue eyes.

"Sorry, I didn't catch your name," she said.

"Sloan," he said.

"Sloan," she confirmed, smiling back, their glance holding.

Gail called from the parking lot, "I'll hang out here and tidy up."

Inside, Dr. Reid was sitting on a couch, perusing an open file, coffee mug in hand. Fillingham must still be in the legal office at the other end, reviewing client cases.

"Dr. Reid," Christine began, "this is Sloan."

"Hi Sloan," Dr. Reid said, standing up. "Did you want to chat?"

"It's confidential?" he asked.

Dr. Reid said, "Absolutely." She grabbed her file and motioned him to follow her. "This way."

Christine had to hand it to the doctor. Regardless of a client's appearance—strung out, hung over, twitchy, greaser, hippie, weekender or biker—as long as they weren't violent or abusive, she didn't blink an eye. Just asked how she could help.

Christine could hear the low rumble of conversation between doctor and client, but she couldn't make out any words. She got busy tidying the kitchen area, washing a few dishes, dumping the grounds from the small coffeepot.

Dr. Reid's office door clicked open. "Gail," she called. "Can you bring me a suture kit from room two?"

"Gail's outside," Christine answered. "I'll get it."

Kit in hand, Christine tapped the half-opened door of Dr. Reid's office.

"Come in," Dr. Reid said.

Sloan sat in a chair in a black t-shirt, a four-inch wound on his forearm puckered open like a mouth, oozing blood. A blood-soaked rag lay on the floor below him. He, or someone else, must have wrapped the cut in a tourniquet to stem the blood flow.

Christina gaped. "Why didn't you say you were injured? We would have taken you to Dr. Reid right away."

Sloan tilted his head up at her, smiling. "And miss the show?"

"Wash up," Dr. Reid said to Christine. "I'll get you to help me with this. Grab the Betadine."

Christine blinked in surprise.

Move it, she admonished herself. This was her chance to get to know a biker and find out about the crimes and the players in the Village.

Christine washed up, placed a sterile gauze pad underneath Sloan's arm and then swabbed the cut with Betadine.

He sucked in his breath at the antiseptic's sting.

"I'll do a local," Dr. Reid said.

He waved her off with his other hand. "I'm okay."

Dr. Reid paused at the cupboard she had opened. "You want me to stitch you up without freezing?"

"Don't like needles," he said. "Got something else?"

"Ibuprofen. Acetaminophen," the doctor answered.

"Codeine? Valium?" he asked hopefully.

Dr. Reid looked at him, eyebrows raised.

"Scotch?" he asked.

"The only alcohol on the premises is rubbing alcohol," Dr. Reid said.

"That'll do," Sloan said.

The doctor told Christine to grab the ibuprofen. Christine handed him two tablets and a glass of water. "Are you sure you don't want the area frozen?"

He swallowed the pills. "I'll be okay if you hold my hand."

"You look pretty tough," Christine commented.

"Only on the outside." He smiled up at her, the lines around his eyes crinkling.

She felt her breath hitch for a second. He was dangerous and unexpectedly charming.

Dr. Reid opened the suture kit and placed a packet of catgut, a needle driver and scissors on a sterilized tray on the counter. "Ready to move up from bananas, Christina?"

Christine's eyes widened. Dr. Reid knew she had first-aid training, so Christine had helped Gail treat clients with abrasions and sprained ankles. Last week, she had practiced suturing by stitching bananas, but she wasn't sure if she was ready to practice on a biker who might be part of the local crime scene.

"I'm a step up from fruit. Good to know," Sloan said.

Dr. Reid addressed Christine. "I'll watch you thread the needle."

Christine pulled on rubber gloves, then pushed the catgut through the needle and tied off the end.

Dr. Reid pulled a chair over so that Christine was facing Sloan.

Christine sat down, needle and thread in hand.

"Tuck in closer," Dr. Reid commanded. "Wipe the area with the topical anesthetic."

Christine shuffled her chair closer to Sloan. He was so close, she could hear him breathing.

"This is cozy," he said.

Dr. Reid stood beside them. "The laceration is straight, knife wound, I'm guessing?" She looked at Sloan, who shrugged.

"Five-inch, non-serrated, boning knife is my guess," the doctor said.

His head jerked back in surprise.

Christine knew that anything longer than two and a half inches was illegal.

Dr. Reid continued, "I'm choosing a running stitch, which is continuous and easier. Christina, what angle should the needle be to the skin?"

"Ninety," she answered.

The doctor nodded. "Place the needle flush to the skin. Press it through from the same side, making sure it comes through the skin on the other side at the same distance from the laceration. When most of the needle is through, use your driver to pull it all the way out."

Christine carefully pulled the needle through the skin. She heard a slight inhale from Sloan, but that was all.

"That's right," Dr. Reid said. "Keep the tension the same, tight enough that the two sides of the wound meet, slightly elevated, without the seam puckering."

Christine carefully sewed two more stitches under the doctor's watchful eyes.

"You look so serious," he said to Christine.

Christine focused on the needle. She didn't want to mess this up.

Dr. Reid regarded the examination table where Sloan had thrown his coat, the gray inside liner stained burgundy-black. "Hydrogen peroxide removes blood stain."

"I'll put that on my grocery list," he said.

"I'm sure we have some around here," Dr. Reid said. She opened the cupboard above the sink and moved bottles around. She turned to Christine. "You okay here for a minute?"

Christine nodded.

Dr. Reid said, "I'll check the other office." She exited, and Christine had a view down the aisle to the kitchen. Fillingham sat on the couch, reading the local underground newsletter, *Satyrday*. Their glance met, Christine's hand poised over Sloan's arm, then the door swung partway closed.

"You work here every night?" Sloan asked.

"Most nights. Shifts are three to three." She pushed the tip of the needle into his skin.

The muscles in his arms tightened. She completed three more stitches.

"What's your story?" he asked.

She looked up. "My story?" She paused. "I'm working at the Trailer Project for the season. I'm a social work student."

"A do-gooder."

She smiled. "Most of the time. You saw me wrestle. I'm not always sweet."

"Look like the innocent flower, but be the serpent under it."

She laughed. "That sounds menacing. Is it Shakespeare or something?"

"My lady is literate," he said.

"Hardly." She looked down at the wound to complete the last stitch. "All I remember from high school English are the witches cackling in *Macbeth*: 'Fair is foul, and foul is fair.'"

"Ah, so you *are* a witch."

She met his glance. "That's unkind. Especially since I'm patching you up."

"Do not denigrate the weird sisters," he said.

She tied off the thread and then trimmed the excess yarn with scissors.

"You have witchcraft in your lips," he said.

She laughed again. "How so?"

"Think about the word 'witch.' Bewitching. Beguiling."

"It's a compliment?" Her tone was skeptical as she taped gauze over the wound.

"I'm under your spell," he said.

The door opened. Fillingham held up a brown bottle of hydrogen peroxide. "I found this in the kitchen. Dr. Reid said you wanted some." He looked at Christine before placing it on the counter.

Sloan looked from Fillingham to Christine. "You two got something going?"

"Why would you say that?" she asked.

He shrugged. "Just a feeling I'm getting." He pulled his sleeve down over the bandage. "That's okay. I like competition. Makes me work harder."

Sloan stood up and addressed Fillingham. "She's beautiful, and, therefore, to be wooed."

Fillingham's brow furrowed.

The biker turned to Christine and bowed. "She is woman, and therefore to be won."

"Let's get a sandwich," Christine said to Fillingham after Sloan roared out of the parking lot. She needed to talk to her partner about what had just happened.

"Can we pick something up for you, Dr. Reid?" Christine asked as she stood at the caravan door.

The doctor poked her head out of a side office. "Egg salad sandwich from Bruno's would be great."

"Dr. Reid, are you okay if I head out too?" Gail asked from the kitchen. "I'll be back in ten minutes."

"Sure. Take a break. Gail, if you are coming back shortly, then maybe Christina and Geoff can mingle with the masses after the two of you eat. Bring the supplies with you."

"Sure," Fillingham said. He picked up the knapsack and shoulder bag from the kitchen floor, and the three headed out.

"How'd it go with the biker?" Gail asked as they reached the east side of Avenue Road.

Christine turned to Fillingham. "What just happened?"

"What?" he said.

"What's going on?" Gail looked from Christine to Fillingham.

"He thinks we're together!" Christine said.

Gail said, "Who does?"

"Sloan," Christine said. "The biker. He assumed that Fillingham and I were together."

Fillingham said. "I think it's a good plan."

"No, it's not," Christine said.

Gail said, "Why is it a good plan, Geoff?"

Fillingham indicated they should start walking, and the trio headed east along Yorkville Avenue. "Sloan said he likes a challenge. A rivalry. He'll be back to court Christine."

Gail nodded. "Makes sense. Sloan is the only biker connection we have. And he's a Grizzly. We should see if it goes anywhere."

Christine threw her hands in the air. "I don't want to act like Geoff's girlfriend."

"It's the role of a lifetime," Fillingham said.

"Not funny," Christine said.

"I see you need some practice," he said.

She elbowed him in the ribs.

Gail said, "All right, all right. Time out. We could call Malo for advice, but we know what he'd say."

Fillingham answered, "Do whatever it takes to lure Sloan in."

"I think I need a drink. One with lots of alcohol," Christine said and headed toward the café.

Chapter 15

Christine's steps slowed as she spotted Deputy Darlow standing outside an unmarked police car near her apartment. When he caught her glance, he gestured to the passenger seat.

How did he know when she left her apartment for work? Or what route she took to the bus stop? He had access to information as senior staff, she reminded herself, including her work schedule. And he had visited her apartment once before to caution her about the dangers of policing.

She got into the passenger seat.

He looked at her with his intense, silent stare.

She reminded herself that he was the parent of a missing girl, not just her superior looking for infractions. "Sir, as I mentioned in last week's phone call, I've been recirculating in the Village to chat with staff and visitors about Kelly. I have no new information aside from the record store and café sightings that I mentioned to you before."

For the past six weeks, Christine had made weekly phone calls to the deputy to update him on the search for his daughter. She called him at his office under the name of Mavis Miller, usually on Fridays.

"Do you have a more recent picture than the school photo?" she asked. "It would help people identify her."

He frowned, looking older and tired. "She wouldn't let us take pictures in the year before she left."

"I thought I would expand my search to the bars on Yonge Street. The venues host rock and roll bands rather than folk. If Kelly likes music, she might hang out there."

"There's drugs there, so it's an option."

"I assume you check the list of daily arrests?" Christine said.

He nodded. "She's smart that way. Even when high, she makes sure she doesn't get caught." He paused. "However, I did see your name on the arrest list."

Christine scowled. Was he being funny? "That was a misunderstanding. They let us go right away." Then a flutter of panic. "It won't go in our file, will it, sir?"

He shook his head.

Christine exhaled with relief. "The Morality Squad is creating a map of Village drug suppliers: the hippies, weekenders, out-of-towners, Americans, bikers and greasers. Do you know the name of Kelly's dealer??"

He looked out the window, thinking. "At first, she hung around with university students. They dressed like hippies, but they were kids from the suburbs. They smoked marijuana. I'm guessing that's not her crowd anymore."

"Of the groups I listed, who might she be affiliated with?" she asked.

He shook his head. "I don't know. The easiest drugs? Free drugs? The hardest drugs?"

"The greasers and bikers seem to sell the harder stuff."

He looked down. "It makes me sick to think about it, but they may be her source." He looked up again. "In the past, Kelly has followed the flow of easy drugs in and out of Toronto, heading from one party to the next. She may be in Kingston or Ottawa for all I know."

"You said you give Kelly money regularly," she said. "That's good. It means she isn't desperate. She has money for food and shelter."

He shook his head. "I'm sure it's gone in a weekend."

"Yorkville is getting busier now that it's June," she said. "Hopefully she'll surface, even if she's been out of town."

He looked ahead. "Once a week, I check Jarvis Street." At night, Jarvis was lined with prostitutes, many of them addicts like Kelly. "I haven't seen her."

Thank goodness, Christine thought. What a terrible thing for a parent to have to do. "We're heading to the church's youth drop-in tonight. Dr. Reid says it's an eclectic group, including many drug users. I'll see if anyone has seen Kelly."

He nodded and started the car. "I'll drop you off a few blocks from Yorkville."

Christine walked onto the lot after her meeting with the deputy.

Julie stepped out from behind the trailer. "Aren't you the sneaky one?" she said, approaching Christine.

Christine stopped in her tracks. "What's going on, Jewels?"

Julie sat down at the picnic table, and Christine reluctantly sat down across from her. Julie was in a snit, and Christine could make an educated guess why: *Fillingham.*

"Would you like a cup of coffee?" Christine pointed to the urn.

Julie shook her head.

Christine poured herself a coffee and waited.

Julie glowered at Christine. She was dressed for work in a white minidress with a silver chain belt, big eyeliner and frosted lipstick. Settling back, she fixed Christine with a flat brown stare. "You've always had your eye on Geoff. From day one."

Christine said, "Don't be ridiculous. We're partners. That's all."

Julie tilted her head. "What's it like to be so desperate that you contrive a romance?"

Christine tried to ignore Julie's remark. "Jewels, I think you got a mixed-up version of the story." Her voice lowered in case there were clients in the caravan. "Geoff must have told you what happened. We got a biker client. He thought Geoff and I were together. It grabbed his attention."

Julie pointed a manicured finger at Christine. "Geoff doesn't know you like I do. The girl who's never had a boyfriend. Who's desperate for love."

Despite herself, Christine could feel tears prick her eyelids. "You're being mean. It's for work. That's all. I'm not thrilled about it either."

"Geoff's a nice guy," Julie continued. "Too nice. He pities you. That's why you're partners."

Christine had heard enough. "You seem worried, Jewels. Concerned someone else is playing with your toy in the sandbox?"

Julie's mouth tightened.

Christine exhaled. This was out of hand. "It wasn't my idea. Or Geoff's. It was the biker's. End of story."

Julie smiled. "I don't believe you for a second."

Christine stood up. "I'm sorry about that. And I'm sorry that you have so little confidence in Geoff's feelings for you."

Chapter 16

"Julie talked to me," Christine said to Fillingham as they walked up Avenue Road, hand in hand, Sarah beside them. It felt funny to hold her partner's hand and walk at his pace. Like she was on a leash.

The trio was heading to the local church's youth drop-in program, which opened its basement nightly for young people to dance, congregate and socialize.

"That's sounds ominous," Sarah said with a laugh. She was wearing low-riding jeans and a floral top. With her short, curly mop, she looked like a cross between a folksinger and a country girl.

"It was," Christine said. "Did she talk to you?" she asked Fillingham.

He nodded but stayed silent. He must have gotten chewed out, too.

"She's not happy about this." Christine raised their linked hands. Sarah said, "That's not surprising."

Dr. Reid hadn't been surprised either. "I knew it!" she had said when Geoff told her they were a couple.

"It's just work," Christine said to Sarah and Fillingham through gritted teeth. She could feel her hand tightening in his grasp.

"Ow!" he said. "Loosen up. Can we talk about something else?"

Sarah gave him a light punch on the shoulder. "Sure. What's this about you juggling on Friday night at the Trailer Project?"

His face lit up as he pointed to himself. "Introducing Geoff, the Juggling Joker."

"Wow!" Sarah said, winking at Christine. "That should bring in the clients."

"That's the hope!" he said.

"Joker's the right word," Christine added.

Fillingham stuck his tongue out at her.

"What did Malo say was our goal tonight at the drop-in?" Christine asked as the trio walked across the sidewalk.

Fillingham said. "See who's in attendance. Check out the hippies and visitors but look for activity by the greasers and bikers."

"What's this about a Russian influence?" Sarah asked.

"Could be a new player in town," Fillingham said.

"Dr. Reid said to befriend women who looked like prostitutes. They're often vulnerable," Christine said.

Sarah nodded. "We can check if they are pimped by their boyfriend. If there is a system going, we could get Morality to follow up."

"Ask who supplies the prostitute with drugs," Fillingham suggested.

Sarah said, "I don't think they will flip on their boyfriends or pimps. They're too afraid."

"Dr. Reid wants us to check for youth in distress," Christine said, "on a bad trip or really high. Youth who look undernourished. Anyone who might need a bed for the night. And let people know the weekly VD clinic at the hospital has started."

"Busy, busy, busy," Fillingham said.

They reached the side entrance to the old stone church, the crumbling concrete stairs littered with cigarette butts and squashed paper cups. Fillingham let go of Christine's hand and headed down the stairs to the basement doors. They could hear the vibration of music through the two wooden doors.

"And don't forget, ladies," he said as he opened the door, "let's have fun!"

"Wow, crowded," Christine said as they entered the wide expanse of the church's open basement. The place was humming, crowds talking, sitting on chairs and beanbags and other groupings of impromptu furniture. Groups were sitting cross-legged on throw rugs and afghans on the wooden floor. Christine smelled popcorn and baked goods, intertwined with the scents of sweat, perfume, patchouli and cigarette smoke.

They moved through the crowd. Christine tried to see if she recognized anyone from her six weeks in the Village, be they Trailer Project clients, café staff or familiar weekenders.

A young woman walked around selling boas to support the legal fund for American draft dodgers settling in Toronto. Fillingham bought three.

He placed a neon-green boa around Christine's neck. "For those green with envy about your boyfriend."

She rolled her eyes. "Any more disgruntled girlfriends hiding in the bushes?"

He looked conspiratorially left and right. "Lots," he whispered.

A smile twitched Christine's mouth.

Sarah waved at a group of women. "I'm going to head out on my own. Shall we meet in an hour by the door to compare notes?"

Christine and Fillingham nodded, and Sarah headed across the floor.

Fillingham took Christine's hand.

Christine said, "You know, we only have to act like a couple in front of Sloan. We don't have to do this now."

He pulled her along. "Maybe. But I was thinking there were advantages to being viewed as a pair."

"Like what?" she said.

"People are less suspicious. More likely to open up. We can befriend other couples."

"I don't know."

Fillingham pointed to the food and beverage tables along one wall. "Let me buy your favor, Christina."

"Pretty sure the juice and popcorn are free."

Fillingham scanned the area. "They have coffee and hot chocolate."

"Now we're talking," she said.

They arrived at the tables staffed by church volunteers, youth wearing jeans, beads and medallions, looking like the rest of the milling crowd. Fillingham and Christine introduced themselves and summarized the Trailer Project services.

"Can we leave some cards on the table?" Christine asked.

The female volunteer, Anna, nodded and made them coffees. She was short, with long, wavy hair and big brown eyes.

"Can you flag us if you see anyone that might need help?" Fillingham asked.

"It's a bit early," Anna said. "We usually get the harder cases later in the night."

"Okay. We'll be back for a coffee refill."

"Check the bathrooms," Anna said. "People go there if they're not feeling well. Or sometimes outside the church by the doors."

"Here." Christine handed Fillingham a stack of cards from her shoulder bag. "Let's split up and check the bathrooms."

Alone, she could ask around for Kelly. On the way to the washroom, she showed the teen's photo to two volunteers. Neither of them recognized her.

Walking away, Christine spotted a man in a dark shirt and white clerical collar. "Reverend McDonald," Christine said when he was within earshot. He was in his late thirties, with shaggy brown hair and a round face. She introduced herself.

"Welcome," he said, enfolding her hand in both of his. "And please call me Dougie. Dr. Reid is a friend of the church. She does wonderful things for youth at the Trailer Project. She is such an advocate."

Dr. Reid had said positive things about the late-night church program, despite the rampant drug use. Originally, it was a place for greasers to congregate, give them an opportunity to dance and socialize. But over the years, the program attracted youth from all walks of life: hippies, drug users, weekenders, tourists, drug dealers and bikers looking to pick up women. Malo said you could buy your drug of choice at Dougie's youth program, from Mary Jane to heroin to LSD. It was a bona fide, church-supported, grant-funded haven for drugs.

"Reverend, Dougie," Christine began, "someone came by our trailer looking for her missing friend, Alice. Have you seen her?" She showed him the photo.

"So many people come through," Dougie said, leaning down to get a closer look. "There was a girl who looked a bit like her here this winter. Tall and thin. I remember because there's fewer people then, mostly Villagers."

Christine felt a flicker of excitement. "When did you last see her?"

"Must have been December or January."

Five months ago. The most recent sighting Christine had found.

"Was she with anyone? A friend? A boyfriend?"

"I'm sorry. I didn't notice." He put a finger on his lip, thinking. "I recall she was missing a bottom tooth."

Christine frowned. Had Kelly fallen? Or had someone punched her?

"Do you have any idea where she is now?"

He shook his head. "You can try the second-floor apartments around the Village. It drives the landlords crazy, but Villagers can be generous, allowing others to crash in their apartment. They often pool resources."

"You mean drugs?" she asked.

He shrugged. "And food. The newspaper. Books. Where to go for a free hot meal. They'd tell each other about the Trailer Project. Things like that. Yorkville can be transitory," he added, smiling at someone going by. "Young people drift in and out."

"Can you let me know if you see her? Call me at the Trailer Project?" Christine asked.

"She's not in trouble?" Dougie asked.

Christine shook her head. "No. People are worried about her." That was the truth.

Dougie nodded and moved on to greet other people.

In the woman's washroom, Christine checked inside the stalls. Graffiti was scrawled over the back door and side of the stalls: peace signs, slogans like "Power to the People" and "No More War." A comment that Jill was a backstabbing bitch. Nothing about an Alice or Kelly.

Two women stood in front of the washroom mirrors. Christine went over to the sink and washed her hands. The mirrors looked old, their reflection wavy, like a fun-house mirror. The bathroom wall was rectangular stone bricks with pipes and vents overhead.

Christine addressed the woman with long red braids. "Having a good time?"

The women nodded but remained silent.

"I work down the street at the Trailer Project," Christine explained, digging in her bag for a business card. "If you've had a fight with your boyfriend, feeling blue, out of money, have problems with alcohol or drugs, we can help you out."

The girl with frizzy blond hair asked, "You some God outfit?"

Christine shook her head. "No. We have a doctor who helps Villagers—no questions asked. We have social workers, psychologists and lawyers, if your landlord is on your case. All free."

Each of the women took a business card.

"Even better," Christine added, "there's juggling on Friday nights. Free coffee and donuts until 3:00 a.m."

"You're a circus?" the braided woman asked.

Christine laughed. "Feels like it some days." She took out a picture of Kelly. "Have you seen this girl? Alice?"

"Why?" the blonde asked.

"Her friend hasn't seen her for a while," Christine said.

"Did you ask Dougie?" the blonde asked.

Christine nodded. "She was here this winter."

"Does she like art?" the blond asked.

"I think so," Christine answered. "Why?"

"Carlos might know," the braided woman said.

"Who's that?" Christine asked.

"He's the artist. Gallery Europa. He paints everybody."

"The art gallery right beside the Boathouse?" Christine said.

The braided woman nodded. "Yeah. People hang there. Watch him paint."

Christine thanked them and left the washroom. She bumped shoulders with someone and staggered. An arm reached out to steady her.

"Christina!" Sloan said.

He was here. Sloan. The Grizzly biker.

"Sorry about that," she said and made herself give him a big smile. "I'm clumsy." She needed to keep him here talking. Get any information she could from him that might help Operation Niagara.

"You following me?" he asked, smiling.

She crossed her arms. "I think, fair sir, that you are following *me*." Her glance strayed down to his arm under his leather jacket. "How are you healing?"

He nodded. "Good."

"No redness, swelling? No temperature?"

"No, ma'am," he said. "I'm the perfect patient."

"Your stitches need to be removed in seven to ten days. Come back to the Trailer for the procedure."

"Will you do it?"

"Sure." She had never removed stitches before, but it couldn't be any more challenging than stitching a biker without a local anesthetic.

"I'm here with Geoff, spreading the word about our services." She paused. "Why are *you* here? I didn't take you for a church boy."

He pressed his hand against his chest. "I'm a creature of God, just like you." His chin started bobbing to the beat of a song as he scanned the crowd. "I like the music, the ambiance."

"It's very social."

"Let's dance." It was a command, not a request.

She hesitated. She didn't want to seem too eager.

"C'mon." He held his hand out.

"I guess I can take a break."

A clutch of twenty people was fast-dancing to the music in the middle of the basement. She couldn't see any Grizzlies, but two men in narrow tailored pants and white shirts were dancing with young women in tight dresses. Greasers.

Fillingham had chatted with three greasers in their shared jail cell after the rumble. The trio didn't sell drugs but told Fillingham that they had friends who were dealers. Marijuana was plentiful. The harder drugs like heroin were more difficult to procure.

When Sloan and Christine neared the group of dancers, he took her hand and pulled her closer. His hold was gentle and loose as they swayed side to side. He twirled her and pulled her back again.

"You're good," she said, smiling.

"I could cha-cha and swing dance if you like."

"Really?"

"My parents used to dance."

"Your parents taught you?"

He laughed. He had an infectious smile, the bottom teeth just a little crooked. "Are you surprised I have parents or surprised that they taught me to dance?"

"My mom and stepdad just drank. And fought." Why was she telling him this?

"My dad broke my mother's arm when I was ten. His shirt wasn't ironed the way he liked it."

She and Sloan had more in common than she thought. They were quiet for a minute, and he turned her under his arm and back around again.

"Is that why you like the Village?" she asked as she swayed in his arms. "For the music?"

"One reason." He smiled. "If music is the food of love, play on!"

"Isn't that from *Twelfth Night*?" she asked.

"My lady is a scholar."

She laughed. "Not quite. I know four books." She held up four fingers and lowered each one successively. "*Hamlet, Macbeth, Twelfth Night* and *Romeo and Juliet*. One for each year of high school."

"You must have been an 'A' student."

She shook her head. She had missed a chunk of school taking care of her siblings when her mom and stepfather were together. "I was a good listener."

He stepped back and held his arms wide. "Life's but a walking shadow, a poor player that struts and frets his hour upon the stage. And then is heard no more. It is a tale told by an idiot, full of sound and fury, signifying nothing."

"You've memorized Shakespeare?"

"Which of the four plays is my quotation from?"

She pointed a finger at him. "It's *Macbeth* or *Hamlet*. I'll say *Macbeth*."

"Correct!"

He pulled her in, and they danced for a few minutes.

He whispered, "Did my heart love till now? Foreswear it, sight! For I never saw true beauty till this night."

She pulled away from him. "That's Romeo! Although I think he fell in love more than once."

He smiled and twirled her. Then they turned together. "I love the name of honor more than I fear death."

"Is that another quote?" she asked as he released her hand to dance freestyle.

He nodded.

She frowned. "It's not familiar, but I'll guess *Macbeth*."

He shook his head.

"*Hamlet*?"

"*Julius Caesar*," he said.

"Cheater," Christine said, punching him lightly on the shoulder with her fist. "I haven't read that one." She could feel her heart banging in her ribs, her adrenaline surging as she role-played with Sloan, trying to keep her demeanor playful while her fear and excitement ran rampant.

She sighted Fillingham on the sidelines beside the beverage table, watching them. "Oops, I see Geoff. Time to get back to work. Thanks for the dance. And the Shakespeare lesson."

"That's my nickname," he said.

"What is?"

"Shakespeare."

She laughed. "I am not surprised."

He took her hand and bowed, turning her wrist to kiss it, his lips warm, his beard scratchy on her skin. "She commands me. I serve her. She is my lady."

She touched him on the shoulder. "I command you to come back to the Trailer Project in a week." Breaking away, she turned and threaded her way over to Fillingham, stopping to hand out postcards and let people know about the Friday night juggling, her heart still banging in her ribcage from her conversations with Sloan.

Her partner was chatting with two blonde women.

"Hey," she said, standing beside him.

"There you are," he said, smiling. "I was just talking about you." He placed his arm around her waist. "I was telling these lovely ladies that not only does the Trailer Project provide medical, legal and tenant aid, but we also have juggling and wrestling competitions on Friday nights."

"Wrestling?" Christine queried, frowning.

"And you're our marquee wrestler!" he added. "The one to beat!"

Chapter 17

"Christine," Fillingham said, "I mean, Christina, is going to be Wonder Woman."

Malo took a deep drag on his cigarette as he nodded. He was perched on a rock beside a cedar. Fillingham, Gail and Christine sat on the grass in front of him. Julie had a shift at the restaurant, and Sarah was back at the Women's Bureau. They were in Bellevue Square Park in Kensington, near where Malo lived.

Their mentor looked like he had just rolled out of bed, his brown hair flattened on one side, his jeans and shirt wrinkled. He wore a worn plaid shirt over a Grateful Dead t-shirt.

Christine shook her head. "I'm not sure about this. Shouldn't we focus on talking to Trailer Project clients and Villagers, gathering information, identifying dealers so we can figure out the supply chain?"

"Sure," Malo said, then took another inhale. As he exhaled, he said, "But it's hard to get addicts out of the woodwork. They'll do it for a hit or if they think they're dying of an overdose. And sometimes they just need to have a fuckin' laugh like the rest of us."

Gail asked Fillingham, "Who are you going to be for the wrestling match? Aquaman?"

"That's a thought," he said.

"I'm not sure how you connived me into this," Christine said.

Gail said, "It's a fundraiser for the Trailer Project. All for a good cause."

"Whose side are you on?" Christine asked Gail.

"Christine may not have agreed," Fillingham said, "but Christina is onboard."

Christine rolled her eyes.

"Malo," Gail said, "what's the update?" Malo usually gave them a summary of Village crimes and arrests.

"A few break-ins," Malo said.

Gail nodded. "We heard the Grab Bag got robbed." The Grab Bag was the variety store that also sold drug paraphernalia.

"A rape in a parking lot on Avenue," he added.

Christine and Gail looked at each other. They hadn't heard about that. That was just up the road from the Trailer Project.

Malo continued, "A biker told this woman he had some heroin, and she followed him behind the car lot, and he and four of his brethren took turns with her."

"Did they get arrested?" Gail asked.

Malo waved Gail's question away. "No one arrests bikers for that low-level shit."

Gail sat up. "A group gang-bang is not worthy of your attention?"

"Nope."

"Why?" she asked. "Because it's a woman?"

"Before you burn your bras, ladies," Malo said, "although I wouldn't mind seeing that, the fact is only five percent of victims report, and of that five percent, ninety-five percent recant or drop the charges. If she goes to court, the defense will ask her why she followed the shithead down the laneway. And if she's a junkhead, no one will believe what comes out of her mouth."

The group was silent for a moment. To the right of Malo, four boys played soccer using twigs to mark the parameters of the goalie net. As they chased each other for the ball, Christine thought about women in Yorkville: the drug addicts, prostitutes and assault victims. Kelly. How the hippies, greasers, bikers and weekenders were always on the prowl for women.

Malo said, "Hospitals have reported more overdoses. Some of the shit was laced with embalming fluid."

Christine asked, "Why would the supplier add a lethal substance?"

Malo shrugged. "Sometimes the seller cuts it with something else that is cheaper. It's a budget decision. They don't always get the ratio right. Other times, it's the buyer's request. They like a bit of excitement with their regular high."

"Is Morality following up with the victims in the hospital?" Gail asked.

"Yeah, yeah, yeah. That's my job." Malo rubbed his hands together. "We have bigger fish to fry." He sounded gleeful.

"What?" Fillingham asked.

"We've identified a new group working out of Bathurst and Steeles, running out of the Kalinka restaurant.

"The Russians," Gail said.

Malo nodded.

Fillingham said, "The Toronto suppliers have competition. So what?"

Malo smiled widely, his bottom teeth tinged brown from nicotine. "It means we're going to get some action. Groups will rise to the surface, be more easily identifiable, as they battle it out."

"We expect violence?" Fillingham asked.

Malo said, "If the greasers or bikers are involved, they react with muscle."

"Christina has a biker admirer," Gail said.

Malo nodded. "The secretary said you met a Grizzly. Stone something? Haven't heard of him. Must be a new member."

"Sloan," Christine corrected.

"Dennis Sloan?" Malo asked, voice tinged with excitement.

Christine said, "I don't know his first name."

Gail said, "He rode a Harley 326."

"Dark hair? Good-looking? Blue eyes?"

Christine nodded.

Malo sat back. "Shakespeare."

Christine said. "That's him."

"Why didn't you tell me this before?" Malo exclaimed.

"I called you at home. Then left a message at Morality like we're supposed to."

Fillingham said, "He thinks Christine and I are a couple. That seemed to rev his engines. He's got a crush on her. So we let it fly."

Malo pondered that. "Not sure what I think about that."

Fillingham leaned back on the grass. The back of his hair was longer, touching the collar of his shirt, darker underneath with lighter strands on top. "Didn't take you for a rule follower, Malo. Sometimes you got to extemporize."

Malo squinted at Fillingham through his cigarette smoke. Malo was their superior, even though he wasn't a sergeant. Christine had heard he refused to sit for promotion exams, saying they were bullshit. That the action happened on the ground, not at a desk. Nevertheless, he was their boss, their mentor, the officer supervising Operation Niagara.

"We don't have to—" Christine began.

Malo interrupted, "It's true, man. Sometimes you got to go with the flow. And if that hooks the big fish, then fuckin' go for it."

Christine swallowed. Having a biker love interest and faking a relationship with her partner were giving her a chronic stomachache.

Malo squatted in front of Christine, shaking his head. "Milkmaid. My wonderful, wonderful, Milkmaid. You just hooked Dennis

Sloan. The vice president of the Grizzlies motorcycle club and the alleged kingpin of their nascent drug trade operations." He took a deep drag on his cigarette and exhaled smoke to the side. "And he has a crush on you. Hot damn! Hot fuckin' damn!"

Chapter 18

"What's in the bag?" Christine asked Fillingham. They were at the corner of Avenue Road and Bloor Street. Since they had become a "couple" a week ago, they usually met up before their shift to walk to work together.

"A silk tie for my dad. It's Father's Day on Sunday." He grimaced. "Commanded to attend the bruncheon."

"Is that so bad?" she asked as they walked north. She had never known her dad, and her stepfather had been an abusive drunk, so it wasn't a day she celebrated. At least Fillingham had a father in his life, although Fillingham Senior didn't seem likeable.

"Can't wait to see what he thinks about this." He rubbed his mustache and goatee.

"Do they know you're undercover?"

He shrugged. "Annie does." Annie was Fillingham's younger and favorite sister.

Christine stopped in the middle of the sidewalk. "That reminds me. I forgot to tell my mom something." She pointed to the public telephone booth on the corner of Avenue Road and Bloor Street. "I'm going to call her. You go ahead."

"Use the phone in the trailer."

She shook her head. "I'll be along in five."

"Do you want me to pick up a latte? Or an Americano?"

There was an advantage to a fake boyfriend. "Latte, please."

"Latte coming up." He leaned forward and gave her a quick kiss on the cheek.

She was getting better at this—the hand-holding, the arms around each other's waists, the kiss on the cheek. But it still felt awkward.

Christine stood in the payphone, the traffic noise from Bloor Street heard through the closed glass doors. "Hello. May I speak with Deputy Darlow? It's Mavis Miller." The secretary put her through to the deputy.

"Miss Miller." His voice was cool. "Just one moment." She heard a mumbling, another voice. "Okay, I'm alone now. Did you check the church drop-in again?" Christine could sense the worry underneath the deputy's impatience.

Her hand tightened on the phone receiver. "I've been back to the church once since last week. Nothing new to report."

"How about the bars on Yonge Street?"

"Those are harder to get to," she said. "They ramp up at the same time as the Trailer Project, so it's difficult for me to leave."

"Go on a different day when you're not working," he suggested.

Christine suppressed a sigh. She was working sixty hours a week. She rarely saw her brother and sister unless she pulled herself out of bed after four hours of sleep to wake them for school and have breakfast with them. Monday and Tuesday were the only days she saw her family.

"I'll try this weekend," she said. "And we're checking the apartments above the stores. Someone may have seen her camped out there."

She heard some mumbled conversation.

"I need to go," he said. "I have a meeting. Thank you for calling. We will speak again." He hung up.

Christine looked at her watch. She was going to call her mom at work to tell her she had given Wayne the money for his field trip and that they were out of peanut butter. But there was no time.

As Christine walked up Avenue Road, she thought it was just as well. Three days ago, she and Phyllis had a fight. Both Christine and her mom had the day off. Donna was lolling around in bed, not getting ready for school, and finally disclosed she was tired because she and Wayne had been staying up late watching TV while their mom was at bingo.

After her siblings went to school, Christine confronted Phyllis. "I thought we agreed you went to bingo on the nights I'm home."

Phyllis moved across the kitchen to put the kettle on the stove for tea. "You're never home."

Christine leaned against the kitchen counter to face Phyllis. "Mom, I'm home two days a week. Go then."

Phyllis sat down at the kitchen table, her hair frizzy and un-brushed. She sighed. "The prizes are the biggest on the weekend."

Christine sat down beside her. "I know, Mom. It's just for now."

Phyllis shook her head. "It's been two months and I have to do everything: dinner, homework, groceries, bedtime. You're never here. I just need a break on the weekends."

Christine sighed. It was hard. Her mom was on shift work. And for five days of the week, she had Donna and Wayne day and night with-out a break. Phyllis and Christine usually split the jobs at home; she helped Wayne with his math and science, played board games with Donna, did her siblings' laundry, made lunches and some dinners. Phyllis did groceries, cooked and tidied the apartment.

"Mom, I know it's not balanced. It's just for a short time."

The kettle whistled on the stove burner. Phyllis got up and poured the boiling water into a teapot. "I don't know how long I can keep going on like this."

"What does that mean?" Christine asked. Was her mom going to start binge drinking again?

Phyllis shrugged.

"Mom, please don't leave Wayne and Donna alone all evening. I know Wayne is ten, but he's not that mature. Just go for an hour or two."

Phyllis faced Christine. "Christine, please don't get killed when a drug dealer finds out you're a cop."

Chapter 19

"Hey, favorite customers," Julie said, coming up to the patio table where Gail and Christine sat. She was talking more to Gail than Christine. Things had mellowed between Julie and Christine since their fight about Fillingham but not completely mended.

Today, Julie was wearing a white halter, navy skirt, red wide belt and white thigh-high boots. A long red scarf banded her hair and trailed down one shoulder. She looked like an American go-go girl. "Can I get you something for dinner?"

"Just coffee today, Jewels," Gail said.

"I'll have the same," Christine added. It was seven o'clock, and she hadn't eaten since noon, but she wasn't hungry.

"You two look glum," Julie said.

Christine and Gail exchanged glances. They had spent the afternoon checking Village rooms and apartments for youth in need. Dr. Reid had sent them on their mission with backpacks full of toiletries, socks, underwear, sanitary pads, syringes, taxi chits, coupons for free ice creams and flyers for the upcoming wrestling match. Plus a bag full of apples. Trudging up the stairs, Gail and Christine could smell the squalor before they reached an apartment: a combination of stale cigarettes, garbage and body odor. At first they had knocked on doors, but no one answered. Turning the handle, almost every place was unlocked.

After saying hello, getting no response, they would wander through the small rooms, finding people draped on couches or crashed on bare mattresses. The places were often filthy, dirt-encrusted dishes, garbage on the floor, stained sheets, aluminum foil in the windows to block the sunlight. Most people were still sleeping, even though it was after three in the afternoon, the rooms dim. Christine squatted beside anyone who roused when she spoke to them, introducing herself, handing them a bottle of orange juice and an apple. Sitting cross-legged beside a mattress, she would offer them her knapsack of goodies. Most people took the orange juice. While Christine chatted to anyone who was awake, Gail checked the rest of the youth, seeing if they were breathing regularly, if anyone seemed unconscious rather than sleeping, who looked blue about the lips. Christine could only ask two people if they recognized Kelly from the photo, as Gail was always nearby. The hippies had sleepily shaken their heads and gone back to sleep.

In their fifth apartment, Christine heard Gail call out from the other room, "Christina, over here!"

Christine hurried into the second bedroom. Gail was kneeling beside a young woman in a sleeping bag, light brown hair plastered to her head, eyes squeezed shut.

"Overdose?" Christine asked, placing her bag on the floor.

The young woman groaned, turning in the sleeping bag.

Gail wrapped her fingers around the girl's wrist. "Not sure." She showed Christine the woman's inner arms. They were free of needle tracks.

Gail leaned closer to the woman's face. "Miss, I'm a nurse. Can you open your eyes? Can you tell me your name?"

The woman did not respond.

Gail said, "Christina, unzip the bag so I can check her out."

Christine pulled the sleeping bag off the woman, who was wearing a t-shirt and shorts. She was curled up, her hand on her stomach.

Gail placed her hand on the woman's forehead. "She's burning up. She must have an infection."

"A stomach bug?" Christine asked. "Food poisoning?"

Gail shook her head. "More like a urinary track infection. But it's not usually this bad. Unless it's gone to the kidneys. It could be appendicitis."

"Should I get Dr. Reid?" None of the apartments had phone lines.

"Wait a sec." Gail turned the woman on her back, gently shaking her by the shoulders. "Hi. My name is Gail. Did you eat something bad? Or take some medication?"

Gail pressed on the woman's sternum, and her eyes opened wide, dark brown with dark eyelashes.

"I'm Gail. I'm here to help. Did you take something?"

The girl shook her head.

"Are you in pain?"

The woman nodded.

Gail continued, "Is it your bladder? Do you have blood in your urine?"

The young woman blinked twice. Before her eyes closed again, she whispered, "Lye."

As they sat on the patio, Gail recounted the rest of the story to Julie, how they had shaken awake the man sleeping on a cot in the corner, asking him if the woman could be pregnant. Lye was used to abort a child; it ended up burning the woman's insides. The man had no idea; he didn't know the woman's name. Neither did the other two university students in the second room.

Christine had run downstairs to the hair salon to call the ambulance.

"Will she be okay?" Julie asked as she set the coffees in front of them.

Gail sighed. "The paramedics said it probably wasn't fatal, given her vitals were stabilizing." She took a sip of coffee. "This is what happens when abortion is illegal and it's difficult to get birth control unless you're married."

Christine and Julie looked at each other. Several of the policewomen, including Christine and Julie, got their birth control from free clinics in the west end who didn't ask questions about marital status.

"Ever been on a sting to shut down an illegal abortionist?" Christine asked the two women.

Julie shook her head, her tray on her hip.

Gail nodded. "Once. Won't do it again. The operating room was filthy. I don't think he washed his equipment. I wonder how many women he botched. And you can't arrest him until the money passes hands. So you're half undressed when you call in the cavalry."

"Did you hear about that nurse who died last month?" Christine asked.

Gail nodded. "My roommate works at the hospital. The woman bled to death."

Julie shivered. "Let's change the topic. Why don't I bring you some croissants to go with your coffee? I'll sneak them out of the kitchen."

Christine said, "We have a budget for food, Jewels. We don't need you to steal."

Julie smiled at them, her mood restored. "And what would be the fun in that?"

After they finished their pastries and refilled coffee cups, Christine and Gail headed to Gallery Europa. It was one place Christine wanted to check, given that Kelly liked art. The woman at the church drop-in had also suggested the gallery. Christine had visited it several times, but it hadn't been open. Many Village businesses kept irregular hours.

Christine followed Gail up the porch stairs and looked at the artwork in the gallery windows. An eight-foot-tall canvas featured a seated young man in a Stetson hat, cigarette between his fingertips, one leg straight, the other leg bent, long hair trailing over his denim jacket. In the other window, a smaller painting of a young woman was set on an easel. Or was it a man? Short, wispy hair, delicate cheekbones, thin frame, wearing an oversized plaid shirt over a white t-shirt. Light green eyes stared at the viewer.

"I know her," Gail said.

"Trailer Project client?"

Gail shook her head. "I've seen her around."

Gail sometimes looked androgynous, like the young woman in the painting. At police college, several cadets made comments about Gail's mannish appearance. Everyone shut up when they saw she was an expert marksman with medical and military expertise. Like Christine, she was strong and easily passed the fitness tests. It was the timed run that gave Christine and Gail problems. They had trained together before classes to meet the minimum pace for the mile.

Gail knocked on the door to the gallery, then pushed open the unlocked door. Christine followed her into a large, mostly unfurnished living area. A woman reclined on a red velour settee, mouthing smoke rings from her cigarette. The rest of the space was occupied by paintings: on the walls, stacked together on the floor, leaning against the chairs, by the front windows.

Christine introduced herself and Gail. "Can we look around?"

The woman swept her hand to encompass the room. "Knock yourself out."

Many of the paintings were portraits—seemingly by the same artist. The subjects were similarly posed with their gaze locked on the viewer. They were mostly young people: folk singer, poet, greaser, addict, hippie, weekender, couples and groups of youth. The background ranged from the studio, a couch, garden and street to the concrete stairs in front of a shop.

Some of the smaller canvases featured the Village cafés and bars. Christine recognized the Toucan and the inside of the Penny Farthing. One showed the backs of three men as they talked on the sidewalk, their leather jackets proclaiming their membership in Satan's Choice motorcycle gang.

As they moved down the room, Gail said, "Quite prolific."

They passed a staircase to the second floor. They'd check the upstairs rooms later. To the left, a half-opened door revealed the smudged mirror and stained sink of a washroom. A few steps farther and they stood in an open room occupying the back of the house, kitchen cupboards on the left and an artist's studio on the right. The back wall featured large windows and a sliding back door that led out to a patio with cast-iron tables and chairs.

A man with a white ponytail stood in front of a canvas, cigarette dangling from his lips, one hand holding a paintbrush as he stared at the painting of an unsmiling young woman with dramatic kohl eye liner and straight dark hair down to her hips. Her chin was tilted down, making her eyes look enormous, and she was leaning forward, holding on to the back of two chairs, her arms straight.

The smell of the oil paints was strong, mixed with the aroma of turpentine.

"Hello," Christine said as they approached the easel. "You must be Carlos."

He studied the painting, shirtsleeves rolled up his muscular arms.

Gail raised her eyebrows, and they looked around. Cabinets ran across two adjoining sides of the studio, countertop cluttered with cans of water, paintbrushes, rags and tubes of paint. The open shelves below were filled with canvases, paint cans and more brushes.

Abruptly, the painter grabbed a tube out of a metal tomato tin, scraped the label with his nail to identify the color, and squirted the paint onto an oval palette covered with smears of dried paint.

Gail took a step forward. "Excuse me. Hi. You must be Carlos Pimenta."

Dr. Reid had confirmed that Pimenta owned the gallery, and his portraits had a devoted following.

The artist slowly turned his attention to Gail.

"We're from the Trailer Project," Gail continued, pointing west. "I'm Gail. This is Christina. We help youth find a place to stay. Get legal help. Food coupons. Medical help. We're going to check with the people here, if that's okay."

He shrugged.

"I like your painting," Christina said. "Her eyes are compelling."

His gaze switched to Christine. "I paint interesting people." He had a slight accent.

Christine nodded. "I can see that. We looked at the paintings in the front room."

"You can buy if you like."

"Maybe," Christine said. She wondered if the paintings were expensive. There was a taste for hippie chic; Dr. Reid said that some Yorkville artists garnered high prices for their work.

Gail said, "We're going to look around."

He shrugged, then picked up his paintbrush and started mixing colors on the palette board.

Gail tilted her head toward the sliding glass door, and they headed outside to the small backyard. A rectangular table with chairs furnished the cement stone patio. Past the patio was a swath of lumpy grass that ended in a row of trees at the back fence.

Gail clicked a switch, and the backyard flooded with light from two crisscrossed rows of plastic lanterns hanging from wires above the patio. Two mugs and an overflowing ashtray adorned one table.

"Ahh!" Christine said as she looked at the oak tree above her. Clay creatures hung from branches and nestled in nooks: a gargoyle, mermaid, frog, three-headed monster and a headless torso with two large breasts.

They walked the length of the small backyard, the long grass tickling their ankles, stepping around stone statues and ceramic sculptures and litter.

"Watch for syringes," Gail warned.

As they made their way back to the patio, Christine could see Carlos applying delicate strokes to the canvas.

"It's restful here," Christine said. Despite the unkempt yard, it felt like a haven from the hustle and bustle of the Village.

Back inside, they walked past the artist. "Were heading upstairs," Christine said.

He did not acknowledge them.

Christine led them up the staircase, one hand on the thick oak banister stained a dark mahogany.

The second floor had three bedrooms and one bathroom. The place was messy, but not as filthy as the other apartments they had visited. One bedroom belonged to Carlos, furnished with an ornate cherry wood dresser and wardrobe, paint-smattered clothes on the floor and canvases stacked against the walls. Some were landscapes, rural farms now only seen north of the city or in east Scarborough.

After a quick step into the bathroom, with its claw-footed tub and antique vanity, they headed into the second room. A man and woman sat on a mattress playing cards, a pile of blankets in the corner, two crumb-encrusted plates beside them.

They chatted with the couple for ten minutes after giving them their spiel about the Trailer Project. The pair seemed healthier than the usual Villagers. When prompted, they confessed to being university students who enjoyed hanging out at the gallery.

Gail headed into the next room.

Christine turned back to the couple and showed them Kelly's photo. "Have you seen this girl, Alice, in the gallery, or anywhere else in the Village?"

They shook their heads. The couple had only been coming to Yorkville for the past two months.

Hauling her backpack onto one shoulder, Christine joined Gail in the other room. Gail was chatting with a young man lying in a swath of blankets. She gave Christine the thumbs-up, so Christine wandered around the room, looking at the larger paintings stacked against the wall and the boxes containing smaller canvases.

On a shelf was a large watercolor sketchbook open to a partially painted scene of the exterior of a Yonge Street bar. Turning the page, she smiled as she recognized the red door of the Toronto Island lighthouse. Christine felt a pang. She missed biking the Island pathways along the lagoon and stopping to chat with Island residents. She pushed her feelings down. She'd be back soon enough. Once they found the illegal drug suppliers and Christine found Kelly.

As Gail continued to chat with the man, Christine found a few sketches of Village scenes. Some were outlined lightly in pencil, others drawn with pencil crayon, and a few were watercolors. Christine recognized the stairs in front of the hair salon and the sign outside the Mousetrap.

She turned the page to a pencil crayon sketch of the interior of a basement bar. Patrons sat on stools around tables, and there was a stage to the right. Was it the Penny Farthing? A man sat on a stool in an unbuttoned sheepskin coat, his dark hair and mustache contrasting the fawn color of the jacket. Sitting erect beside him on a stool was a lean young woman with long hair, head tilted as she looked up at her companion.

Kelly.

Gail finished her chat, and she and Christine grabbed their knapsacks and headed downstairs. Christine urged Gail to go ahead in case Dr. Reid needed her, saying she was going to check in with the artist again.

Gail left. Christine returned to the studio, sketchbook in hand. Carlos was washing paintbrushes at a stainless-steel sink.

"You can't get anyone to help you wash up?" Christine asked.

He shrugged. "No one cleans my brushes but me. They're mink."

"I found a drawing of a Village bar." She held up the sketchbook. "Do you know these people?"

"I didn't draw that."

Christine's shoulders sank.

"It's the Penny Farthing," he said.

Christine perked up. "Do these patrons look familiar? Have you seen them before?"

"No." He added, "He's probably the entertainment."

"Why do you say that?"

"The guitar."

"What guitar?" she asked.

"At his feet."

Christine looked closer at the crosshatching under the table where the man and woman sat. The dark shadow could be a guitar.

"Have you seen the girl around the gallery? Or around the Village? I have a picture." Christine showed him Kelly's photo.

He shrugged. "They come. They go. I pay no attention. I paint."

Christine thanked him for his time and headed down Yorkville Avenue toward the trailer. Her fingers felt tingly—she was getting closer to Kelly. Or at least following her trail. Maybe Kelly was still with the guitarist. Many bands played regular gigs at Village venues or the rock and roll taverns on Yonge Street. If Christine could identify the man, find out where he was playing, maybe Kelly would be with him.

Christine also needed to find Dennis Sloan. Christine, Gail and Fillingham had a quick meeting yesterday with Malo on a patio on Augusta Street. Malo was still excited about Shakespeare's visit to the Trailer Project and made them come up with ways they could find him.

"We just need this one," Malo's thumb pointed at Christine who sat across from him, "to give him a warm welcome."

Fillingham said, "What's that mean?" He was in khaki pants, t-shirt and tan leather vest. Leather bracelets wrapped his wrist.

Malo answered, "See what's on his mind. Empathize with him. Have a little pillow talk about the pressure of his job with the new competition."

Gail frowned. "We're not prostitutes."

Malo looked at Christine. "Do what you need to do."

Christine's eyebrows rose. "I'm not a prostitute."

Malo waved his hands in surrender. "Doris Day, I don't give a shit how you do it, but get him to tell you about his distribution system, if he uses greasers as middlemen, how many pushers he has under his wing, any detail to build a drug case against him."

"Will the charges stick?" Gail asked. Biker gangs had their own team of lawyers that defended them in court.

"If we have enough evidence. The closer you can get to him, Christina," Malo said, "the more you hang out, the more players you meet, the more likely you'll hear about an incoming shipment or the name of his supplier."

"That's a tough assignment," Fillingham said. "She's not under-cover in the Grizzlies. It's not like she sees him every day. Talk about drugs is going to make him suspicious."

Gail said, "I agree with Fillingham. Christine's connection with the Grizzlies is a long shot. We should focus on finding the drug pushers and their chain of command, as well as address other Village crime like break-ins and assaults."

Malo shook his head. "Our mandate is the big fish, and in this story it's Shakespeare. And we have Christina, his muse, in the wings."

Chapter 20

"Hey," Christine greeted the bartender. On the way to work, she had trundled down the basement steps of the Penny Farthing, the venue in the painting. It was dark and smelled musty. No wonder they called it the Dungeon.

"We're not open yet," the bartender said as he placed glasses on a shelf. His long brown hair was tied back into a ponytail. "Try upstairs."

"I'm from the Trailer Project on Avenue."

"The mobile home in the parking lot?" he asked.

"Yes. We help youth with housing, addiction, food."

"Cool." He paused, glass in hand. "How can I help you?"

"I'm looking for a girl who hangs out here. Alice? She's sixteen, brown hair."

He shrugged.

"She hangs out with a guy who played guitar here. Tall. Dark hair. Sheepskin jacket."

He scratched his face. "You mean Maurice?"

"Is that his name?"

"He's out back cleaning the pool."

She leaned forward. "He works here?"

"He plays guitar and sings a couple of nights a week. And does other jobs. Sets up the equipment for performers. Takes care of the pool. Unloads deliveries."

Christine headed upstairs and outside to the backyard patio with its sunken pool filled with young people in bathing suits sipping drinks. A tall, thin man with a beard and mustache was at the back by the open shed.

Christine introduced herself. He nodded as he placed a jug of pool chemicals on a shelf.

"I'm looking for a girl named Alice Dodgson. I heard she hangs around here. And she likes your music."

He stared at her for a moment. "The bitch didn't like my music. She liked my money. Stole a week's worth of tips from my guitar case."

"Are we talking about Alice? Brown hair. Brown eyes. Missing a tooth?"

He nodded. "That's her."

"When did you meet?"

"A year ago. She would come to watch my set. We'd get high together. Fun times. Then she was high all the time. Or itching to get high. She stole my weed. Then my money."

"When did you see her last?"

"November. December."

"You haven't seen her since then?"

He shook his head. "Good riddance."

"Do you think she's in trouble?"

"She will be if I see her again." He hung a net on a hook inside the shed. "Let me know if you find her."

"What is that?" Fillingham said, loosening his hold on Christine's hand.

"Wait!" She pulled him back.

They stood at the bottom of the stairs leading to the trailer entrance, staring at a package taped to the door.

"Nobody's inside yet," he remarked. The interior of the caravan was dark.

They were usually the first ones to arrive for their shift. They would open the mobile home, tidy up, brew the coffee and put out food. Dr. Reid arrived at three o'clock or soon after, whenever she could get away from the hospital.

"Do you think it's dangerous?" she asked. The Trailer Project hadn't been picketed, but an evangelical group had questioned them about the free condoms, venereal disease clinic and sterile needles distributed to addicts. They were earnest young men and women; Dr. Reid ushered them off the property after a polite chat.

"It's too small for a bomb." Fillingham bounded up the stairs.

The item was wrapped in brown kraft paper and crisscrossed with black duct tape to stick it to the door.

"Should we call for a unit to check it out?"

He shook his head. "It's probably a joke. I'll take it off."

"We should use gloves," she added. The container could contain a death threat or a toxic substance. "And cover our eyes."

They headed inside to the kitchen to find gloves. He pulled on washing gloves and grabbed a pair of scissors.

Sliding his sunglasses over his eyes, he unpeeled the tape and pulled it off the door. Placing it on the picnic table outside, he cut through the paper and tape.

"A book," she proclaimed.

"Or a journal." He carefully unpeeled the tape from the outside of the leather book.

"What's this?" a female voice asked.

They turned. It was Gail.

Christine said, "We found this book taped to the trailer door."

Gail arched her eyebrows. "Maybe it's a list of Yorkville's dealers and their pecking order."

"That would be convenient," he said.

With fanfare, he removed the last strip of tape. He held up a brown leather book embossed with a title in gold lettering: *Shakespeare's Sonnets.*

Gail and Fillingham looked at Christine.

"It's from Dennis Sloan," Gail said.

Much to Malo's chagrin, Christine hadn't seen Sloan since their meeting at the church two weeks ago. He hadn't come back to get his stitches removed. Fillingham hazarded Sloan had taken them out with his teeth.

"Is there a note?" Christine asked.

Fillingham riffled quickly through the pages. "No, but he's book-marked a page with a ribbon." He theatrically cleared his voice and read out Sonnet XXVII.

The archaic English was challenging. She hadn't heard Shake-spearean English since high school, but she caught the gist of the fourteen lines. Tired from work, the writer lies down in bed and thinks of his beloved as a "jewel hung in the ghastly night." And his body and mind, "For thee...no quiet find."

Christine could feel herself blush from embarrassment and trepi-dation.

Fillingham snapped the book shut. "Dennis Sloan, Shakespeare, after a hard day of cracking heads, selling heroin and running over people with his motorcycle, lays his head down on the pillow and thinks of Christina."

Christine grimaced.

Gail said, "Well, he's hooked. Malo's going to explode with hap-piness." She handed the book back to Christine. "You don't look overjoyed."

"Would you?" Christine asked. Her stomach felt leaden. Having a biker infatuated with you was frightening, even if he was their best chance to shut down drug use in Yorkville.

Gail placed her hand on Christine's arm. "We'll come up with a plan to keep you safe. And figure out when you bail out. No job is worth getting hurt."

Christine gave Gail's hand a quick pat, feeling relieved.

"Plus," Fillingham said, "as Aquaman, I can take Sloan out like this." He snapped his fingers. "Wrestle him to the ground until he cries 'uncle.'"

"Or octopus," Gail responded with a smile.

Chapter 21

"You're Wonder Woman!" Donna squealed as she stared at Christina in the bedroom they shared. It was a Friday morning, and her siblings were home because it was a school professional development day.

Christine gave her sister a smile. Donna thought it wonderful that Christine was dressing up as a superhero, even if Christine herself thought the costume was chintzy. The blue shorts felt like underwear, and she wasn't sure if the strapless top would stay up. Fillingham had picked up the costume from a party store, alongside his Aquaman outfit, for the wrestling match tonight.

Christine adjusted the gold cummerbund and clipped it tight.

"Can I try on the cape?" Donna asked.

Christine grabbed the red, blue and white striped garment off the bed and threw it over her sister. Donna tried to swat herself out of it as Christine held her in. After a few light punches from Donna, Christine let go and Donna slid the cape around her shoulders.

After grabbing a comb from the side table between their beds, Christine teased the crown of her hair as Julie had taught her. She had put her hair in her mom's large foam rollers last night, and now it waved on her shoulders like in the comic series *Wonder Woman*.

Staring at the mirror hung on the back of the bedroom door, she placed the gold headband with the red star around her forehead.

Christine grabbed the rope off the bed—the Lasso of Truth. Fillingham had insisted she practice lassoing him today, since this could be part of the show, just like Wonder Woman lassoed criminals and forced them to divulge their deceptions. A canvas clasp attached to the shorts held the lasso.

Wow, Christine thought as she looked in the mirror. She felt both ridiculous and powerful. Like Wonder Woman, she looked strong and voluptuous with her thigh and arm muscles, broad shoulders and full breasts underneath the corseted top. It reminded her of what she felt like when she put on her police uniform: confident, competent, with a mission to help people. Except this superhero outfit exposed way more skin.

"Donna." Christine turned to her sister, who was lying on her bed with the cape wrapped around her like a blanket. "Wonder Woman needs your help."

Donna sat up. "Sure."

"I need to learn to lasso." She held up the golden coil. "Can I practice on you outside?"

Donna scuttled to the edge of the bed and stood up. "Let's go."

"I'll change first."

"No!" Donna yelled. "You can't change. You're Wonder Woman. That's why you're lassoing me."

"I don't want to go out—"

Donna crossed her arms, frowning and pouting at the same time.

"Fine," Christine said.

Donna smiled gleefully and handed Christine the cape.

Christine strode down the sidewalk in front of her apartment, cape floating behind her, Donna jogging alongside. She felt her face burn with embarrassment as they headed to the park. Looking straight ahead, Christine forced herself to walk confidently, knowing that tonight she would be Wonder Woman, wrestling Yorkville youth in her partner's hare-brained scheme to promote the Trailer Project.

At least she was better at roping, Christine thought as she exited the subway station that afternoon. She had thrown and rethrown the lasso at Donna in the park, the loop sliding down her sister's back or landing on either side, but never over her head. A man stopped to give Christine instruction. He had worked as a cowboy on a ranch in Alberta before migrating to Toronto to work in an abattoir. He was between forty and fifty, eyes webbed with wrinkles, nonplussed by her Wonder Woman costume. After fifteen minutes of practice, with the cowboy demonstrating the counterclockwise throw and then coaching her performance, she finally looped a succession of throws over Donna's head.

Christine's costume and rope had been in a bag by her feet as she rode the subway—there was no way she was wearing it to work. She had five hours of her shift before the eight o'clock match. Fillingham was borrowing a wrestling mat and had rustled up floodlights, a speaker system and microphone so he could announce the night's events. When he had told her yesterday he paid for the items himself, she teased him about using his dad's credit cards.

Fillingham said, "Actually, my father cut me off when I joined the police force."

Christine and Fillingham had been sitting at the picnic table in front of the caravan as they chatted before their shift.

"But–but I thought you were rich," she stuttered. "You always have money."

He shrugged and sipped his coffee.

"But you have two cars," she said.

"My grandfather gave me his sports car in his will, and I got the other one as a university graduation gift."

"You're Richie Rich," she said.

"A misnomer."

"Geoff, you paid my mom's gambling debt. That was thousands of dollars!"

He waved her concern away. "I can get my hands on money when I need it. The bank manager and I have our own side agreement. In one year, I access my grandfather's trust fund."

"So you *are* rich. Or almost rich." She wiped her brow. "Phew."

"It's not my money you love, Christina," he said. "It's the charisma. The charm. The Nordic good looks."

"Humility," she added.

"That, too."

Christine was thinking about her almost-rich partner as she waited for him on the top stair of the church steps on the corner of Bloor Street and Avenue Road. The sun beamed on her shoulders and she pulled her circular Jackie O sunglasses out of her purse. Another lovely June day, perfect for the wrestling fundraiser tonight.

A hundred feet away, she spied three points of a pitchfork in the stream of pedestrians walking toward her. A man emerged from the crowd in an orange shirt, green tights, black shorts and gold belt with a stylized A at the clip. Aquaman, a.k.a. her partner, Fillingham. And it wasn't a pitchfork. He was holding a trident.

Fillingham strode toward her, ignoring the curious glances, his blond mustache and beard and longer hair making him look like the superhero of the sea. Spying Christine, he crossed the street and ran lightly up the stairs to sit beside her.

"Is that metal?" she asked, pointing at the trident.

"Nah," he said, placing it on the stairs beside him. "It's a broom handle, and the rest is painted cardboard."

"Thank goodness. I wouldn't want to get stabbed while I am pinning you to the ground."

He raised his blond eyebrows. "I'll let you win tonight, only because the crowd will love it. And the donations will flow in."

"Did you let me win the other twenty times we've wrestled?" she said.

He pressed his hand to his chest. "I *am* a gentleman."

She shook her head.

"And where, Princess Diana of Themyscira, is your Wonder Woman costume?"

She tilted her head toward the bag at her feet. "I'll put it on later."

"Aquaman has a few moves that are going to surprise even Wonder Woman."

"What moves?" she asked.

"You'll find out when you hit the mat." He stood up.

Christine reached into her bag and pulled out the rope. "I could use the Lasso of Truth on you."

"Okay, my princess," he said, offering his hand to help her stand up. "Let's first rescue the undernourished, addicted, homeless and itchy youth of Yorkville. Then we can wage war on each other."

"A busy day ahead," she said, hooking her arm companionably in his.

"Did I mention we will have to kiss and make up on the mat?"

"You tell that to Julie," Christine said.

He shook his head. "Good point. She's a fiercer foe than Wonder Woman and Aquaman combined."

Chapter 22

It was a busy afternoon. Fillingham set up the wrestling area with mats and seating for spectators. Staff came out of the trailer to watch him juggle a menagerie of plastic and wooden sea creatures: fish, whales, dolphins and a nautilus shell. He had another routine where he waved his trident like a martial arts weapon and then a cheerleader's baton.

Whether it was word of mouth or the flyers they had distributed in the Village, many people dropped by during the afternoon to ask about the evening's events. Sarah had made donation boxes that she and other volunteers would circulate amongst the spectators to replenish the Trailer Project's supply of condoms, bandages, skin creams, taxi chits and food stamps.

The increased interest in the event meant the staff was busy with clients who complained of a bad drug trip, malnutrition, a broken toe, anxiety and a landlord who had turned off the tenants' electricity. Now that the team had worked together for two months, they had a smooth system going, and with the help of two law students, they had served thirty clients by dinnertime. Fillingham had wanted Christine to change into her Wonder Woman costume, but she hadn't had time.

At seven o'clock, Fillingham poked his head inside the caravan. His tanned face was lightly sweating, the damp hair clinging to his neck.

"You better eat something, Princess, then suit up. We're got a lineup of contestants."

Christine peeked outside. About twenty people were standing around. "Gail," she said, "Batman and Catwoman are here."

Gail was washing her hands at the kitchen sink. "Ah!" she said. "The DC comics crew." She was wearing a referee's shirt from her hockey league with a large peace sign necklace. A client had put a daisy behind her left ear.

Christine ate the peanut butter sandwich she had brought with a glass of milk. The first bite stuck in her throat; she was nervous. She had to remind herself she was Christina—fun-loving and easygoing! Wrestling her boyfriend—what a blast!

Gail sat across from her on the couch, eating her meat pie. "You'll be fine, Christina."

"Can you tell I'm nervous?"

"You've practiced with Geoff. And you're a good wrestler. You'll know how to handle the contestants. It's meant to be fun, promote the Trailer Project, rustle up a few dollars for consumables."

"You're right," Christine said. She stood up and headed to the empty law office to change; the legal students were chatting with people outside. Donning her Wonder Woman outfit, she crossed her fingers that she wouldn't fall out of the corseted top. The rigid supports felt firm. Her tan boots weren't the red color of Wonder Woman's comic book outfit, but hopefully no one would notice. She belted her gold cummerbund and snapped the bracelets on her wrists. In the tiny trailer washroom, she teased her wavy hair before placing her gold headband around her forehead. With a dash of heavy eyeliner and crimson lipstick, she was ready to go. Back in the kitchen, she tied her cape around her neck and checked that the Lasso of Truth was secured to her hip. She could hear the music outside already, the bass vibrating from the two large speakers on the lot.

She slammed the door of the caravan closed and stood at the top of the stairs, hands on hips, her cape thrown back.

"Wonder Woman!" several people exclaimed.

She descended the stairs to a burst of applause, The Beatles blaring through the speakers. She headed toward Aquaman, who was juggling balls on the mat. Gail and Sarah followed her out, alongside two volunteers with donation tins.

Forty people milled about, clapping at Aquaman's antics, sitting on the benches and watching from the sidewalk. She could smell pot and cigarette smoke.

When Fillingham saw her, he threw the three balls high in the air, somersaulted and landed on one knee in front of Christine, catching the three balls in his hands.

"My princess—Wonder Woman!" he said.

She tried not to roll her eyes at his excess, and she let him grab her hand as he stood up. He bowed low to kiss the back of her hand and made his way up her arm, making loud smooching sounds as he went.

She grabbed him by the back of the neck and guided him toward the middle of the mat, accompanied by hooting and hollering. "Manners, my good Aquaman. Have you forgotten etiquette during your time undersea?"

Gail turned on the mike and introduced herself. As she outlined the evening's wrestling agenda, people began filling up the benches, couches and chairs Fillingham had arranged around the three sides of the mat.

Behind Gail, Sarah stood with a donation box around her neck and chatted with a line of candidates who were interested in wrestling the superheroes.

Fillingham had dragged a picnic table over to the mat edge, where he had placed his trident and juggling paraphernalia. Gail handed him the microphone.

"Welcome to the match of the century," he said to the audience, "the marquee wrestling match between Aquaman, King of the Seas," he placed his hand on his chest, "and Wonder Woman, the greatest female superhero on Earth." He gestured with one arm to Christine.

Christine took over. "Greetings and thank you so much for coming. As Gail mentioned, we will select audience members to wrestle both superheroes. Each match will last three minutes, with a point allotted for pushing someone out of the inner circle and three points for pinning someone to the ground. It's all in the name of fun, so make sure not to get any demerit points for bad behavior!"

"As well as being superheroes," Fillingham added, "we have secret identities as staff at the Trailer Project." He pointed to the caravan, where Dr. Reid stood in the open doorway. "I would like to introduce you to the eminently skilled and friendly Dr. Reid. If you have a rash in your nether regions, a cough, need someone to talk to or have no place to stay, Dr. Reid, myself, Wonder Woman, Gail, Sarah-Jane and our law students can help you out."

He gestured to Sarah, who had a donation box hung around her neck painted with fish, octopus and dolphin art. "We encourage everyone to donate to the Trailer Project in gratitude for the excellent entertainment you will see today," he flashed a smile, "and to help us provide additional care kits to youth. Every dime or quarter counts—no donation is too small."

The volunteers passed the donation boxes down the line of seated people while Fillingham met the first wrestling candidate in the middle of the mat, Gail positioned between them.

Fillingham was great—he pirouetted, danced around, made faces and squealed when someone grabbed him. He wrestled without having the other person lose face, letting a woman force him to the ground, then asking her to marry him as she sat on top of him.

Christine was next. It was getting darker, a soft dusk, and the lights on the caravan and the floodlights illuminated the ring. There were at least a hundred and fifty people on the lot. She felt relaxed, since she had laughed so much at Fillingham's antics. Gail had whispered that they had collected a hundred dollars in donations so far.

As Christine stood in the middle of the mat, Gail took the microphone. "As a special surprise, guess who we have in the house?" With a flourish, she pointed behind her. "Catwoman!"

Julie! Dressed in a black leotard, cat ears and whisker makeup.

Christine looked over at Fillingham, who was sitting on a front-row bench. He shrugged to show he hadn't known Julie would wrestle. As the two competitors faced each other, Christine whispered, "What's going on?"

"Nothing," Julie said, her candy-red lips smiling. Even in cat makeup, with dramatic eye eyeliner and a black nose, she looked sexy.

"Okay," Christine whispered, "at the end I'll throw you into the crowd. Fillingham will catch you."

Julie frowned, then nodded.

Christine let Julie grab her, come behind her and force her down on her knees. When Julie grabbed her by the hair, Christine let out an "Ow!" and Gail stepped in to call a foul.

The two women stood up again, facing each other, Julie lifting her eyebrows, smiling. Julie was fighting dirty. Was this payback for being Fillingham's pretend girlfriend? Christine prickled with annoyance.

Christine let herself be tripped by Julie's sweeping foot. As Julie neared, Christine grabbed her by the waist, and they somersaulted together.

"Tie match!" Gail yelled, smiling.

After getting up, Christine and Julie clinched, arms on each other's shoulders. Christine said, "We need to wrap this up. Slide your arms forward, and I'm going to lift you onto my shoulders."

"Be careful!" Julie hissed. "I'm not feeling well."

Julie let herself slip forward and Christine hauled her onto her shoulders. She turned in a slow circle to show the crowd, and with a yell, "Wonder Woman!" She lifted Julie straight above her in the air.

Fillingham stood up. With a grunt, Christine tossed Julie into Fillingham's waiting arms.

"Winner!" Gail yelled, pointing at Christine.

Julie lay clasped in Aquaman's arms, smiling up at him, and then they smooched.

After a few seconds, Christine kicked Fillingham in the leg. He released Julie, who stood up and waved at the audience before disappearing into the crowd.

Christine wrestled two more people, one young man who was athletic and thought he could trip her up. He was a good sport, though, and Christine let him have a point.

And then it was the finale: Aquaman vs. Wonder Woman.

It was dark now, almost ten o'clock. The place was humming: the music playing, the crowd buzzing. After encouraging spectators to donate and reviewing Trailer Project services, Gail introduced the competitors again. "And for the final match of the evening, on my right, in green and yellow, with the ability to breathe underwater and in air and commanding the powers of the sea and its creatures: Aquaman!"

Powerful applause while Christine gave a thumbs-down.

"And on my right in red, gold and blue, endowed with superhuman strength, the ability to stop bullets with her bracelets and drive anyone into submission with her Lasso of Truth: Wonder Woman!"

The applause was thunderous. Christine reminded herself she was Christina, and smiling ear to ear, she went over to each side of the mat, waved to the audience and shook a few well-wishers' hands.

"The match will be ten minutes long," Gail said. "Same rules as before. Good luck." She looked at each of them, winked at Christine and backed off to the edge of the mat.

Christine and Fillingham faced each other, both crouching, hands held in front of them. They had practiced a fun routine, each of them doing silly holds and somersaults. When she turned around to the audience, Fillingham was going to jump on her back. Later, he would stand on her shoulders. She would then throw him in the air and catch him in her arms.

They hammed it up. He held her down on the mat, and she slammed her fist down in frustration as he won a point. The next time she got him down, but he rolled her over and then she rolled him over again. For a point she swiped both his feet, so he went sailing in the air with a thump to jump up again and throw himself in her middle to push her out of the circle.

They gestured to the audience between points, trying to solicit their support. For a finale, she grabbed him from behind as he kibbitzed with the audience, swung him around and around in the air and threw him into the audience.

This last part was tricky. They hadn't prepped the audience. Fillingham was unconcerned, but Christine was worried he'd take a tumble. Five sets of arms raised and a young woman screamed and fell off the bench, but all was okay. Aquaman pretended to be unconscious as he lay across the laps of three spectators, and Gail came over and raised Christine's hand in the air.

"Winner of the first annual Yorkville superhero wrestling contest—Wonder Woman!"

Christine's hand was still in the air, held up by Gail, when a man walked onto the mat waving a hundred-dollar bill.

Dennis Sloan. Shakespeare.

The spectators quieted as he showed the bill to the audience, circling around the two women to the four sides of the mat until he faced Christine.

"I challenge Wonder Woman to a match," Sloan said.

She shook her head. "We've had our last match."

"Don't you want a hundred-dollar donation to the Trailer Project, Wonder Woman?" he asked loudly.

The audience started cheering and hooting.

Christine didn't want to fight Sloan. She couldn't win the match and risk bad feelings. And Malo would kill her if she messed up their lead. But she couldn't bear the thought of Sloan getting the upper hand.

"We're happy to take your donation," Christine exclaimed.

He shook his head. "Not so easy. You need to work for it."

"Then I decline," she said, turning away.

She halted when he pulled on the lasso attached to her hip.

"How about you lasso me?" he asked. He looked at the crowd. "What do you think? Can Wonder Woman lasso me in three tries for one hundred dollars?"

The audience on all three sides of the mat chanted, "Lasso! Lasso! Lasso!"

She looked at Sloan, her smile tight. What was he up to? Was he trying to make her look bad? Upstage her?

Gail gave her a nod. She should do it.

Christine addressed the crowd. "I'm rusty, since I've been spending my time wrestling. But if this gentleman could bring himself to accept five tries, Wonder Woman is up for the challenge!"

An explosion of applause. Sloan nodded his agreement, and Gail walked him to a spot fifteen feet from Christine.

Christine grabbed the lasso, feeling its stiff, prickly texture. "Turn around," she yelled to Sloan above the crowd's noise.

The money was for charity, Christine reminded herself. They could buy food, condoms, transit tickets and needles for addicts. And Malo would be ecstatic that she was connecting with the vice president of the Grizzlies.

"That's okay," he said, both hands gesturing. "I enjoy looking at you."

"I don't want to ruin your rugged good looks," Christine said.

He smiled and slowly turned around.

Christine began swirling the lasso like the cowboy had instructed until she felt a rhythm and let it go.

The rope hit Sloan in the middle of his back. He looked over his shoulder. "Lost your focus, Wonder Woman?" he asked.

She needed to throw higher. Sloan was much taller than Donna.

The second throw hit the back of the head. He gave his dark curls a rub.

"Shakespeare!" a female voice yelled. "Are you okay?"

Sloan looked over at the woman and gave a thumbs-up.

Christine glanced at the woman sitting in the second row of benches.

Kelly?

She had long, thin hair, hard to see the color in the dark, but it looked light brown. She was thin, her cheekbones high, dressed in a baggy long-sleeved shirt and loose jeans. She might be a teenager, but she looked older, purple circles under her eyes. The woman looked from Sloan to Christine, and then she smiled. She was missing a lower tooth.

Kelly!

Christine had to go. Stop Kelly from leaving. Grab her and convince her to stop so she could talk to her.

Gail's voice bellowed from the mike. "Throw number three. Go ahead, Wonder Woman."

Christine stared at Gail in alarm.

Gail tilted her head toward Sloan.

Darn! Christine pulled her gaze away from the audience. She'd have to look for Kelly after. *Concentrate, Christine.*

This time, Christine swirled the rope at a higher height, going round and round until she felt a rhythm, the rope almost slipping out of her hand, as the cowboy had instructed. *One, two three. Release!*

The golden rope went sailing into the air. Sloan turned his head slightly as the rope looped over his head and around his shoulders.

Quickly, Christine tugged, and the slipknot tightened.

The rope slid down Sloan's chest, and he turned around to face her. He tugged on the rope so that Christine moved toward him. She pulled on her end until they met in the center.

"Wonder Woman prevails!" Gail bellowed.

Christine waved at the cheering crowd, desperately scanning for Kelly.

"I'm all yours," Sloan said.

"Your money is mine." She loosened the lasso, and it slid to the ground.

Sloan made a show of pulling the hundred-dollar bill out of his vest pocket and delivering it to Christine with a flourish and a bow.

Christine waved it in the air, then handed it to Sarah to place in the donation box.

Christine scanned the dispersing crowd. Kelly wasn't in the second row anymore. Christine quickly walked over to the group of exiting youth, greeting the crowd, accepting donations, scanning left and right for Kelly. Where was she? Had she left? Was she still in the Village? What was Deputy Darlow going to say when Christine explained that Kelly had been ten feet away and slipped through her fingers?

A voice beside her said, "Can we go somewhere for dinner?"

Christine looked into Sloan's deep blue eyes, which looked indigo in the dark. "I'm still working."

"This is work?" he asked, pointing to the mat.

"This was a publicity stunt for the Trailer Project."

"An ice cream. Come on. I'll have you back within the hour."

Christine saw Fillingham talking to the crowd, laughing.

Sloan followed Christine's glance. "Want me to ask your boyfriend if it's okay?"

"No. I'll let Dr. Reid know I'm on break."

As Christine returned from her chat with the doctor, she was tingling, from the adrenaline of the performance, from successfully lassoing Sloan, from her fear of being with a motorcycle gang member. Kelly seemed to know Sloan. The biker could be her means of finding Kelly and the source of Village drugs.

Sloan throttled the motorcycle engine. "Get on, Wonder Woman."

Christine looked around the yard, catching Fillingham's glance as he moved the benches. She thought they were going to a café on Yorkville Avenue, not a motorcycle ride.

She was close to something. She could feel it. Christine mounted the bike behind Sloan, still in costume, placing her feet on the pegs.

"Hug me tight," Sloan said. "We're going for a ride."

Chapter 23

Sloan steered down University Avenue, accelerating in bursts as he weaved around slower cars. Christine leaned into the biker, her eyes partially closed as the buildings and cars blurred beside her.

He slowed, and they stopped at a light on Lake Shore Boulevard. "All good, Wonder Woman?" he asked, smiling as he turned to her.

Christine nodded. "Where are we going?" She hoped her tone wasn't as anxious as she felt. Was she being kidnapped? Was he going to hurt her?

Christine had practiced her moves in her head as she sat on the back of the motorcycle. If he grabbed her from the front, she would use an inside-out move to break his hold. But what if he pulled a knife?

"You'll know soon," he said. When the light turned green, he gunned the motor, then eased into the slower traffic filled with couples returning from dinner, teenagers driving their parents' station wagons and taxi cabs. They continued west down the Lake Shore, passing the winged angel at the Exhibition gate holding the victor's crown high.

The muffler rumbled at a quieter volume as they passed Sunnyside Beach. Christine recognized the pavilion. She took her siblings to the pool there in the summer to swim.

They drove farther west toward the Humber River. He geared down and eased into a parking lot filled with cars. People were walking along the boardwalk or watching the water from their cars. Christine slackened her grip around Sloan, thinking they would stop here, but he steered around the concrete parking blocks and drove over the grass to a jetty of boulders bordering the lake. Cutting the engine, he dismounted. He held out his hand to help Christine off the bike, then tipped his chin toward the shadowy pile of rocks.

They climbed to the top of the boulder pile, taking their time to find their footing in the dark, Sloan holding her hand when she had to jump across a gap. Sitting on two rocks at the apex, the view was resplendent. The boulders jutted out like a peninsula into Lake Ontario so that they were looking back toward the city. Christine recognized the shape of the King Edward Hotel and the pointed tower of the Canada Life Insurance building. The windows of the bank buildings and businesses twinkled, ivory checkerboards accented by the red and green lights on the top of the taller towers. The city lights reflected in the water like lines of colored rain.

"This is beautiful."

He grinned. After a moment of silence, he patted his pocket, withdrew a package and offered her a cigarette. She shook her head. He lit it, inhaling audibly, the match quickly blown out by the gentle wind.

He pulled something from his pocket. "Want something else to celebrate your victories on the wrestling mat?"

She looked at the pills in his palm. "Uppers?" She was getting better at identifying pills. She tried to get clients who were high or on a bad trip to tell her the name or color of the drug as the information helped Dr. Reid choose treatment.

He nodded.

"No thanks," she said. "No ice cream kiosks up here?"

"Sorry about that." After a minute, he pulled a metal flask from the inside of his jacket and offered it to her.

Christine paused. She could have a drink, instead of seeming so prissy, rejecting Sloan's offers.

She nodded, and he handed it to her. She took a swig and gasped as the whisky burned her throat. They handed the flask back and forth companionably as they gazed at the skyline, hearing the occasional call of a cormorant and the rhythmic lap of waves against the boulders.

She shivered. He took off his leather jacket and placed it around her bare shoulders, the inside liner warm from his body.

"Now you're an honorary member," he said, smiling.

"Is that all it takes to be a Grizzly?" she joked. "Wrestling a few people?"

"You are a superhero. That helps."

This was her chance. "What would membership involve?"

"For you, just being beautiful."

"What do you do as a member?" she asked, keeping her tone casual.

"A variety of stuff," he said.

"What is your typical day?" she asked. "What did you do today?"

"Aside from getting lassoed by Wonder Woman and losing a hundred dollars?"

"It *is* the Lasso of Truth," she said, smiling.

He gave a long smoky exhale. "Today I organized some supplies. Bought some items for our office. Solved a few problems."

"Are you in your office a lot?" she asked.

He shrugged. "Some weeks more than others. If there's a meeting or a problem. Sometimes just for a drink. There's a bar and a pool table. A barbeque out back."

"You sound busy."

He shrugged. "I come down here." He pointed to the boulders. "I read. Go for a ride on my bike. Travel to Montreal, up north, whatever I feel like. If something needs to be done, I take care of it."

Should she ask him about Kelly? She didn't have the picture on her, but she could ask about the woman who had called out his name tonight.

"Any other woman offered a membership," she asked, keeping her voice teasing, "other than Wonder Woman?"

He shook his head.

"No women in the Grizzlies?"

"A few guys have girlfriends who ride with us sometimes. Some have wives at home."

"I heard a woman call your name when I was lassoing you. Young. Light brown hair. She was in the second row. Do you know her? She looked familiar."

There was a long pause as he stared at her. "Nope."

Christine looked down, breaking eye contact. She shrugged out of his jacket and handed it to him. "I better get back for cleanup. And there'll be a lineup of clients to serve after the match."

"You sure?" he asked.

She nodded. "I don't make my schedule."

"You could with me, Juliet."

"Christina," she said.

"You seem like a Juliet to me." They both stood up, and he held her hand as she made her way down the boulders to the ground.

"I'm not a noble woman," she said. She laughed as they reached his motorcycle. "Although today I am Princess of Themyscira."

"Are you not betrothed to another?" he said as he got on the bike.

"I have a boyfriend," she said, getting on behind him. "Geoff."

"Juliet had Paris," he responded, "before Romeo."

He gunned the engine before she could answer. With a squeal of tires, they headed back to the trailer.

"You awake?" Donna whispered loudly.

Christine opened one eye to regard her sister in the twin bed three feet away. "I am now."

"Good. Let's cuddle."

Christine closed her eyes but lifted her blanket for Donna to slide in. She gave Donna a kiss on the head before they both moved onto their sides. Donna's hair smelled fruity. She must have had a bath last night.

Christine and her sister hadn't cuddled on the weekend in a while, since Christine tried to sleep in until nine or ten just to get six hours of sleep. Wayne had slept in his sofa bed last night, so Christine was back in her room. This morning Christine was extra tired after the wrestling match and the droves of people they had served last night. She would try to fall back to sleep for another hour with Donna and then get up to make pancakes for the family.

Trailer staff had been so busy last night that Dr. Reid told them to leave everything as it was, and they would clean the next day. Dr. Reid hadn't been pleased that Christine had been gone for over an hour with Sloan and had put her to work finding three youths a shelter for the night. Thank goodness Sarah was there, as well as two volunteers and a law student, since they were overwhelmed with clients.

Fillingham had driven her home at three thirty in the morning. They had stopped at a phone booth on Bloor Street so Christine could phone Malo about her conversation with Sloan. Malo had instructed them to pass on information right away, no matter what time of day or night, either on his home phone, or, if there was no answer, to leave a message at the Morality Squad desk.

"Who is this?" Malo had asked. He was awake. She could hear the burble of voices in the background.

"It's Christina. Operation Niagara."

"Milkmaid."

Christine recited her conversation with Sloan, about what he did, his unscheduled life.

"Hot damn!" Malo said.

"What?" she asked. "Is any of that important?"

"He's there for the drop. When the drugs come in from Montreal."

"You know that from my conversation?"

"Could he stash it at headquarters?"

"Wouldn't that be stupid," she said, "if the clubhouse was raided?"

"Yeah, it would be. And Sloan is not a stupid guy. Just a second."

Christina could hear him talking to someone else. "I fold."

Was he at a poker game?

"Keep at it," he said. "Keep feeding lover boy your farm-girl charm and see what else he offers up."

He hung up. Christine pretended she was still talking and turned her back to Fillingham, who was waiting in the car outside the phone stall. She quickly dialed Deputy Darlow's number.

"Yes." It was a male voice.

"It's PW Lane, sir. I'm sorry to wake you. I think I saw Kelly tonight."

"Where?"

"She was watching a wrestling match at the Trailer Project. I tried to follow her, but she got lost in the crowd."

"Just a second," he said. She could hear rustling. He must be going somewhere else with the phone. "I'm going to drive down and look for her. Did you see which way she was going?"

"I'm sorry. There was a large crowd. She was sitting on the bench, then she was gone. She was wearing a long white top and light-colored pants."

"At least she's in the city." He paused. "How did she look?"

Christine didn't know what to say. "Thin."

"Anything else you noticed?"

"Could she be affiliating with a motorcycle gang? The Grizzlies?"

"I hope she isn't. But they may supply her with drugs."

"I'll search the Village tomorrow, sir, in case she is still around."

"I'm going to drive around Yorkville and see if I can find her."

Christine sighed as she got into the car. The long nights, her mission to find Kelly, the stress of hanging out with a biker, were getting to her. She closed her eyes as Fillingham drove her home, envisioning being back on Toronto Island patrol.

Chapter 24

"Just in time," Dr. Reid said from the open door of the trailer. "These are for you." The doctor held out rags and a bottle of rubbing alcohol and directed Christine to take them.

Christine grabbed the materials and stood in front of the long white caravan with Fillingham.

They had seen the words painted in two-foot script on the trailer's side as they headed into work. In large black lettering that looked like calligraphy was the quotation: "*O, she doth teach the torches to burn bright.*" The sentence was interrupted by the two doors, so it took the whole forty feet of the mobile home to complete.

Immediately, Christine had thought about Dennis Sloan. Had he done this after he dropped her off and the program closed for the night?

"You recognize the quotation?" Dr. Reid asked.

"*Romeo and Juliet,*" Fillingham said.

Christine could feel herself blush. Malo would be exhilarated, but it made Christine sick. She was getting in deeper, and she wasn't sure how to navigate her way out, nail Sloan for his alleged drug empire and extract Kelly while keeping herself sane and safe.

Fillingham grabbed a rag, and the two of them set to work wiping off the paint. It didn't come off easily, and Christine got them rubber gloves. This was going to take a while.

"Juliet, you are one busy woman," Fillingham said, scrubbing at the siding.

"How's that?"

"You get around."

She stopped rubbing, rag in hand. "What's that supposed to mean?"

He pointed to himself. "Me. Hawk. Shakespeare. How many boyfriends can you juggle at once?" He whistled. "Quite the libido."

She strode over and pushed him so that he went stumbling into the side of the stairs. While he struggled to regain his footing, she grabbed him in a headlock, bending him over. "You think I want this?" she said as she backed up, dragging him over to the wrestling mat still out from the previous day.

"A biker takes me for a motorcycle ride, and you think that's fun?" she hissed in his ear. He mumbled something, and she clinched his neck closer.

She continued, "Every second, I'm wondering: is he going to try something? Will he rape me? Or maybe just beat the crap out of me? Slice my face? Is he taking me somewhere to meet with five of his buddies? Is he getting suspicious about my questions? Those are the fun thoughts going through my head when I'm with Shakespeare."

"Okay." Fillingham gasped. "Okay. I got it."

She loosened her grip and could hear Fillingham breathing deeply, catching his breath. She kneeled on the mat, still holding him around the neck. "I do not want to be your girlfriend."

"I know." His voice was hoarse.

"And I'm not with Hawk. He's married. So I have no boyfriend, for which I thank God every day."

"I was joking."

"It's not a joke."

"I can feel that, *Christina*."

His recitation of her name reminded her she was supposed to be working right now. As Christina—Trailer Project staff. She loosened her hold, and Fillingham sat down on the mat, his neck ringed red.

Christine sat down facing him. "This is not easy for me."

"I know. I was out of line. I was joking to lighten the mood. But it's not a funny situation. I get that." He stood up and held out his hand.

She got to her feet, and Fillingham opened his arms for a hug. "Let's make up before Dr. Reid comes out and orders us to clean the septic. "

The last thing she felt like doing was hugging Fillingham, but she obediently leaned in for an embrace. She rested her head on his shoulder, her breath calming. They stayed there, neither moving, as the anger drained out of her. It felt good to be held, even if it was role-playing. Fillingham was her partner. He was on her side, even if he sometimes acted like a jerk. She could depend on him. He had her back.

Fillingham leaned out of the embrace and went to kiss her on the cheek. Christine turned her cheek to him, and somehow their lips met. They stood there kissing for several seconds.

The Trailer door banged open. Gail's' voice said, "Can you two stop smooching and get to work?"

After Christine and Fillingham finished erasing the graffiti, Christine busied herself cleaning inside the mobile home while he worked outside. She volunteered for the physical jobs: mopping floors, wiping down cupboards and taking out the garbage while Gail, Sarah and Dr. Reid dealt with clients. She wanted to keep busy, keep her mind off her kiss with Fillingham.

It was accidental; they sometimes kissed on the cheek in greeting, or Fillingham would kiss her on the forehead. No big deal. The kiss was a mistake. That's all. And they held the kiss because they were surprised.

She wasn't backstabbing Julie. She had no designs on Fillingham. She thought Julie and Fillingham made a cute couple. Of course, Christine liked Fillingham. He was funny and energetic and a good partner. But that was it.

After an hour of cleaning, her thoughts circling, Christine moved into the trailer's kitchen. Head in the small fridge, she pulled out leftover sandwiches, dry muffins and outdated milk cartons and dumped the old food in the garbage. She cleared out the rest of the food and wiped the inside of the fridge. She took out the shelves and soaped them up in the sink. The more she cleaned, the calmer she felt. She'd be happy to spend the entire day making the caravan ship-shape if she could avoid her uncomfortable thoughts.

"Christina," Gail said.

Christine turned from her position at the sink. "What's up?"

"Someone's asking for you. They're outside at the picnic table."

Christine nodded. The staff made connections as they roamed the Village, and a client sometimes asked for a specific person.

"I'll be right there." Christine dried her hands on a tea towel while Gail went down the aisle to a medical office.

Christine descended the stairs, a ready smile on her face for the person seated at the picnic table.

She stopped dead. *Kelly!*

She looked gray, as though her skin never saw the sun, dressed in long sleeves and pants as if she were always cold, even in summer. Her hands were clasped on the picnic table. It was the same girl from last night.

The teenager turned, staring intensely at Christine with her wide brown eyes.

"I, um, hi. I'm Christina." Christine sat across the picnic table from the young woman.

"I know." Her voice was flat.

"Can I get you a coffee?" Christine pointed to the urn. She needed a moment to gather her thoughts. And she had to keep Kelly here as long as possible.

The teen nodded.

"Black?"

She nodded again.

Christine handed her the coffee and poured herself a cup. She tried to calm her racing thoughts as she spooned sugar into her cup. She had Kelly Darlow, a.k.a. Alice Dodgson, in front of her. Deputy Darlow's missing daughter. If Christine played her cards right, Kelly could be home with her parents today. And Christine's secret mission would be completed.

After taking a sip, Christine said, "I'm sorry. I didn't catch your name."

The teen ignored her. She scanned the yard, eyes lighting on the couches and beanbag chairs Fillingham had set back in order, the lava lamps and coffee table. She was constantly moving, her toe jiggling as she crossed her legs.

"How can I help you?" Christine asked.

"I need money," the girl said.

"Okay," Christine responded. She opened the manila folder in front of her containing forms for resources and services. "Did you need help with groceries? Your rent?"

"I need cash." She glared at Christine. Her eyes were fringed with long, dark eyelashes.

"What do you need it for?"

The woman placed her coffee on the picnic table. Her wrists were so thin. She must weigh a hundred and ten pounds, even though she was almost as tall as Christine. "What the fuck does it matter?"

Christine raised her eyebrows at the profanity but calmly said, "It matters to the Trailer Project. We're not a bank that gives out money. We provide services and resources. What do you need?"

Kelly leaned back, arms crossed. "I know who you are."

Christine froze. What did she mean?

"You've been looking for me," the young woman added.

Christine felt a whoosh of relief. Kelly had heard that Trailer Project staff were looking for her around the Village. She didn't know about Operation Niagara.

"I need five hundred bucks," Kelly said.

"Five hundred? That's a lot of money."

"You're the one looking for me, *Christina,*" she said. "Not the other way around." She stood up and stepped out of the picnic bench. "You got a week. Find the money, or I'm going to disappear." She regarded Christine with a flat stare. "Forever."

Chapter 25

"This sandwich is terrible," Julie said, tossing it back into the paper bag.

Fillingham, Julie, Sarah and Christine sat around the cast iron patio table in the backyard of Gallery Europa, shaded by the oak tree and surrounded by concrete and wooden sculptures. After checking out the art gallery last week, they had come back for a return visit. Carlos didn't care if they ate outside his place, so they had picked up dinner and met in the backyard. They could get together with Julie and discuss information they had gleaned from clients and customers that would be forwarded to Malo. Plus, the trees and grass blocked the noise from the Village.

"Geoffrey," Julie said, "can you get me the soup from Le Café?"

"Sure," Fillingham said. "Are you sure you're okay?"

Julie looked wan, despite wearing a bright red minidress with matching crimson lipstick. And a line of dark roots showed in her hair.

Julie gave him a smile, then patted his hand.

He turned and headed toward the pathway at the side of the gallery that would take him back onto Yorkville Avenue.

"Too much shimmying in the front window?" Christine asked.

Julie shook her head, then looked down. A tear dropped into her lap.

"Julie!" Sarah said, moving into the chair beside Julie. "What's wrong?"

Julie shook her head again and sniffed several times as another tear ran down her cheek. Sarah looked at Christine, who shrugged.

"Is it Sal?" Sarah asked. They all knew the owner of the Toucan was a bit much, pressuring the waitresses to hustle more business.

Julie shook her head again. She patted at the mascara smeared under each eye with her fingertips, then gave a long exhale.

"Is it the job?" Christine asked.

Again, Julie shook her head. She looked more composed now. She took a tissue from her purse and blew her nose, removing some of the pancake makeup.

"No," Julie said. "Other than hustling for the customer dollar and being creative with his taxes, Sal seems clean. The bartender sells weed, bought off a kid from East York, but I haven't seen evidence of organized criminal activities."

"We're working long hours," Sarah said. "That takes a toll."

It must be hard to be Julie on her own at the Toucan while the rest of them worked at the Trailer Project.

Christine felt a pang of guilt. Neither she nor Fillingham had mentioned their accidental kiss. Christine was happy to pretend it had never happened. For a minute, she had considered what it would be like to be Fillingham's girlfriend. The fun-loving guy dating the too-serious woman. Richie Rich romancing the girl from Parkdale. Ridiculous.

"I'm a bit emotional," Julie said.

"Things can feel overwhelming," Sarah said, leaning toward Julie. "Especially in our jobs."

Julie waved her hand in negation. She took a deep breath. "I'm pregnant."

Christine's mouth dropped.

Sarah placed her hand over Julie's. "We're here for you, Julie."

Christine asked, "What did Fillingham say?"

Julie's eyes widened in alarm. "I haven't told him." She pointed a finger at Christine. "You can't say anything. Either of you!" She pointed at Sarah.

Sarah said, "Okay, Julie, we won't say a word. You tell him when you're ready."

"You think I am going to tell him?" Julie spat out, one hand on her chest.

Christine was taken aback by Julie's anger. "I... I...think he'd want to know."

"Do you?" Julie turned to Christine. "Do you really! In your vast knowledge of men, that's what you figured out. That a boyfriend wants to hear that his girlfriend is pregnant."

"I...mean...he cares for you," Christine said.

"We have fun."

"It's more than that," Sarah said.

Julie shook her head. "It isn't, really. Do you think Geoffrey Fillingham III wants a shotgun wedding with a woman from work?"

"Julie," Sarah said. "Geoffrey loves you."

Julie shook her head, her hands clasped tightly in her lap. A blue jay squawked loudly in the oak tree above them.

"Does the doctor," Julie said, "does Dr. Reid, can she help me?"

"Help you with what?" Christine asked.

Julie said, "I don't want it. I need it to go away."

Sarah met Christine's glance.

Sarah said gently, "You know that's not legal. Even in the hospitals. It's only allowed if the mother's life is in danger.

"I don't care," Julie wailed. "I'll get it somewhere else."

"Julie," Christine said, "it's dangerous. All of us have seen it."

"They're not all like that." Julie sat up taller.

"It's too risky," Christine said.

"Help me." Julie grabbed each of her friends' hands. "You both have to help me."

"What's all this?" Fillingham had entered the backyard unseen. "Having a séance without me?"

Julie laughed loudly, releasing her friends' hands to take the bottle of ginger ale from him. "Just horsing around. You know the girls."

He smiled. "Up to mischief is my guess."

Julie looked at both her friends, silencing them. She stood up and gave Fillingham a hug. "You know us so well."

"Did I do something to offend you guys?" Fillingham was washing apples at the trailer's kitchen sink later that week.

"You mean more than normal?" Gail said.

"Very funny. Everyone is so quiet. Down at the mouth."

Christine met Gail's glance. Christine said, "Everything's good."

Fillingham raised his eyebrows in disbelief. He patted the apples dry with a tea towel, deposited them in a bowl, then went outside to place the food on the picnic table.

"You're acting weird in front of Geoff," Gail said to Christine in a low voice. She was standing in front of the kitchen cupboard with a clipboard, inventorying food, while Christine sorted through a box of donated bakery items on the coffee table.

Christine brushed icing powder off her hands. "I can't help it. I don't think Julie has told him. I hate keeping secrets from him; he's my partner." She lined the basket with wax paper and placed the croissants inside. "We have to talk to Julie."

"We already did," Gail said.

Gail, Christine and Sarah had gone over to Julie's apartment and sat around her kitchen table with warm cups of tea in their hands.

"I need it gone," Julie had cried, her face blotchy from tears. "Can't Dr. Reid help me out?"

Gail said, "Dr. Reid said abortions are tightly controlled in the hospitals and only used in high-risk situations for the mother. There are no legal methods for a woman to get a safe abortion."

"I can't tell Geoffrey," Julie said. "I can't tell my parents. I'm going to lose my job. My life is over." She sobbed into her hands.

For policewomen, pregnancy resulted in automatic job termination, married or not.

Sarah reached over and rubbed Julie's back, her brow furrowed with concern. Christine found a tissue box and proffered it to Julie.

As Julie wiped her face, Christine said, "Maybe you can go out of town for a while. Stay with a relative or friend. Take a leave of absence until the baby is born."

"I don't know anyone to stay with," Julie cried.

Christine said, "There are organizations that have places out of town for pregnant women."

Sarah said, "You have to be careful. Some of the Christian organizations are quite strict. I've spoken with a few women who feel their treatment there was abusive. They were castigated the whole time for sinning, and their babies were taken, even if they wanted to keep them."

Christine reached for Julie's hand, but Julie pulled away. "You don't get it. All of you. I'm not having this baby. It's not wanted. I don't want it inside me. It's ruining everything."

Sarah said, "There are people who want babies, Julie. It will be easy to find a nice family for adoption."

"I want to get rid of it. Now," Julie said. Her brown stare was fierce.

"There's no legal abortion," Christine repeated.

"Then I'll do it illegally," Julie responded, her eyes wide and wild. "I will. They're around. People talk. The Morality Squad gets calls about them all the time. Some of them are doctors."

"Julie," Gail said tersely. "Those are backroom abortionists. We know about them because they botch the job. We just found a girl from the Village who was hemorrhaging from a self-induced abortion. It's dangerous to do this yourself. Or go to one of these quacks. They're not trained. It's easy money for them. There is no way you want any of those guys touching you."

Julie grabbed Gail's wrist from across the table, pulling Gail's arm toward her. "You must know somebody. You know lots of women—smart women."

Everyone was quiet for a few seconds.

"You're political," Julie continued, grabbing Gail's other hand. "You're always talking about women's rights. You must know someone."

Gail shook her head. "I don't know anyone safe. There was a female doctor performing abortions last year, but she was scared that she would be jailed and lose her license, so she stopped. There's a new clinic in Montreal, but it hasn't opened its doors."

"You've got to help me!" Julie wailed.

Sarah wrapped an arm around Julie's shoulder. "We'll find you a place to have the baby, somewhere safe, with kind people."

Christine and Gail left Julie's apartment to head to work. They could hear Julie's sobs through the closed door as they walked down the hall to the elevators.

Christine sighed as she grabbed another basket for the bakery goods. There were many reasons she was acting "weird" in front of Fillingham. Julie's pregnancy was a loaded secret. It wasn't that Fillingham would necessarily marry Julie, but he wouldn't desert her either. That much, Christine knew. And he would want to know. She and Fillingham both had been abandoned by their parents to a certain extent, and he wouldn't do that to someone else.

Fillingham had criticized Christine about her tendency to keep secrets and explained that it wrecked the trust between them. Which of course made Christine feel even more guilty about Julie and the search for Kelly Darlow.

Kelly. Christine went outside and placed the croissants and muffins on the picnic table. Christine had called the deputy about Kelly's appearance at the Trailer Project and again to let him know she had checked the Village all week with no sign of the teen. On the phone, Christine had asked, "Why didn't Kelly ask you or your wife for money, like she usually does?"

"I think she knows how desperate we are to hear from her. Now that she knows you are looking for her, she can get money without having to contact us directly."

"If you give her the five hundred dollars, won't she come back again for another payment?"

He sighed. "Maybe. And I know it's used for drugs. But it's our only connection with her. And maybe one time we can build on that. Give her some food. Pay for lodgings. A haircut. Get her to come home for a visit."

"Sir, if we include more people in the search, police, social service agencies, addiction centers, maybe you'd have more luck in getting her help."

"My wife does not want the notoriety, Constable. It is not helpful to our family or to Kelly." His tone was clipped. Final. They ended the call with a time to meet so Darlow could give her the money.

Now Christine was wearing a hidden money belt filled with folded twenty-dollar bills for when she met Kelly again. And she was carrying a boatload of guilt regarding her secrets about Julie, Kelly and the memory of Fillingham's kiss.

Later that afternoon, Christine walked solo around the Village, circulated amongst the cafés and throngs of people, distributing flyers and showing Kelly's photo to visitors. There were no seats on the Toucan patio. The place was bustling. Christine saw Julie in passing and received a quick wave before Julie took a customer's order.

Christine continued along Yorkville Avenue, enjoying the sun, chatting with groups as she passed by, setting aside her guilt and stress for a few moments. The Village was an energizing place, full of music, poetry and youth enjoying food and a glass of wine on a patio. On a summer afternoon, it was glorious.

As she walked west, she spotted four motorcycles parked on the sidewalk. The street had no parking. It was a one-way road clotted with eastbound traffic, cars stopped to gawk at the youth in colorful clothing on the sidewalks and patios.

Was that Shakespeare's bike amongst the motorcycles? Christine edged closer, wishing she had Gail with her who was knowledgeable about machines. The bike was a Harley-Davidson with a blue gas tank and back fender, like Sloan's. She approached the vehicle, scanning the crowd for Sloan, her stomach knotted. She couldn't wait for Operation Niagara to be over.

"Don't touch!" a voice yelled.

Christine turned. It was a boy, maybe ten or eleven, in bare feet, dirty white shorts and a t-shirt. There weren't many children in the Village. No babies or toddlers. Families and commitment didn't fit the Yorkville lifestyle.

"Are you on guard?" she asked.

The boy crossed his arms. "No one can touch the motorcycles."

He had a space between his front teeth, hair an unwashed tangle.

"What's your name?" she asked.

"What's it to you?"

"I know a place where you can get free chocolate milk. And sandwiches." Christine pointed west toward Avenue Road. "It's the Trailer Project. Have you seen it?"

"They got free cigarettes?" he asked.

"Kid," a voice called.

The boy and Christine turned.

Dennis Sloan was wearing a white t-shirt, jeans and leather vest with the Grizzly logo on the back. His blue eyes looked bright in his tanned face, framed by his dark hair.

"Protecting the bikes, sir," the boy said. "Like you said."

Sloan tousled the boy's long hair. "Good job." He passed the boy two single dollar bills. "We're good here."

The boy slipped the money into his shorts pocket and disappeared into the crowd.

Christine raised her hands in the air. "I didn't touch anything. I was checking if the bike was yours."

"Looking for me, Christina?" he said, smiling, his teeth white against his black beard and mustache.

"Actually, I was." She zipped open her purse and grabbed the book of sonnets. As she pulled it out, a piece of paper fell to the sidewalk. It was a photo of Kelly, the one Christine had showed around the Village.

Sloan picked up the photo, pausing, before handing it to Christine.

Christine's breathing quickened. "Do you know her?"

His glance was unreadable. "No."

"Her name is Alice. A friend came to the trailer looking for her, saying she hadn't seen her or a while."

He said nothing.

She proffered the leather book. "Thanks for the sonnets. I didn't get through them all, but most of them."

He shook his head. "It's a gift for you."

"I can't take it," she said, smiling. "I could tell the book was well read, well loved."

"Keep it." His tone brooked no argument.

"Oh, okay." She needed to do better, keep the repartee going. Malo had a list of questions she was supposed to ask Sloan the next time they met.

"I have a favorite poem," Christine said.

"This wasn't a homework assignment," he said, smiling.

Christine opened the book to Sonnet CXXX. "'My mistress' eyes are nothing like the sun.'" She looked up at Sloan. "He's being funny, right? Because most sonnets describe the women as beautiful."

He nodded.

"Her hair is wire, her breath isn't great, and she doesn't tread lightly," she said. "Realistic, right? He's saying that she's a real woman, a real person, not a goddess."

"That's what I think about you," he said.

She joked, "That I don't tread lightly?"

He shook his head. "You're fresh. Real. Honest."

Yes, she was honest as they come. Time to change topics. "Nice day to be in the Village," she said. "Are you taking the day off?"

He shrugged. "I choose my schedule."

"I'm working today, as you can see." She showed him a handful of postcards she was handing out.

"I did a little work this morning," he said. "Came here to relax."

"Are you sticking around?"

"Why? Wanna go somewhere?" he asked.

She shook her head. "I work until three." She paused. "But maybe another day. Are you in town for a while?"

Malo had said to check for any trips out of town in case Sloan headed to Montreal.

"For a couple of days."

Christine said, "Sunday?"

He shook his head. "It'll have to be earlier. Saturday?"

"Saturdays are busy, but maybe we can have coffee around dinner-time."

He nodded.

"I should head back to the Trailer."

"*Alea, iacta est*," he said, staring at her.

She was so close to him, she could smell his leather vest, the smell of gasoline. It reminded her of Hawk. "Is that from Shakespeare?"

He shook his head. "'Til we meet again."

Chapter 26

"Duck!" Fillingham said. The three policewomen lowered their heads as the boom of his twenty-eight-foot boat swooped across the boat's cockpit.

"I think he's trying to kill me," Christine said to Sarah and Gail sitting beside her.

Gail stood up. She was in shorts, deck shoes and a baseball cap. "I'll see what he's up to." Gail loved to sail, like Fillingham.

Gail joined Fillingham at the helm while Christine and Sarah held on to the rails and made their way to the bow. To their right, an airplane taxied on the Toronto Island Airport runway, its drone mingling with the wind. As the boat reached the outer harbor, Christine tucked her hair into the neck of her jacket. It was the first day in July, but the lake air was chilly. She was glad she had brought a windbreaker.

Sarah patted the place beside her, and Christine sat down close so they could chat without having to yell above the wind. This was a good idea, the four of them getting out, away from Yorkville, shaking off the stress of their undercover jobs. Too bad Julie wasn't here. Fillingham said she was visiting an aunt in Ottawa. Christine wondered if Julie was scouting a place to stay during her pregnancy.

Christine sighed as she thought of Julie. It was clear Julie hadn't confessed her pregnancy to Fillingham; there was no way he would be so light-hearted.

Christine shook her head. She didn't want to think about secrets today. She wanted to enjoy the blue sky, the smell of fresh water and the Lake Ontario horizon that never seemed to end.

The four officers had already talked shop before they set out on the water. Fillingham had ordered food from the yacht club kitchen, and the group had lunched on a picnic table by the docks. Strawberries, grapes, cheese, bread, deli meats, olives and wine. A delicious spread.

"No wonder women like you," Sarah had said, gesturing to the food on the table.

"I am resourceful," he said.

The women toasted Fillingham with raised wine glasses as he beamed at them in his white captain's hat.

Christine smiled. Things seemed back to normal between her and Fillingham. If they could just get through Operation Niagara, return to Island patrol, then all would be well.

"What's the latest from Malo?" Fillingham asked as he popped a grape into his mouth.

Gail said, "He's following up on the info we gave him about break-ins, vandalism and assaults, but he's all about the drugs."

Sarah said, "Cleaning up all criminal behaviors would be good for the Village."

Fillingham said, "He thinks it all starts with the drugs. Nail the suppliers and all related crimes go down."

Gail said, "Any news from your greaser friends?"

Fillingham shook his head. "I haven't seen them since the drop-in. They seem a low-level operation. A part-time business."

Gail said, "Even if greasers get the hard stuff from the bikers to sell, there's no way they're snitching. They'd lose their kneecaps."

Christine added, "Malo said that Grizzly activity has increased. New member initiations. Their club has been renovated. They bought a cottage in the Kawarthas. They're flush. And it's not from their usual income sources of racketeering, prostitution or loan sharking. It's evidence they may have ventured into the drug business."

Gail said, "The Grizzlies identified a need in the market, an opportunity with so many youth heading to the Village for drugs."

Sarah said, "I always thought of bikers as drinkers, not drug users."

Christine said, "I don't get the sense that they use. Malo said some clubs have a rule against it in their by-laws. Weed is fine, but anything that goes into your arm is grounds for expulsion." Certainly, Sloan wouldn't put a needle in his arm.

"What's Malo's next step?" Gail asked Christine.

"I told him Sloan was busy Sunday and wouldn't be in the Village, so they're following that lead."

Fillingham wiped his mouth with a linen napkin. "No more shop talk. Time to take you ladies for the voyage of your life."

"How's the Women's Bureau?" Christine asked Sarah as the boat headed west out onto Lake Ontario. The two women were sitting on the bow of the sailboat as Fillingham and Gail steered in the stern.

"Not bad. I don't mind ticketing when the weather's nice."

"Any places for Julie come up?" Christine asked. Sarah had contacts in social services.

Sarah stretched her legs out in front, her striped shirt billowing with the wind. "There's a few houses in Toronto run by churches, but I think Julie wants to get out of town."

"Ottawa?" Christine asked.

"I'm not sure."

"How does adoption work?" Christine had been thinking about this, not only for Julie, but also regarding Hawk's situation.

Sarah said, "The pregnant woman or mother consents for adoption and signs the necessarily legal papers."

"If Children's Aid is involved with a family, they can remove a child and put it up for adoption, correct?"

Sarah frowned. "It depends. They would make a case for removal with documented visits over months, even years. Maybe have the child fostered first while the parents get help."

"But if the judge decides it's in the best interest of the child, the child can be removed permanently from the home."

Sarah nodded. "It's very sad and traumatic. The children never want to leave, even if they are living in neglect. I hated being called to removals."

Christine nodded. Policewomen were called to assist child welfare in these situations. They were tortuous scenes, the child screaming, the parent yelling or sometimes silently crying.

"And how about if a mother wanted to find the adopted family of her child?" Christine was thinking of Remi and Layla, Hawk's family.

"Occasionally, the adopted family allows this, but it's rare. The philosophy is that it's better to cut the ties so that everyone can move on. They make this clear in the consent form."

"Where is adoption information kept?"

"The agency would have it. And the court."

"So, the information is physically in a file somewhere?"

Sarah nodded, her curly short hair whipping around in tendrils around her sunglasses. "We had cabinets under lock and key in the agency I worked at. Only the supervisor could go in. And the court papers are closed to the public."

"Could they get accessed?"

"I guess the police could file for access if it involves a case. But they would have to petition the court."

"Sixteen!"

Christine looked over her shoulder at Fillingham. Sixteen was her badge number.

He motioned for her to come back and steer the boat.

Christine stood up, stumbling a bit as the boat hit a wave. Looking down at Sarah, she said, "You may want to put your lifejacket on."

The next day, Christine walked quickly along Bloor Street, eager to meet up with Fillingham at the church stairs. Her mood had improved since their sailing afternoon. Gail had reminded Christine that it was Julie's prerogative to tell Fillingham about the pregnancy, even if he was Christine's partner and friend.

Last night, Christine and her mom had baked before Phyllis went to bingo. Donna had helped, but Wayne said he'd just eat the butter tarts once they were ready. So Christine had a container of home-made tarts for Fillingham and the Trailer Project staff.

As she crossed the intersection of Avenue and Bloor, she spotted a woman with long brown hair and baggy clothing sitting on the top steps of the church.

Kelly.

Christine slowed, trying to think. Kelly didn't look at her, but Christine sensed she was aware of her approach. Kelly was there for the cash, of course. Touching her waist, Christine felt the money belt underneath.

She tried to think of a phrase that would get Kelly to stick around or get help. Go home to a family who missed her. Who wanted to help her. Christine was worried that Kelly would grab the money and run.

Settling near Kelly on the stairs, Christine said, "Hi, Alice. It's nice to see you again."

Kelly tossed her head, pushing the greasy strands of hair away from her face as she glared at Christine. She was in a man's long cotton shirt that billowed around her thin frame.

Kelly didn't seem high, just agitated.

"Give me the money." Kelly stuck out an arm toward Christine, showing fingernails bitten down to the quick.

"Let's chat first," Christine said.

"Do you have my fuckin' money or not?"

"I do. I do. I just want to say hello. See how you're doing."

Kelly leaned forward, her brown eyes large in her face, deep circles hollowing her eyes, acne trailing across her forehead and down her cheek. "How I'm doing? You want to talk? Like we're buddies? Sorority sisters?"

Christine raised both hands in the air. "I'm just asking how you are. Maybe there's something the Trailer Project can help you with."

"You can give me the five hundred dollars."

Christine lifted the hem of her shirt and unzipped the wallet pouch one inch to show the wad of bills.

Kelly huffed a laugh. "You *do* know my dad."

"What do you mean?" Christine said.

Kelly gave her a baleful look. "I know Christina doesn't have five hundred dollars lying around unless you stole it from work. I've seen the dump you live in."

Christine froze. How would Kelly know where she lived? She pushed the thought to the back of her mind. It was best to come clean. "Your parents care about you. They want to help you."

She snorted, her head falling back, showing her long, sinewy neck. "You don't get it."

"Get what?"

"You don't know one fucking thing about my family."

"So tell me," Christine said. If she could keep Kelly talking, connect with her, figure out how to help her, then maybe she would stick around.

"I'm not the prize horse," Kelly said. "The apple of everybody's eye. I never was."

Christine blinked. Did Kelly have a sister or brother? Deputy Darlow had described Kelly as an only child. Maybe the Darlows had high expectations of Kelly, expectations their daughter couldn't meet.

"My stepdad didn't understand me," Christine offered. "Or like me."

"But your father did," Kelly said, staring at her.

Christine frowned. "I never knew my father."

"You do." Kelly smirked.

What game was Kelly playing? Did she know Christine's mother had gotten pregnant by a man engaged to someone else? And then never saw him again.

"I don't know what you're talking about," Christine said.

"You and me," Kelly said, a smile playing around her mouth, "have got more in common than you think." She paused and added, "Sis."

Christine's head jerked back.

Kelly pointed at herself and then Christine. "That's right. You and me. Half sisters. Can you believe it?"

What was Kelly talking about? How could they possibly be related?

Kelly stared at Christine, her smile widening. "Bit of a shock for me too when I found out, snooping around my dad's den. He had forgotten to lock his desk drawer, for once. And I knew he kept cigars there. And there it was!" She paused dramatically. "The scrapbook."

Deputy Darlow—her father? Kelly must be high. Delirious.

"It was a loving record of a little girl as she grew up," Kelly said. "Pictures of her as a baby. Then toddler. Riding a red tricycle. Out in the park on the swings. A report card from her grade two teacher. A perseverance award from grade eight graduation from Parkdale Elementary School. Her wrestling team certificate. A shot-put ribbon. Even an eight-by-ten glossy of her graduation from police college."

Christine shook her head. This wasn't making sense.

"The girl in the picture, Christine Lane, it said on the report card, looked like me. She was taller and heavier. And wasn't wearing very nice clothes. But I knew it, by the time I turned the last page, that you were the one. My sister. The one he loved better."

Christine shook her head again. "I have no idea what you're talking about. I never met Deputy Darlow before I started on the police force."

Kelly's head tilted. "He was following your life."

"You must be mistaken."

She scratched her arm. "No, I heard my mom and dad fighting about you. About the money he sent every month to your mom—Phyllis."

"We didn't get any money."

"Maybe *you* didn't. Your mother did." She sighed and smiled at Christine, showing the missing bottom tooth. "Is that enough chatting for you? Can I have the money now?"

Christine stared at Kelly, her jaw slack with shock. Mechanically, she withdrew the money from her waist wallet and handed Kelly the five hundred dollars.

Kelly grabbed the wad, and it quickly disappeared into the folds of her clothes. She stood up. "Now you know how I felt all this time; no matter how hard I tried, I was never quite good enough."

Christine knew she shouldn't let Kelly leave. At least set up a time to meet again, ensure that she stayed in town, implore her to call home, but no words came out.

Kelly walked away and disappeared behind the church. Christine stared blindly at the cars driving by on Bloor Street.

"Hey, Christina." It was Fillingham. "Who was that?" He stood in front of her, his chin pointed toward the church.

Christine stared at him mutely.

"The girl you were talking with," he added.

Christine shook her head. "No one," she managed.

He frowned. "What's going on?"

She looked at his clear, frank gaze, the concerned blue eyes. How many lies were between them? And now this.

"I just, I don't." She blinked. "I don't feel well."

"You're really white." He sat down beside her. "Lower your head. You look like you're going to faint."

"I might be sick," she whispered, closing her eyes as her head rested on her knees, wishing she had never been assigned to Operation Niagara, that she was back on Toronto Island bike racing her partner to the Centre Island Pier, the loser stuck with sweeping the kitchen floor.

Chapter 27

"Come on," Fillingham urged Christine. "I'll give you a juggling lesson. It'll make you feel better."

It was two days since Christine had met with Kelly on the church stairs. Christine had done nothing with Kelly's proclamation that they were stepsisters. She hadn't talked to Phyllis or Sarah or Fillingham. She was numb. And incredulous. In a million years, she couldn't envision her mom with the deputy. Phyllis had said Christine's father married his wealthy fiancée. Had he just let Phyllis raise Christine on her own?

"Go ahead," Gail said. "I'll call you if we need help."

There were two people sitting on the kitchen couch for services. One youth had just finished with the law student, and Gail would take the second client. Dr. Reid had been called into the hospital, so they were on their own for the last hour of their shift.

It was two o'clock in the morning, Friday night, or rather early Saturday morning. They had been busier in the evening, but things had been winding down since some businesses and music venues closed. Christine and Fillingham headed outside.

Across the street, a lone couple sipped coffee on the outdoor patio of a closed café. Groups of youths walked south down Avenue Road, probably heading to Bloor Street to find an all-night bus or taxi home. And cars still turned onto Yorkville Street as visitors and gawkers checked out the scene.

Fillingham pulled out a mat and placed it several feet away from the couches. The mat was lit by a soft white glow from the trailer lights, but he dragged a side table over with a lava lamp for additional light.

"No grapefruit," Christine requested. Fillingham liked to juggle from the bowl of fruit on the picnic table, and the heavier citrus fruit had hit her on the head and shoulders more than once.

"Yes, my sad, sad girl, we are going back to basics. Guaranteed success to elevate the mood."

She smiled. Things were less strained between her and Fillingham, although Christine had been fuzzy and distracted since meeting Kelly. Deputy Darlow—her father? Kelly—her stepsister? Maybe Kelly was a consummate liar, intent on hurting anyone in her path to getting high. But why would she make up stuff about Christine and her father? What was her game?

Shaking her head to dispel thoughts of the Darlows, Christine sat on the couch as Fillingham grabbed three rubber balls from his box of juggling equipment. He demonstrated juggling with two balls and how you introduced the third into the series. As she watched him grab a ball from behind his back, she thought how lucky she was to have him as a partner. As a friend. And that this thing with Julie's pregnancy had better resolve fast.

"Your turn." He caught the balls in the cradle of his arms. He tossed two of them at her. One hit her in the arm, the other her chest.

"Ow. Give me a warning." She picked the rubber balls off the couch. Quickly, she threw all three at her partner.

One hit him on the shoulder while the other two went flying past him toward the trailer.

"Temper, temper," he said, wagging his finger. "We only have three rubber balls, so unless you want to upgrade to bowling balls, I suggest you find them." He picked up the ball beside him.

She looked behind the stairs. There it was—a patch of white under the picnic table. She crouched and peered underneath.

"Geoff!" she yelled. "Someone's passed out under here."

She could hear him running over. It was shadowy under the table. She could just make out a person, a woman, lying on her stomach. "Get a flashlight!"

Christine tried to reach the person through the bench seat. "Hey, can you hear me?" She tapped the person on the shoulder. "My name is Christina. I'm here to help."

She didn't smell alcohol. Or marijuana, or even cigarette smoke. A heroin overdose?

"Hey," Christine said, moving closer to shake a shoulder. "Wake up."

A small groan.

Christine exhaled. The person was alive.

Light ricocheted around Christine. Fillingham was back. The beam lit up the person for a second before veering off. It was a woman, face turned away, in a dark dress and white boots. Nice clothes—well dressed. Probably not a junkie. Maybe she had been at the table waiting for help and fainted, slipping under.

"Can you grab a blanket, and we'll roll her onto it, then slide her out," Christine said. The two picnic tables were chained together, so it would be difficult to lift them off the woman.

Fillingham ran into the trailer and was back in less than ten seconds. Placing the flashlight on the ground, they half lifted, half pulled the woman onto the cover and tugged the blanket until she was out from under the table. They gently turned her on her back.

"Julie!" Christine and Fillingham said in unison.

The woman's eyes fluttered in her ashen face.

"Julie, honey," he said, leaning over her. "What happened?"

Julie's eyes opened and closed several times. Her eyeliner was smudged, her hair tangled.

"Are you hurt?" he asked. He quickly checked her head for bumps with his fingers, looking for contusions. "Can you move your hands?" He raised her right hand in the air. After a few seconds, several fingers twitched. She moved her left hand.

"Great," he said. "Now your legs. Bend your knees for me."

It took a full minute, but one, then the other leg bent.

"Go get Gail," Christine said.

Fillingham ran inside the trailer, and she could hear him thumping down the aisle.

Christine leaned over Julie. "Julie, did you do anything? Did you take anything?" Had Julie been so depressed that she took an overdose? Was this about her pregnancy?

Julie didn't answer.

Gail came running out and kneeled beside Julie. She checked Julie's carotid artery and then pried open her eyes. Standing up, she said, "Let's get her inside. Can you bring her in on the blanket?"

Julie and Fillingham lifted the blanket and brought Julie into the medical room. They placed her carefully on the examination table.

"She's bleeding," Gail said.

"What? Where?" Christine asked.

Gail pointed to rivulets of red down Julie's leg.

"Is she stabbed?" Fillingham asked.

Julie's eyes were open now, but she seemed unaware, staring blankly into space.

"Everyone out!" Gail said, swooping her arms at Christine and Fillingham.

"I'm not going anywhere," he said.

"Out," Gail repeated. "If I need anything, I'll call you."

"No," he said.

"You're delaying her treatment," Gail said.

Christine pulled on Fillingham's arm. "We'll be right outside the door."

They waited for five minutes, hearing Gail ask Julie questions, a quiet voice responding.

"Let's sit on the couch in the kitchen," Christine said. "We can watch the door from there."

Fillingham couldn't stand still. He sat down. Stood up.

"Geoff," Christine said. "Let's close the Trailer Project for the night. We'll be ready to take Julie to the hospital or go home with her. Turn off the lights outside, and I'll tidy the kitchen—"

Fillingham bolted outside. She could hear him shuffling the furniture, snapping lids on containers.

Christine's stomach was roiling with anxiety. Julie was bleeding. She may have been assaulted. Or was she hemorrhaging from a miscarriage?

Fillingham should pull his car around in case they needed to drive Julie to the hospital.

"Geoff! Christina!" Gail's voice called out.

Christine opened the trailer door and called for Fillingham. The partners hustled down the aisle to the examination room.

Gail was at the open door. Julie was still on the examination table, eyes closed, a blanket tucked around her.

"She needs to go to the hospital," Gail said.

"No!" Julie said, her eyes flaring open.

"Julie—" Fillingham said, approaching her.

"I won't go!" She looked at Fillingham, then at Christine. Her voice was shrill, desperate. "I'll refuse service."

He turned to Gail, face scrunched in confusion.

Gail's voice was gentle as she placed a hand on Julie's arm. "Tell him, and then we'll go."

"I can't," she whispered and turned her head away.

"Tell me what?" he asked.

"You tell him," Julie directed Gail.

"Geoffrey, Julie was pregnant."

"Pregnant?"

"She's hemorrhaging," Gail interrupted abruptly. "From a self-induced abortion." She addressed Julie. "You need to get checked out at a hospital. Make sure that your uterus is empty. Monitor your bleeding."

"I won't go," Julie sobbed. "I'll be fired. For the abortion. For being pregnant."

"Julie," Christine pleaded, moving closer. "Don't worry about that." She looked over at Fillingham for support.

Fillingham was staring at Julie in shock.

"Julie," Gail said. "You're still bleeding."

Shaking her head, Julie said, "I won't go! I won't go! I won't go! You can't make me."

"What do we do?" Christine whispered to Gail.

Gail shook her head as if to clear her mind. Turning to Fillingham, who hadn't said a word since he received the news, she said, "Get your car."

Wordlessly, he turned and left.

"Where are we going?" Christine asked.

"My place," Gail said.

"Why?" Christine asked.

"My friend," Gail explained, "my roommate, she's a doctor from Poland."

"Can she help Julie?" Christine asked.

"I think so."

Julie agreed to go to Gail's place. They bundled her in the back of Fillingham's car with Gail beside her. Christine hopped in the front with Fillingham.

Gail said, "I'm in an apartment building on Earl Place, near Church and Jarvis."

Without speaking, he squealed out of the parking lot. They got there in five minutes.

Standing in front of Gail's building was a tall woman with straight, dark hair. She was holding on to a wheelchair.

Gail got out and addressed the woman. "Petra, where did you find that?"

"From the building superintendent," Petra said.

Gail and Christine slid their hands under Julie and deposited her into the wheelchair. Julie's head lolled back. She looked like she might pass out again.

"Blood pressure eighty over forty," Gail told Petra. "Pulse sixty-five. Vaginal hemorrhaging. I've palpitated the abdomen for blood clots. I think all tissue is out."

The roar of an engine caused Christine to turn. Fillingham was driving away.

Gail shook her head. "Let's get her inside."

Christine pushed the wheelchair into the elevator as Gail punched the button for the fifth floor. Petra was leaning over Julie, two fingers pressed against Julie's neck to check her pulse.

Gail introduced Christine to her roommate. Petra gave a neutral hello in accented English.

Inside, Petra directed them into a bedroom. A plastic sheet had been thrown over the double bed, then a bedsheet. A doctor's bag and a tray of equipment sat on a side table.

"Should I stay?" Christine asked.

"Wait!" Petra said, extending her hand. She turned to Julie, who was looking at them sleepily from the bed. "Julie, hello, I'm Petra. I'm a friend of Gail's. I'm a doctor. What is your blood type?"

Julie blinked several times.

Petra repeated the question.

"'A' positive," Julie whispered.

Gail said. "I'm 'O.' I can donate if needed." She turned to Christine. "Can you go to the kitchen, get some coffee going? The pot's on the stove, and you'll find everything you need in the cupboards above."

Christine hesitated.

Gail waved her away. "It's okay. Give Petra time to check Julie out."

Petra was leaning over Julie, stethoscope in one hand, as Christine left the bedroom.

Christine went into the kitchen. Mugs were in parallel lines in the cupboards. In the cutlery drawer, the spoons nestled in with each other. The sink was clean, the countertop clear, and the small table was covered by an embroidered linen tablecloth. Their place was kept as tidy as a military barrack.

Christine filled the coffeepot with water, her stomach churning. She was terrified for Julie, but Gail was a good nurse. Christine had seen it at the Trailer Project. If Gail had faith in Petra, then so did Christine. And Gail wasn't stupid. If it became life or death, Gail would call an ambulance, regardless of Julie's wishes. And where the heck was Fillingham?

As the water heated on the stove, Christine wandered restlessly around the apartment, one ear out for the conversation in the bedroom. Solid teak furniture anchored a Persian carpet. A bookshelf by the window contained texts in English, Polish and Russian, the subjects ranging from architecture to literature to medical textbooks.

The hutch displayed framed pictures, glassware, a silver beer stein and a porcelain teapot with matching creamer and sugar bowl. Several of the photographs captured stunning scenery: a dazzling sunset over water, the misty peak of a mountain, the humped backs of whales beside a boat rail. Gail in a white navy uniform in front of a ship. Petra and Gail hoisting drinks in an outdoor beer garden. A photo of them kissing.

They were a couple. How had Christine missed it? She scanned the apartment. It was a one bedroom. Christine shook her head. What did it matter? Gail and Petra were helping Julie, keeping her alive.

Christine set three cups of coffee, creamer and sugar bowl on a tray and stood outside the open door of the bedroom. She could hear the roommates talking in another language. "Can I come in?"

Gail sat in a chair beside the bed, her arm on a pillow, a tube of blood running from her arm into Julie's. Julie's eyes were closed. She seemed asleep.

Petra handed a black coffee to Gail, then added cream and sugar to a cup for herself. Christine placed the tray on the bottom of the bed and grabbed the last cup of coffee, adding cream and sugar too.

"How is she?" Christine asked.

Petra sat down on a chair beside Gail. "She is stable. I believe the fetus was miscarried and the placenta and tissues expunged. I gave her Valium. She sleeps now. I will get a doctor friend to order a blood-clotting prescription for her."

"I thought you were a doctor," Christine said.

"I was," Petra said, "in Poland. I cannot practice here yet."

Gail said, "Petra is a nurse's assistant until she can write her exams."

"How do you have all this equipment?" Christine said, gesturing to the IV and tray of medical tools.

Gail looked at Petra, who gave a slight incline of her head. Gail said, "Petra sometimes helps people without insurance. New immigrants. Refugees from Poland. Russia."

"Is that what you were speaking?" Christine asked. "Polish?"

Gail said, "Russian. Petra's family moved to Poland after the Russian Revolution. And I studied Russian when I worked in navy communications."

Christine shook her head. All that mattered was that Julie was getting care. "She'll be okay?"

Petra nodded. "I believe so, as long as she does not hemorrhage again. Or get septic."

"Can I talk to her? I know she's asleep."

Gail nodded.

Petra said, "I will find something sweet to go with our coffee," and left the room.

Christine sat down on the other side of the bed. Julie lay on her back, head tilted to the side, so marbly white, she looked like a statue.

But she was alive. Christine reached for Julie's arm under the blanket. "Julie, you're tough. You'll get through this. We'll help you get through this."

Christine sat for a few more minutes, holding Julie's hand. Then she stood up.

It was time to find Fillingham.

Chapter 28

Petra lent Christine her car to find Fillingham.

Christine was shocked that he had dumped them off at Gail's and driven away, as if he had been their taxi driver and not a fellow officer, partner or boyfriend.

Turning onto Davenport Road, Christine headed for the tony neighborhood of Forest Hill, where Fillingham had a house bought for him by his parents, who lived nearby. She had visited him at home once and hoped she remembered where the place was. It had a distinctive triangular-shaped front and was farther back from the road than the other houses, more modest in size.

Her intention was to batter the door until he came out, even if the neighbors complained about a four-in-the-morning noise disturbance.

The car crunched to a halt in the gravel driveway. Christine opened her door and stepped out.

He wasn't home. Not only was the house pitch-dark, but his Buick wasn't there. His MG sports car sat at the back of the driveway in front of the garage.

Where could he be at this time of day? A bar? All closed. A friend's? Would Fillingham wake up a private-school buddy or yacht club pal to hash out his feelings about Julie's pregnancy and abortion? Unlikely.

The water. That was where he'd be. He was a water person through and through, a boater and sailor all his life. He was on or by Lake Ontario whenever he wasn't at work. The sound of the crashing waves, the offshore breeze, the smell of the lake would be calming.

Christine headed back downtown. Where exactly would Fillingham be? If it were daylight, he'd be on his racing schooner, leaning halfway off the boat to steer its complex rigging. But it was night, and the water taxi to the yacht club didn't start until seven in the morning.

If he wasn't at the club sailing, maybe he would be by the water. At a beach? The eastern beaches? Sunnyside? People often parked in the beachside lots to gaze at Lake Ontario through the windshield while they ate their lunch or chatted with a friend.

After checking three parking lots in the western beaches and Ashbridge's Bay in the east, Christine pondered returning to Gail's apartment. Finding Fillingham was a needle in a haystack. He could be anywhere in Toronto or out of town. Maybe he had changed his mind and went to Gail's.

It wasn't quite dawn yet, but the sky was lightening, the deep darkness and chill fading. Christine stopped at a red light on Lake Shore Boulevard at Leslie Street. Cherry Beach was five minutes away. Maybe she should look there. On the way, she could check the yacht club parking lot to see if her partner was waiting for the first water taxi over to Toronto Island.

As she drove down Cherry Street, Christine scanned for Fillingham's car. Spotting the sign for the RCYC parking lot, she turned in.

A few cars were scattered over the rectangular lot. *There!* Christine located the gray Buick parked by the dock, facing the island airport and the cityscape.

Christine drove up beside the car.

Fillingham stared straight ahead at the water.

Christine took a deep breath, exited the car and stood beside his window.

Bending down, she tapped on the glass. "Fillingham," she said loudly, "roll down the window."

He ignored her.

"Please. I have an update on Julie."

He blinked. Slowly, the window cranked down. "Is she okay?" he asked, not meeting her eyes.

"Petra thinks she's stable," Christine said. "They stopped the bleeding."

He glanced up at her for a second, blue eyes fierce and cold, before returning his glance frontward. "She should be in a hospital."

"She won't go." She paused. "It would wreck her career."

Fillingham's hands tightened on the steering wheel as if he were driving, the knuckles white. "How far along?" he said through gritted teeth.

Christine paused. "I'm not sure. Eleven? Twelve weeks?"

His head swiveled toward her. "You knew." It was a statement, not a question.

"I...I told her to tell you...that you'd want—"

"How long have you known?" His voice was slightly louder.

"I thought she'd—"

"How long?"

"Two weeks," she said.

He opened the door, and Christine shuffled back a few steps. They faced each other.

His blue eyes were marble-hard as he looked at her. "You knew Julie was pregnant and didn't think I'd want to know."

"I implored her to tell you," Christine said, her voice almost a wail.

"So," he said, crossing his arms, "after being partners, saving each other's life—"

"I...it wasn't my..."

"Paying off the loan shark, keeping my mouth shut about Hawk, saving your brother. This is how you pay me back?"

"I wanted to tell you. You have a right to know." She could feel him moving away from her, closing himself against her. Shutting her out. He was so important to her. Her friend. The person who put a smile on her face every day. The one human being she could spend the whole day with and still look forward to seeing the next day.

"If I had known," he said, "Julie wouldn't have done what she did."

Christine didn't have an answer to that.

He continued, "Your secrecy nearly got her killed."

Was he right? Was this her fault?

"What other secrets are you keeping?" he asked.

Her mouth opened. She felt stuck. She was losing him. His friendship. His caring.

He shook his head. "You are unbelievable." He turned to open the car door.

"Wait!"

He paused, hand on the driver's door handle.

"There's one thing."

He turned around.

"I was asked to look for a missing person while we were undercover in Yorkville." Her confession whooshed out in one breath.

He frowned. "By Malo?"

She shook her head. "No. By Deputy Darlow."

"Darlow? Who are you searching for?"

"Darlow's teenage daughter."

"Why didn't Operation Niagara know about this?" he asked.

"The deputy wanted to keep it private. His daughter Kelly is a runaway. He's trying to find her and get her to come home."

"You've been looking for her for the past three months?"

She nodded.

"Did you find her?"

She nodded again. "She's an addict. She wanted money, so she approached me, but she took off after that."

He looked at her silently.

Christine could hear her own rapid breathing. She tried to read his expression. Fed up? Angry? Sad?

He looked over to the water, the sky lightening to show the outline of trees on Ward's Island.

Facing her, he asked, "Why you?"

"Why me, what?"

"Why did Deputy Darlow pick you to look for his daughter? You said he disliked you, that he thought you were incompetent and was picking on you."

She opened her mouth to say she was surprised too but then saw the icy glint in his eyes. She couldn't lie anymore.

"I...I'm his daughter," she said.

"What!"

"He's my father. My biological father."

Fillingham's eyes were wide with disbelief.

"I don't know him. He was never in my life. He married someone else. You know I never knew my father."

His head tilted, brow furrowed. "Your dad is not a dead World War II soldier? He's a Toronto deputy chief."

She nodded.

"When did you find this out?"

"Two days ago."

He shook his head as if he couldn't absorb the information and opened the driver door.

"That's it," she said. "I've told you all my secrets. There's no more. I promise."

He got into the car. "I'm done here." He looked up at her through the open window. "I'm done with you." The engine roared to life, and the car sped out of the parking lot in a crunch of flying gravel.

Robotically, Christine got back into the car and headed back to Gail's. She felt frozen, as if her thoughts and feelings were packed in ice as she steered through the streets, dawn pinking the buildings.

She found Gail beside Julie's bed, a cup of coffee in her hands. Julie was still asleep, her breath even. The hum of water spray came from the bathroom where Petra was showering.

"You found Geoffrey," Gail acknowledged as Christine sat down in a chair. "He called. He's coming by."

"That's good," Christine responded, although she wasn't sure she could hold it together if she was in the same room with him. He was so angry.

"He asked that you not be here," Gail added.

Gail's comment felt like a slap.

"He blames me for not telling him," Christine said. "Among other things."

Gail shook her head. "That was Julie's responsibility."

"Tell that to Fillingham." Christine sighed. Her brain was so fuzzy, and she was so upset, she could hardly think. "How's Julie holding up?"

"Stable. Rest, liquids, antibiotics, pain medication is the regimen for the next couple of days."

"She'll pull through, right?" Christine asked. "She's not in danger?"

Gail sighed. "Petra thinks she will be fine—meaning she will recover from the abortion. We don't know if there is damage to the uterus."

"What does that mean?" Christine asked.

"She may not be able to have children," Gail answered, her expression grim.

Christine rubbed her face in fatigue and glanced at her watch. Six o'clock in the morning. Phyllis would be getting ready to leave for her early shift at Records. Christine had successfully avoided her mother for two weeks. All she could think about were Phyllis's lies. Her omission that Deputy Darlow, Christine's boss, a man Phyllis saw visiting her in the hospital, was her father. Christine couldn't deal with that right now. She needed to survive Operation Niagara, support Julie's rehabilitation and figure out how to repair her relationship with Fillingham.

"Go home," Gail said. "Get some rest."

Gail offered the car again. Christine would return later to check on Julie.

As Christine inserted the key into the side door of her building, she felt overcome by exhaustion. She had been up all night, fueled by anxiety for Julie and the adrenaline of searching for Fillingham. But now she could hardly lift one foot above the other to ascend the stairs.

Inside her apartment, she saw evidence of her mom's morning routine: the washed teacup in the drying rack and the ashtray in the sink with three stubbed-out cigarettes. Phyllis had probably assumed Christine hadn't returned home because she was working overtime.

Phyllis. Christine did not know about how to deal with her mom: the subterfuge, the lies, the photos, the money from John Darlow. But she kept returning to the fact that Phyllis had stuck around for twenty-five years while John Darlow had been absent. That seemed to be the singular point of consideration.

Lunch boxes sat on the counter filled with peanut butter and jam sandwiches. Both siblings were attending summer camp at the community center. Opening the fridge, Christine found two apples. She added the fruit and the last two chocolate chip cookies to the lunch boxes.

She quietly opened the door to her and Donna's room, where Wayne had been sleeping for the past two months. Once Christine had started Operation Niagara, it made more sense for him to sleep in a room when Christine was working rather than on the sofa bed, since she woke him up when she came home at three thirty. Wayne wasn't keen on sharing a room with his little sister, and he preferred being in a room with the TV, but he had more places for his comics and baseball cards, so he was appeased for now.

Even though her stomach was roiling from fatigue and too much coffee, she couldn't help but smile at her sleeping siblings. She had missed them. They were growing so big, so old, without her. She couldn't wait to be in a more normal routine with them.

Donna was flung on her back, the sheet wrapped around her, one arm up in abandon. She looked energetic even when sleeping. Wayne lay prone on his stomach, sheet and comforter piled on top so Christine could only see his left foot and the end strands of his hair.

After gently shaking each of her siblings awake, Christine returned to the kitchen and placed cereal, milk and bowls on the table. Sometimes she cooked eggs or pancakes for Wayne and Donna, but that was on her days off, and right now her energy was ebbing quickly. As soon as she could, she hustled her siblings out the door, after ensuring they had water and hats for the hot weather.

When the door clicked closed behind them, Christine didn't bother opening up the sofa. She collapsed on its cushions, her six-foot length barely fitting, even when she placed her head on the arm. She curled into the sofa, closing her eyes, wishing away the events of last night as if they had never happened.

A tear trickled down one cheek, followed by another. She shouldn't be crying, she admonished herself. Julie's experience was tragic—not Christine's.

But she was sad—for Julie. And panicked by her own conversation with Fillingham.

It wasn't her fault, Christine thought, as her sniffling became louder. The deputy had commanded she keep Kelly's search secret. Did Fillingham expect her to go against her superior, knowing she could get fired? If he were in her shoes, would he have told her he had a separate mission while undercover?

Christine exhaled. He would. He would have told her. He didn't revere the hierarchy of the force. Maybe because he had money and would survive if fired. With a university education and his family name, he had options Christine did not.

There had been secrets between them before, and Christine had sworn to be above-board in their relationship. She sat up, grabbing tissues from the coffee table to wipe her cheeks. Fillingham couldn't leave her. He couldn't abandon her. He was the best thing about her job, at the Trailer Project, on Island patrol. He was the reason she smiled every morning on the way to work, thinking of ways to prank him or new ideas for competitions.

She had to fix things. She could go apologize now. Say he was right. She needed to be more forthright with the important people in her life. Work as a team, not on her own.

Or maybe she should wait. Give him time. She could write him a letter. Or call him before their next shift to apologize. Tell him that their relationship was the most important thing to her.

Her fingers tugged at the roots of her hair. What should she do?

Her hands fell to her side, and she looked up at the living room clock. Nine thirty. She'd never sleep with her racing thoughts. She flung open the curtains, squinting against the light. The sky was a deep clear blue, like beach glass. Sometimes Lake Ontario looked this color when Christine rode along the Island boardwalk, the blue of the sky merging with the water so that the two elements blended into one.

Toronto Island. That was it. She could go down to the Island, have a cup of tea with Mrs. Polotov. The older Islander knew Fillingham well. She could help Christine pick a strategy that would induce her partner to forgive her, thaw the ice in his eyes and make him smile at her again.

I won't mess it up with Fillingham again, Christine promised herself as she drove Gail's car to the ferry docks. She'd be honest from now on. And she would fix this, no matter what it took.

Chapter 29

The drone of the ferry engine almost lulled Christine to sleep as she sat in the open-air cabin heading to Ward's Island. She had forgotten how calming it was to sail to Toronto Island.

Exiting the ferry ramp, Christine walked east toward Mrs. Polotov's house on Third Street. It was relatively quiet. Certainly quieter than Centre Island, with its hordes of visitors heading to the amusement park. For a moment, she thought of Hawk. Did he have a place on the Island? She didn't even know if he was working at Centreville. Resolutely, she pushed thoughts of her old boyfriend aside.

Nearing the community center, Christine spotted circles of children in summer camp eating watermelon in the field, supervised by local teenagers. Most of the adult men and some women would be at work on the mainland. Christine spotted a housewife hanging her laundry on the clothesline to dry in the sun.

Other than waving at Jimmy DiAngelo as he headed toward the tennis courts, Christine was grateful not to meet anyone she knew as she headed up Third Street. Reaching Mrs. Polotov's small blue cabin, she headed to the backyard to see if the older woman was pruning her wildflowers or gathering herbs. The yard was empty, watering can and gardening equipment stored away in the shed. A butterfly of panic batted in Christine's throat. What if Mrs. Polotov wasn't home? Maybe she was visiting friends or her daughter in Vancouver.

"Christine! Is that you?"

Christine jogged to the front yard, smiling. "I thought you were communing with the roses."

"That was earlier," Mrs. Polotov said from the front porch. She motioned Christine up the stairs. "Aren't you a sight for sore eyes."

Christine leaned into Mrs. Polotov's open arms for a hug, bending to rest her head on her friend's shoulder. After a few moments, Mrs. Polotov pulled back to look at Christine.

Christine tried to smile, although her lips were wobbly. Mrs. Polotov looked at her with such affection, Christine could hardly handle her kindness.

Mrs. Polotov motioned for Christine to come in. "Are you working on the Island today?"

Christine shook her head as she stepped inside. "No. I thought I might pick up a few shifts, but my new assignment involves long hours, so I haven't been back."

"Iced tea?" Mrs. Polotov queried, already heading to the small kitchen ten feet away.

"Yes, please," Christine answered.

"Make yourself at home, love."

Christine relaxed into the soft comfort of the tapestry couch, inhaling the scent of lilies from the two vases on the side tables. The small room was cozy, with floral rose wallpaper, paintings of island scenes, macramé plant hangers, a packed bookshelf and a bag of Mrs. P's knitting by her chair. Over the past year, Christine had sat here many times, cup of tea in hand during her work breaks.

It wasn't that Mrs. Polotov fed her tea and sweets, which was lovely, or allowed her to shelter from the outside elements for a few minutes on her patrol. She was nonjudgmental but discerning, able to see different viewpoints. The Islander had listened to Christine's secrets: her mother's gambling debt, Phyllis's drinking habit and Christine's romance with Hawk.

Christine offered to help when Mrs. Polotov entered the living room with a silver tray of desserts and blueberries, but the older woman waved her off. Returning with a glass pitcher of iced tea, she sat down beside Christine on the couch and poured them each a glass.

Mrs. Polotov updated Christine on Island news. The Binghams had left after their lease expired. The residents had submitted a new petition to Metro Hall to protest the demolition of Island houses. Centreville was attracting more visitors than last year. And the aphids had attacked her roses, again.

"And how are you?" Mrs. Polotov asked, taking a shortbread cookie from a plate on the coffee table.

"Okay. Tired, actually. I've been up all night."

"Oh, my goodness. Let me top up your tea." She filled Christine's glass. "Were you on night shift?"

"Partly. My shift ends at three."

"You couldn't sleep?"

Christine's lips pressed together as she thought of Julie's body underneath the picnic table. Thank God they had gotten to her and Petra had treated her.

"My friend got sick. I think you know her—Fillingham's girlfriend, Julie?"

"The petite bombshell."

Christine gave a small smile. "That's her. She became ill, and we had to take care of her."

"Has she recovered?"

Christine nodded. "I think so. She's improving. It's just that..."

Mrs. Polotov waited, hands in her lap.

Christine took a deep breath. "I kept a secret, a couple of secrets from Fillingham." She looked down. "And now he won't talk to me."

Mrs. Polotov blue eyes stared intently at Christine.

"One was a secret about Julie," Christine continued, "that I thought Julie should be the one to tell him. Another was about the job we are doing. I had a separate mission that I didn't tell him about. And the last one," she hesitated, unsure of how to explain her relationship with Kelly, "was about my family."

The Islander tilted her head sympathetically. "Christine dear, this sounds complicated, impacted by your allegiance to your friends and family."

Christine exhaled. "He's my friend too. An important friend. He expects the truth."

"That's our Geoffrey," Mrs. Polotov says. "He is up-front."

"I haven't been honest," Christine said.

"Do you think you should have been?"

Christine frowned. "Yes. No. I think so. We spend so much time together. He knows me almost better than anyone. He's asked me to be honest, and I haven't been."

"It sounds like you're sorry. That you realize where you should have been more forthright."

Christine clenched her hands together. "I do." A single tear went down her cheek.

"Dear," she said, turning her body toward Christine, "the other thing we know about Geoffrey is that he has a good heart. A light heart. I can't see him bearing a grudge."

"Normally, I would agree with you. He's a happy guy. An upbeat person. But not this time. I've crossed a line. Again. I think he's given up on me." She ended with a sniff, batting the tears from her eyes.

The older woman grabbed a crocheted box from the wooden side table and offered Christine a tissue. "What did he say?"

"He said we're done." Christine's face crumpled. Mrs. Polotov put an arm around her as Christine cried into her tissue.

After a minute, Mrs. Polotov stood up and closed the living room blinds. "I'm going out in the garden for an hour or two. Lie down. Get some rest. Things will look different when you wake up."

As her friend pulled a knit afghan over her, then turned on a fan, a seed of hope sprouted in Christine's heart. Fillingham needed time. They all did. Everyone was so worried about Julie last night, no one was thinking straight. She would make it up to him. Be the friend he wanted her to be. She wouldn't give up on their relationship. She wouldn't let him go.

Chapter 30

The first inkling that things were different was that Fillingham wasn't waiting for her on the church steps. Her pace slowed as she scanned the busy intersection of Avenue Road and Bloor Street, searching for his blond shaggy hair and outrageously colorful shirt.

She had dressed carefully in yellow bell bottoms and muslin peasant blouse, dabbing concealer under her eyes to hide the sleeplessness of the last two nights since she had seen her partner. Lingering in front of the church, she gazed west, where Fillingham usually parked his car. She checked her watch. It was getting close to the start of the shift; Gail would wonder where she was.

Sighing, she turned and walked up Avenue Road, surveying left and right for her partner's jaunty gait.

Fillingham showed up at the Trailer Project at two minutes to three. Gail had made coffee in the urn, and Christine had washed some fruit and placed a bowl on the picnic table.

Entering the caravan, he greeted everyone, not meeting Christine's eyes. There was a pause in which no one said anything as they stood in the kitchen.

Addressing Dr. Reid, he said, "I'll make a pile of peanut butter and jam sandwiches."

Dr. Reid's glance switched from him to Christine to Gail. "You three are quiet today. Everything okay?"

He smiled, although his eyes remained cool. "All good." He opened the fridge.

"I'll set up the patio furniture," Christine volunteered, wanting to escape outside. She wiped down the couch cushions and the beanbag chair and plugged in the lava lamps. She retrieved the broom and swept the outdoor carpet and then the entire lot.

A few people approached the trailer. Christine poured a young woman a coffee and helped her complete her housing application. She handed out muffins and apples to youth walking by.

As the afternoon wore on, Fillingham came out to make a fresh pot of coffee, nodding at her, then went inside. His politeness was worse than anger.

Christine headed into the caravan at dinnertime, unable to avoid her partner any longer.

Dr. Reid was in her office with a client, door closed. Christine could hear Gail's voice behind a curtain in the medical area.

Christine stood in the kitchen with Fillingham. "Hey," she started, "I wanted to—"

"I'm heading out for dinner," he said. He grabbed the knapsack filled with Trailer Project resources. "I'll check in with people while I'm there."

"Do you want company?" she asked.

He met her glance for the first time. "No." His tone was clipped, definitive.

She blinked several times, trying to keep her composure. "Oh, okay. Have fun."

She turned the sink water on, soaping up the coffee cups. After wiping down the kitchen counter, the coffee table and the cabinets, she headed down the aisle to the medical storage cupboards.

Gail's client left, so Christine stepped inside the medical room to give it a wipe too.

"Smells clean in here," Gail said.

Christine nodded, switching to vinegar water to wipe the window.

Ten minutes later, Dr. Reid came down the aisle, walking her client out. She joined Gail for a cup of tea on the couch.

"Want to join us, Christine?" Dr. Reid asked.

"I'm okay," Christine said as she wiped the window. "I'm on a roll."

She saw Dr. Reid and Gail exchange glances. Christine headed down toward the other end of the trailer, spraying the inside windows and wiping them dry with a rag.

The trailer smelled like meat. Christine looked over at the kitchen. Dr. Reid was stirring a pot on the two-element stove top, probably a stew. She often brought dinner, sometimes made by her husband, who liked to cook, or her mother who lived with them.

"Christina," Gail asked, "did you bring dinner?"

Christine shook her head.

Dr. Reid flicked her fingers. "You two head out for a bite. It's almost eight o'clock—time for a break. I'm going to have my dinner. Things are slow."

"We can wait until Geoff gets back," Gail responded.

Dr. Reid shook her head. "The law students should show up soon. Go ahead."

The two women headed out, pausing on the sidewalk.

"Where'd you want to go?" Gail asked.

"I don't feel social," Christine said.

"Let's pick up a sandwich at the deli and walk in Ramsden Park. It's still light out."

Christine nodded. She wanted to keep moving. Whenever she paused for reflection, she became sad.

They didn't talk much as they ate their corned beef on rye sandwiches on a bench, washing them down with ginger ale. Placing their waste in the garbage, they headed for the pathway into Ramsden Park.

It was refreshing to be walking alongside grass, trees and flowers. A jogger huffed by. A group of teenagers played Frisbee.

"I'm glad Julie is recovering," Christine said. Petra had said she could return to work in a couple more days if she felt well enough.

"Me too." Gail walked along, her gait slightly bow-legged in her jeans.

"Did you check with Malo?" Gail asked.

"About what?"

"About Christina and Geoff breaking up. Did he agree that was a good move?"

Christine's mouth pursed. "I haven't talked to him."

"Well, you look like you've broken up, so unless you make amends in the next twenty-four hours, you need a story to tell Dr. Reid and the rest of the Village."

Gail sat down on a large rock on the edge of a playground, and Christine joined her on an adjacent rock.

Christine said, "I don't think I'll be forgiven in a day."

"Why?" Gail said. "We all kept the secret: me, you, Sarah and Julie. Why is he mad at you?"

"It's not all."

Gail crossed her arms. "It's not all, what?"

"Not all the secrets."

"Okay," Gail said hesitantly.

"I've kept information from Fillingham. From you and the others."

Gail waited.

Christine clenched her hands together to push down a rising wave of emotion. *Keep it together. Don't cry.* "Before we went undercover, Deputy Darlow met with me."

"He's the one who's always breathing down your neck? The one who wants you fired?"

Christine nodded. "He asked me to work on an additional operation while undercover."

Gail frowned. "That's strange."

"He wanted me to find his missing daughter. She's a sixteen-year-old drug addict who hangs out in Yorkville."

"Why wouldn't he tell the Operation Niagara team?"

"I asked the same question. But he wanted to keep it private. I assume he's embarrassed. The family is old money." Christine paused. "Whatever the reason, I should have told you guys. You could have helped me find Kelly."

Gail said. "It's hard when your senior officer commands your silence." Being in the military, she understood the hierarchy of command better than most.

"Thank you for being understanding. Fillingham thinks I'm full of lies: about the job, about Julie, about my family."

"What else have you lied about?" Gail gestured to Christine. "You're an honest person, Christine. Of all of us, you're the one with the biggest conscience."

"He wants nothing to do with me."

Gail tilted her head. "I can't believe that. You guys are like Mutt and Jeff. Frick and Frack."

"He's not forgiving me this time." Her voice quavered.

"He's upset," Gail said. "Give him time to come around. He'll bounce back." She glanced at her watch. "We should head back. Check in with Dr. Reid."

They slid off their respective boulders and walked to the path.

"There's one more thing I omitted to tell him and the team," Christine said as they walked beside each other.

"There's more?" Gail asked.

"You can't tell anyone. Especially anyone on the force. But I'm Deputy Darlow's illegitimate daughter. Kelly Darlow is my stepsister."

Chapter 31

During the next week, Christine told her friends about her undercover work for Deputy Darlow, her meetings with Kelly and Kelly's disclosure about being her stepsister. Gail found it shocking that Christine hadn't asked Phyllis if she had sent Darlow baby photos or received money from him, to confirm Kelly's version of events.

"You're not even curious?" Julie asked. Gail, Julie, Sarah and Christine sat on the patio behind the gallery, eating their dinner. The day was still warm, the late-day sun twinkling through the branches of the oak tree.

It was Julie's second day back at work. She looked pale, despite the bright orange lipstick and the salmon and red paisley scarf draped over her white minidress.

Christine shook her head.

"Really?" Julie continued. "You're basically police royalty, the brat of the brass, and you're not going to work it in your favor?"

Christine leaned forward in her chair, both hands on the cast-iron table. "You can't tell anyone—especially anyone else on the force. And maybe Kelly was lying about us being siblings to throw me off her trail."

Gail said, "Did it seem like she was lying? From what you told me, she was envious of her dad's devotion to you."

"Devotion?" Christine said, louder than she meant to. "Ignoring me for twenty-five years is devotion?"

"He didn't ignore you," Julie interjected. "He couldn't go public. He had married into that prissy, old-money family, so he had to keep you under wraps. But it sounds like he asked about you. That he followed your progress. That he and Phyllis had an arrangement."

"He was really concerned when my mom and stepfather gambled our rent money away."

Sarah said, "He visited you in the hospital, twice, when you were injured on the job."

"That was to tell me to follow orders next time or else."

Julie said, "You and Geoff got commendations."

Christine held up a hand. "Enough! He's never been my father. He wasn't there during the rough times. It doesn't matter if Kelly is speaking the truth. Let's change the subject."

There was silence. Julie took a spoonful of her banana split. She licked her lip and said, "Geoffrey broke up with me."

"What?" Christine and Gail said together.

Julie looked down. "It was inevitable."

Sarah leaned over, putting her hand over Julie's. "I'm so sorry, Julie. I know you really liked him."

Julie said, "Not enough to tell him the truth about the baby, evidently."

"Is that why he broke up with you?" Christine asked.

Julie nodded, pushing the dish away. "The same reason he's broken up with you, it seems. We are untrustworthy and untruthful."

"He has a point," Christine said quietly.

Gail gestured widely with both hands. "Does he? Why should he control what we do with our bodies?"

Sarah said, "Geoffrey views it as a lack of trust."

Julie stood up. "I better head back. Saturdays are always busy. Sal has me working the hostess desk for a few days, since he knows I haven't felt well."

"That's big of him," Gail said.

Julie pulled her white vinyl purse over her shoulder. "He's okay. Slick, but has a soft spot for the waitresses."

They waved goodbye to Julie and continued eating their sandwiches. Christine wasn't dying to get back to the trailer. This past week with Fillingham had been excruciating. He wasn't mean, nor did he ignore her. He joked with everyone, like usual, and offered to pick up pastries or colas for people when he was going into the Village. Most of the time he was out of the caravan, checking on Villagers or driving to the hospital to pick up medical supplies. There were no more wrestling sessions, Frisbee-tossing, hand-holding, or meeting before work at the church. Dr. Reid had asked what was going on; Gail had told her the couple was going through a rough patch.

When Fillingham looked at her, really looked at her, Christine felt nothing from him. No anger. No resentment. It was like they were strangers, working side by side, as if their friendship and feelings had been extinguished like a candle.

Sarah said, "Did Geoff want us to pick him up food?"

Gail shook her head. "No. He said he'd head out when we returned." She paused, then addressed Christine. "You should tell him."

Christine put down her sandwich. "I told him I'm sorry. Ten times."

"Not that," Gail said.

"Then what?" Christine asked.

Gail and Sarah met glances.

Sarah said, "The other thing."

Christine frowned. "What other thing? I told him about Kelly. About Deputy Darlow. That I was sorry about Julie. There's nothing else."

Sarah said, "Tell him how you feel about him."

"Feel about him? He's my partner. He's on our team. He's my friend."

"It's more than that," Sarah said, her brown eyes widening as she looked at Christine.

"I don't..." Christine started.

"I thought you pledged to be honest," Gail said.

Fillingham was the best thing in her world since Hawk. And Hawk was married.

"It's not like that." Christine shook her head.

"Are you sure?" Sarah asked.

"It's just...it's just..." Christine said.

"What?" Gail asked.

"He brings me joy," Christine said.

"Oh, is that all?" Gail said.

Chapter 32

The roar of a motorcycle outside the caravan made Gail, Christine and Fillingham look up from their tasks. Fillingham met Christine's glance, then looked away.

Christine swallowed but without comment exited the motor home and greeted Sloan with a wave. Malo's latest instructions swam in her head. She needed to get a time and date when Sloan was heading to Montreal. The last information she had given Malo hadn't checked out. Sloan had stayed in town all day. If they could figure out when Sloan was returning from Montreal, then they could swoop in and catch him with his inventory. They didn't have the budget to watch Sloan or other key members twenty-four hours a day. And Malo was worried the Grizzlies would figure out they were being watched and change their routine.

"Want a coffee?" Christine said after Sloan shut off the engine.

He shook his head, still sitting on the bike. "Got somewhere fun for us to go." He smiled, wrinkles appearing around his deep blue eyes. With his dark, glossy curls and bad-boy magnetism, he was compelling, but all Christine could feel now was fear. And the need to get Operation Niagara over with.

"We're pretty busy," she said, looking back at the trailer. She spied Fillingham at a window before he stepped out of view. "Can we chat here? Or get a coffee in the Village?"

Sloan grabbed her wrist. "Pretty please," he said.

Christine pulled her wrist away, but he held on, the smile still in place.

"I'm working," Christine said. "I can't always get away. I'm not like you."

"No, you're not," he said enigmatically.

Christine took a step back, and he pulled her in sharply so that she banged her knee against the bike.

"Ow, you're hurting me."

"Get on the bike."

Something had happened. She paused.

"If you're thinking about pulling one of your wrestling moves," he said, "not only will I kick your ass, but I'll kick the ass of Alice, too."

Kelly. He knows Kelly.

He let go of her arm. Opening his hands wide, he said, "But it's up to you."

She stared at him, trying to read him. Was Kelly in danger? Did he know they were half-sisters? That she was a cop? Or that Kelly's father was a police officer?

"Where's Alice?" she asked.

He patted the back seat of his bike. "Waiting for you."

"You're taking me to see her?" she asked.

He nodded. He was so amicable in his menace. Christine's fingers were cold with fear. Would he hurt Kelly—a girl already so fragile, damaged and hardened?

Darlow would not forgive Christine if she stayed here and Kelly was harmed. And who knew if Christine would have a job after that?

He started the engine and gunned the throttle.

Christine walked to the back of the motorcycle behind Sloan. Fillingham was at the window again. She raised one arm straight in the air, the universal sign for help that her partner had taught her during swimming lessons.

"Get on!" Sloan yelled over the engine roar.

She looked back at the window, but Fillingham had moved away. Had he seen her distress signal? Did he care?

After throwing her leg over the seat, she huddled forward, feeling the smooth leather of his jacket under her arms, inhaling the scents of exhaust fume and cigarette smoke. With a skid of the back tire, he roared out of the parking lot and headed down Avenue Road.

She leaned forward as Sloan accelerated, tightening her grip on his jacket. The scenery beside her blurred into a gray line from buildings along Avenue Road and then changed to green as they drove down Rosedale Valley Road.

Was he taking her to Kelly? She didn't know this Sloan—the menacing one who grabbed her arm and didn't care if it hurt. She only knew the flirt, the one who quoted Elizabethan sonnets and compared her to the evening night.

Sloan sped down Bayview Avenue, weaving in and out of cars heading downtown. Were they going down to the lake? Ashbridge's Bay? The eastern beaches? She would be so relieved if he parked beside the ice cream stand at the base of Coxwell Avenue and ordered them a double scoop.

But she didn't think that would happen. He continued on past Queen Street until he looped onto Eastern Avenue. The smell of baking bread was strong as they roared past the Weston bakery. Christine didn't know the east end of Toronto like she knew the west. Was he taking her to his place?

They passed a gas station and a used car lot before the road became more residential, bordered by semidetached houses and small businesses.

"Where are we going?" she yelled.

He didn't respond. He either didn't hear her or was ignoring her.

They were nearing the eastern beaches when he swerved left into the driveway of a bungalow surrounded by a fenced, paved yard. The front door was bricked up, the two windows on either side fitted with metal bars.

Christine's stomach dropped. It wasn't a house. It was the Grizzlies' clubhouse. A large black flag mounted over the side door waved the Grizzly crest.

Sloan braked, and they slowed to a stop near the side door. Christine quickly slid her leg off the bike seat. Should she make a run for it? To the south was the road. Behind the house was a small patio dotted with tables and chairs and the hulking outline of two barbeques. The entire property was bordered by a ten-foot barbed wire fence.

As if sensing her thoughts, Sloan grabbed her upper arm. His head tilted toward the side door, which looked like it was made of steel.

"After you," Sloan said with a small smile on his face, urging her toward the door.

Christine had never been so reluctant to enter a building. No one knew where she was. Even if Fillingham had sounded the alarm, he would assume that Sloan had taken her to the Village or to the western beaches, like he had before. He and Gail would search those locations first.

So here she was, a lone woman entering the headquarters of a brutal motorcycle gang that reputedly controlled much of the drug distribution in Toronto. And she was an undercover police officer. With an addict stepsister who knew her identity, needed rescuing and also threatened Christine's safety.

He came beside her to unlock the door and the deadbolt lock. After pushing open the door, he elbowed her forward into the smoky room.

To the left was a bar. The tall, balding man behind the counter sported a long, gray beard. He was wearing a leather Grizzly vest over a black t-shirt. Behind him was a mirrored wall with shelves of hard liquor bottles. To the right of the entrance was a rectangular room with a pool table and dartboard on one side and four round wooden tables with chairs on the other. One table was occupied by two men in their late twenties. The wall beside the tables was decorated with Grizzly paraphernalia: crests from over the years, a framed leather jacket, a pennant which ran along the top of the wall, framed photos of club members on their bikes and head shots of the executive members.

"Boss." The bartender addressed Sloan.

"Shakespeare," said one of the younger men with long, dirty-blond hair. "Who you got there?"

"No one for you to be concerned with," Sloan said.

The man turned back to his companion.

Christine scanned the room for an exit. The two windows to her right had been bricked up but still sported dirty beige curtains. Two oil lamp scones bordered either side of the bricked windows, their lights flickering, giving off a burned residue that combined with the cigarette smoke to make the air gray. An overhead fluorescent light lit up the pool table. Beyond the pool table at the back wall was a small kitchen with a sink in between two barred windows, the only source of natural light. The kitchen windows were open, the curtains fluttering against the metal bars.

As they stood at the entrance, Sloan called, "Alice!"

After a few seconds, Kelly appeared in the doorway to the adjacent room. She looked thinner, maybe because she was wearing fitted clothes: a halter top with Capri pants, big earrings and makeup, like a girl trying to play at being an adult. Except she looked older, with her wide, sunken eyes, muddy gray skin tone and missing tooth.

Kelly flicked a glance at Christine but then concentrated on Sloan.

Shifting a step sideways, Christine looked into the shadows of the windowless room behind Kelly. She could make out a far wall, the edge of a couch and a railing, which could be stairs to the basement. No door in sight.

"Where's my stuff, Shakespeare? Can I have it?" Kelly asked.

He tilted his head, his hand still holding Christine's arm. "You haven't delivered the goods, Alice."

"I told you," Kelly said, sidling closer to Sloan, "my parents will come through."

Sloan pointed to a phone on the bar's wooden counter. "Make the call."

"What's going on?" Christine said, trying to keep her voice light.

Sloan addressed the bartender. "See this woman here, Joe? She's full of surprises."

Joe stared at her, eyes flat and amused at the same time. "How's that, boss?"

Christine swallowed. Did Sloan know she was a police officer? Surely that would stop him from assaulting her? Or worse?

Sloan continued, "Christina here can wrestle, stitch you up if you've been in a fight, help you with your landlord problems, and surprise, surprise. She's worth a bit of money."

Christine frowned. He knew her family didn't have money. She had told him a few stories of her life growing up, trying to connect with him.

"I think you've been misinformed." Christine said, turning to Sloan. "I'm just a social work student, working a summer job to pay for school."

"Alice," he said, looking at the young woman now at the bar. "Do we have Christina confused with someone else?"

Kelly shook her head, her thin brown hair trailing on her shoulders. "No. She's my sister. My stepsister. I saw the proof in my dad's desk."

Christine's stomach turned over. Sloan knew she and Kelly were related. That couldn't be good.

Sloan walked over to the bar, pulling Christine alongside him. "Let's give good old Dad a call, shall we?"

He shoved Christine down on a bar stool and then picked up the black receiver, holding it out to Kelly.

Kelly grabbed it. "If I call, will you give me something right now? Before the money comes?"

He pulled a small package out of his pocket filled with brown dried leaves and placed it on the heavily shellacked bar counter.

"How about some henny?" she asked.

"You don't want it?" Denny said, reaching for the bag of marijuana.

Kelly put out her hand to stop him. "No, no, that's good."

She grabbed the phone and quickly dialed, her thin finger hooked in the rotary holes, eyes on the weed. "It's me," she said into the phone. After a pause, she said, "Fine. I'm fine."

She shook her head at something the other person said. "Dad, guess who I have sitting beside me?" A pause. "No, guess."

Kelly looked directly at Christine. "My sister. Isn't that a laugh? My stepsister is here. In the same city. But you knew that, right? ... She's fine," Kelly added through gritted teeth. "Your precious firstborn is fine."

Christine was trying to figure out what was going on.

"There's just one thing. I need a bit of cash." She exhaled. "I know, I just got some. But I need something extra. No. Not the regular amount. I need more. To keep quiet about *her*. Five thousand dollars," she said, looking over at Sloan, who nodded confirmation.

"Get the money together, and then your illegitimate bastard stays a secret."

There was a pause as Kelly listened, her leg jiggling impatiently as she leaned against the bar counter. "Daddy, you want all your friends, Grandma, Grandpa, your coworkers, your buddies at the curling club to know that one daughter is a drug addict and the other is a love child born to another woman when you were married to Mom?"

She waited a few seconds. "I didn't think so... A couple of days?" she asked Sloan.

Sloan said, "Tuesday. He's got until Tuesday to make the payment."

"Daddy, you have two days." She held the phone away from her, staring down at the receiver. "Fuck!" She looked up at Sloan. "He wants to talk to her first," she gestured toward Christine, "before he'll go to the bank."

Sloan nodded. Kelly dropped the receiver, and Christine grabbed it as it hung down from its cord.

Kelly's thin arm snaked across the bar counter to grab the baggie of marijuana; she slipped out of the room.

"Hello," Christine said into the phone.

"Is that you, Christine?" It was John Darlow.

"Yes."

"Are you okay?" he asked.

"Yes," she said.

"Do they know you're a police officer?" he asked.

"I'm not sure." She almost added "sir" at the end of her response.

"I'm guessing Kelly hasn't let that cat out of the bag, or that I'm deputy chief, because they wouldn't have targeted you. And there goes her drug money."

Christine remained silent. What would happen if she told Sloan she was a cop? Or that Kelly was Darlow's daughter? Would he hurt her or let her go? Either way, Kelly would take the brunt of his anger. Christine was certain about that.

"Are you in danger?" Darlow asked Christine.

"Not if you bring the money." What if Darlow said it was too much or that his daughters weren't worth it? That he couldn't be blackmailed?

Sloan nodded at her comment.

"I don't care about the money," Darlow said. "I want you and Kelly to be safe."

"Safe as a duck on water if you come up with the five thousand," she said.

Sloan frowned at her choice of words. She had been scared to add them, but if Darlow could figure out that they were in the clubhouse near Lake Ontario, then maybe he would send help. Sloan leaned over and hung up the phone.

The sound of a motorcycle revved loudly outside, then with increased volume as it drove near the door. After a few seconds, the engine cut out.

There was a pounding on the wide steel door, heavier than a hand, as if someone were hitting the steel door with a heavy object or kicking it with a steel-toed boot.

Sloan said, "What the fuck? Are we expecting anybody, Joe?"

The big man shook his head.

"Open the door," Sloan said to Joe.

Joe pulled out a bat from behind the bar and approached the wide steel door. Sloan flicked two fingers at the seated men who got up from their table and moved to the other side of the entrance.

Slowly opening the door, Joe propped it ajar with his foot, the bat ready in his hands.

Fillingham stood at the door with a wide smile on his face, flanked by a dead-serious Gail. Ten feet away, Christine spotted Gail's yellow motorcycle.

Thank God. Christine's friends had hopped on Gail's bike and followed her here.

"Hello," Fillingham said amiably. He looked past Joe to Sloan and Christine at the bar counter. "Yep, my girlfriend's here. Hey, honey," he said, waving to Christine.

Joe looked back at Sloan. The blond club member guffawed. "Snatching someone else's snatch, Shakespeare?"

Sloan gave a little smile, but his eyes never wavered from Fillingham. "This is none of your business."

"Oh, I think it is," Fillingham said amicably. "You okay, sweetie?" he said, directing his question at Christine.

"Yes," Christine managed. Thank God. Thank God for her partner. For Gail. She wasn't alone anymore.

His glance bore into hers for a second, then he addressed Sloan. "Where my girlfriend goes is my business. You can relate to that, being a businessman and all."

"What's with the mutt?" Joe said, looking at Gail.

Gail ignored the jibe. "We're here to give Christina a lift back to work."

"She's busy," Sloan said. "I'll bring her back later."

"I'd rather she come with me now," Fillingham said.

Christine took a small step toward her friends.

Sloan put out his arm, blocking her. "Listen, chump," he said, "in my clubhouse, people follow my orders. Give us a wave goodbye, then you and the dyke head back to the Village to help out hippies with crabs."

Christine looked at the group, Gail and Fillingham outside the door, Joe and the other two bikers bracketing the doorway on the inside. Should she make a run for it? Knock Sloan down with an elbow to the head? But what would happen to Kelly?

"Alice!" Sloan called.

Kelly came into the poolroom, blinking sleepily. She stopped beside Sloan, scanning the tableau of people.

"Alice," he commanded.

She looked over at him, expression dreamy.

"Suck my dick," he commanded.

Immediately, she dropped to her knees in front of him. She reached for his jeans, unbuttoned the metal button and unzipped his pants.

Sloan stood there, smiling at Fillingham.

"Stop!" Christine said, her hand out toward Sloan. "I'll stay. Tell her to stop."

Seconds ticked by. Sloan took a moment to look around the room, met the glances of Gail, Fillingham and the now-smiling Joe before he zipped up his pants.

Kelly stayed on her knees for a few more seconds, then stood up.

"Okay, fun's over." Gail stepped inside the house, gun in hand.

Gail had a gun! Christine was shocked and then relieved. It wasn't a police gun; women weren't issued one. It must be the one Gail was given on the navy base in case it was attacked. She must have stored it in the trailer or on her motorcycle. The police were in control. They hadn't found evidence of drug trafficking, but she and Kelly would be safe.

"Put down the bat," Gail instructed. The bartender slowly lowered his arm and placed the bat against the wall. Fillingham walked inside and retrieved it. Upon Gail's order, the bartender backed up until he pressed against the bar beside Sloan. She ordered the other two members alongside the bar. Kelly moved over beside the pool table. Christine walked over to stand beside Fillingham.

"Hands in the air. All of you," Gail said. The four men slowly lifted their hands in the air, as did Kelly.

"A gun?" Sloan said incredulously. "You bring a fuckin' gun to get the girl? Are you nuts?"

"I could give a fuck about either of your whores," Gail said. She looked at Sloan. "*Ya zdes za narkotikami.*"

"What is that? German? Russian?" Sloan asked. "What the fuck are you saying?"

"I want the drugs," Gail said.

"I don't know what you're talking about." Sloan shook his head.

Gail looked at him balefully for a moment. She turned to Fillingham. "Loverboy. This is your chance for revenge." She opened the door wide with one hand, eyes still on the gang members. "See the Harley over there, the blue one?" He looked outside and nodded.

Gail added, "Take the bat to it."

"Hold on!" Sloan said, stepping forward.

Gail straightened her arm with the gun. "Take one more step and I'll shoot you. And it won't be in the leg."

"Yippee!" Fillingham said and ran out of view. After a second, the sound of crashing metal as something heavy toppled over and repeated banging.

"Stop!" Sloan yelled. "Stop! I'll talk to you. Tell him to stop."

Gail leaned back, her eyes still on the gang members in the room. "Geoff!" she yelled. "That's enough. For now."

After a minute, Fillingham returned, panting, smiling, bat clenched in one fist. "I slit all their tires, too."

"Well, that's a good boy," Gail said and let the door close.

"I just want the girl," Fillingham said to Gail.

"And you can have her." She pointed her finger at Christine, then Kelly. "Both of them. Not my type."

What was Gail playing at? Fillingham was still acting like the avenging boyfriend, here to rescue Christine from the evil motorcycle henchman who had taken a fancy to her. Gail was on a totally different tack. Had Malo told her to do this?

Gail cleared her throat. "I asked a question."

"I'm small potatoes." Sloan waved his hand dismissively.

"According to my boss, you're the commander."

"Who's your boss?" he asked.

"Someone who believes that the Halloween candy should be shared."

Sloan shook his head, crossing his arms. "The guys in Montreal trust me. Clients are happy. Payments are in on time. They're not looking for anyone new."

"We're not asking permission," Gail said. "Enough chit-chat. Where's your stash?"

Sloan frowned. "Stash? Why would I store my shit here?"

Gail said, "Because the building's like Fort Knox."

"You got in," the bartender said.

Gail smiled. "I'm persuasive."

Fillingham addressed Kelly. "Where does he keep the drugs?"

Kelly looked back at him, her gaze unfocused. "What?"

Gail waved her gun. "Where are the drugs?"

Kelly shook her head.

Sloan said, "Think I'd tell an addict where the shit is kept? I'm not a moron."

Suddenly, Sloan stepped away from the bar and grabbed Kelly, pressing her in front of him, his arm around her neck. "You need to tell your people, Russian mafia, KGB, pretty sure you're Romanov's bitch, that they're not welcome here. In my clubhouse. In my business. In Toronto."

"You don't think I'd shoot the girl to get to you?" Gail said.

"She's a cop," Kelly yelled, pointing at Christine.

Everyone swiveled to look at Christine.

Suddenly, the bartender reached behind him, and a bottle of vodka sailed toward Gail's head.

Fillingham yanked Gail back. The glass bottle sailed past her and smashed against the oil lamp on the wall. The glass lamp and alcohol bottle exploded into a thousand shards, littering the floor. A second and a third bottle sailed by, smashing first on the wall, then the floor. Oil and alcohol splattered over the wallpaper and onto the wooden floor.

A shot rang out, and everyone crouched.

Gail stood there, gun pointed at the ceiling.

A lick of flame fluttered across the alcohol, and oil spilled on the floor and climbed up the wall. The bottom of the cotton curtains whooshed into flame.

"Fuck!" Sloan said. He threw Kelly down. Her head hit the side of the pool table with a thunk, and she dropped to the floor in a collapsed heap.

Sloan took off into the living room, and Christine could hear him thumping down the stairs to the basement.

Joe stood up and reached behind the bar. Christine launched herself at him, grabbing him around the neck as she pulled him down. Her knee in Joe's back, she looked up to see the fire dance across the wall, curling the wallpaper and licking the shelf of the cue sticks. The place filled with gray-black smoke.

Gail yelled, "We have to get out of here! We can't control the fire." She pointed her gun at the bikers. "Not you. Don't move."

Christine got off Joe, and the bartender sat up. The bikers crouched on the floor, glances flickering from Gail's gun to the encroaching fire.

Christine crawled over to Kelly and grabbed her under the armpits while Fillingham grabbed the teen's legs.

As they lifted her up, Christine said to Gail, "There must be an exit from the basement. That's where Sloan went."

"Where does the basement exit come out?" Gail asked the bikers.

The bartender had his shirt over his mouth, trying to breathe.

"Shoot them," Christine said.

"Next door!" roared the blond biker. "At the back of the gas station."

"Any drugs on this floor?" Christine asked.

His glance swung over to the pool table.

"Get it!" Gail yelled, her gun pointing at the table. "Or I'll shoot you and leave you here."

The three bikers ran over. The bartender gave two kicks to the side panel of the pool table, and the wood splintered. Canvas bags spilled out.

"Bring it over," Gail commanded.

She grabbed the three bags over her arms, guns pointed at the bikers. "I'm going to open the door on the count of three. Oxygen is going to flame the place, so everyone jump through and get the hell away from the door."

"One. Two. Three!"

The door opened. The fire whooshed. The group staggered blindly through the billowing smoke and flames, spilling onto the ground beside the broken motorcycles, their skin and clothes sooty as they coughed and gasped. The steel door slammed shut behind them,

Outside, six officers screamed at them to stay where they were, guns pointed at the group. The wail of a fire engine could be heard in the distance.

On her hands and knees, Christine inhaled the fresh air in huge lungfuls, her arm touching Kelly, who was splayed out on her back beside her. Kelly was safe, as were Gail and Fillingham. Gail was identifying themselves as police officers, placing her gun on the ground, yelling at them to check the gas station next store. And that they needed an ambulance for the girl.

After a bit more talking, the three gang members were handcuffed, the canvas bags seized as evidence.

Christine squatted beside the unconscious Kelly as the clubhouse, its pennants, crests and memorabilia incinerated, the air pungent with the sweet, skunky smell of burning marijuana.

Chapter 33

"Did we have to meet at midnight?" Julie asked as she, Christine and Gail approached the shadowy figure sitting on the swing in Bellevue Square Park.

"Too spooky?" Malo's voice could be heard from the swing. The lit end of a cigarette pinpointed where he was.

"No," Julie said as she sat down in the adjacent swing. "I need my beauty sleep."

"Ah yes, our little Marilyn Monroe."

The dark surrounded them like cotton batting, except for one area of the playground bathed in a circle of light that receded into concentric rings of shadow.

Christine sat down at the base of one slide, and Gail took a seat on a bench. Behind them was the hulking outline of the hospital two blocks away.

Malo took an audible inhale on his cigarette. "Where's your better half, Marilyn?" he asked.

From her vantage point across from Julie, Christine could only see the lower part of her face and body where the light hit it. "We're not together," Julie said evenly, as if the phrase had been repeated several times.

"Is that the way it landed?" He nodded. "Undercover can do that." He turned to Christine. "You still playing Juliet to Sloan's Romeo?"

"No," Christine said perfunctorily. Sloan had been captured two blocks away from the Grizzly headquarters with two large hockey bags of heroin and cocaine. Thank goodness. She wanted him behind bars and never to see him again.

Malo raised his hands in the air. "The summer of love is loveless?" He laughed, then began coughing.

Gail said, "Can we start the meeting? We're tired and want to go home."

Yesterday was filled with paramedic checks, searching for Dennis Sloan and accompanying the arrested bikers to the station. The ambulance took Kelly to the hospital. Christine found a phone to tell the deputy, but he already knew. Firefighters attended the clubhouse for hours. After extinguishing the fire, they found a fireproof vault in the basement that specialists were trying to open. And, of course, there had been interviews. And paperwork. Reams of paperwork.

Malo turned to Julie. "You did some good work, Marilyn, out of the Toucan."

Julie laughed, sounding bitter. "Not as exciting as the takedown on Eastern Avenue that everyone else was invited to."

Gail spoke up. "Julie, there was no time. Sloan grabbed Christine and took off. I could barely keep them in view. Fillingham and I hopped on my motorcycle seconds after they left."

Julie shrugged and looked away.

"Ah, yes. Christine," Malo said. "The beating heart of Operation Niagara. A woman whose wrestling skills and sonnet knowledge were honey to a Grizzly bear." He shook his head. "I would not have picked you as the Village Athena."

Christine frowned. She knew she wasn't sexy, like Julie, but she was presentable, even more so since her makeover for Operation Niagara. And she had flirted with Fillingham as his undercover girlfriend and with Sloan. She wasn't a block of cement, for goodness' sakes.

"I think you're trying to say 'good job,'" Gail said dryly.

Malo gave a low whistle. "Wish I had been there for the showdown: drugs, guns, motorcycles, bats, exploding vodka bottles. You burned down a fuckin' bikers' den. Exciting shit!"

Fillingham's voice said, "What's exciting?" He approached the playground and stepped into the yellow light. He was clean-shaven, his hair back to regulation length above the ears, sporting jeans and a polo shirt.

Christine would miss Village Geoff, the one who put flowers in her hair, coached her on her Frisbee throws and wore outrageous shirts to work.

"Yesterday's finale, man!" Malo answered.

Fillingham stood at the monkey bars opposite Malo and Julie, leaning against the metal poles.

Malo tossed his cigarette into the sand. "Have to say I didn't really have faith in this team. Didn't think you'd pull it off."

Gail said, "What you're trying to say, Malo, is 'good job!'"

"Ah, yes, Gail," Malo said. "Our nurse turned SWAT team commando. Getting the upper hand on the Grizzlies. Pretending to be Romanov's bitch. *Ty supergeroy.*"

"I'm no superhero," Gail said.

"Kind of turns me on," Malo said.

"Gross," said Gail.

"You are bad asses," Malo said.

"My bad ass has third-degree burns," Fillingham said.

Christine said, "I'm still coughing up black ash."

From the swing beside Malo, Julie said, "Are we done with Operation Niagara? Interviews recorded. Reports filled out?"

He nodded. "All of you," he pointed at each of the officers individually, "are getting commendations. All the way up the pipeline from the deputy chief's office."

Everyone looked at Christine, who lowered her eyes to avoid their glances.

Malo continued, "The brass is fucking delirious. Operation Niagara has taken down a major drug distributor. The city councilors and developers are pissing themselves with happiness."

"So we're done?" Gail said.

Malo stretched his arms over his head. "Get some well-deserved R and R. I know you guys were pulling long hours."

"One week off, according to my sergeant, before I head back to the Women's Bureau," Julie said.

Malo said, "While I have you here, there's something interesting coming down the chute."

"More undercover?" Gail asked.

Malo nodded excitedly.

Gail and Julie shook their heads simultaneously.

"We're going back to the WB," Julie said.

Malo grabbed his chest as if broken-hearted.

"I'm heading back to Island patrol," Christine said.

"PC Fillingham?" Malo said. "You up for some bad shit?"

Fillingham smiled. "Nah. I've got an interview at the Harbor Police in September."

The Harbor Police. The separate nautical force that Fillingham had been angling to get into for years. And after three consecutive years of applying, he had an interview.

He was leaving her. And Toronto Island patrol. Christine stared at Fillingham, but he didn't meet her glance.

"Congratulations," said Julie softly. "I know that's something you've always wanted."

"You're all refusing," Malo complained as Gail and Julie stood up.

Gail said, "It's not an order, Malo. You're just fishing for interest."

Christine didn't want to move—to leave this spot on the bottom of the slide—to have the group venture into the future separate from each other. Operation Niagara was over; they'd never be a team again.

"Do you want a drive?" Julie asked Christine. She and Gail had come together.

Christine shook her head. "It's a twenty-minute walk home. I need the fresh air."

Fillingham raised one hand in farewell and silently headed down the park path, disappearing into the shadows as he reached the road.

As Christine headed toward Bathurst Street, she was filled with a bittersweet sadness. Part of undercover work had been exciting. Village life, with its music and cafés, was vibrant. And the team had laughed a lot together, at the superhero wrestling match, in their day-to-day interactions. And it was satisfying to help people find housing, a counselor or food for the next week. No wonder Sarah had been a social worker.

But she felt old, her heart heavy, from Julie's abortion, the sick danger of hanging around a motorcycle gang member and her sadness about Fillingham. She was a better actor now, a better liar, as her partner would attest. Thanks to Operation Niagara, she had lost her relationship with Fillingham. And gained a father she didn't want and a stepsister who would sell her to the highest bidder.

Chapter 34

"I'll get it," Christine said as the phone rang in the kitchen. The four of them, her mom, Donna and Wayne, had been sitting on the couch watching *The Pig and Whistle* show. Phyllis loved polka songs and old Quebec ballads; the show always put her in a good mood.

"Hello," Christine said into the receiver.

"It's Deputy Darlow. I mean, John Darlow, your—"

"I know who you are," she said, keeping her voice low.

"We should meet."

"Is this about work, sir?" She stood by the wall phone, refusing to sit down and get comfortable.

"No. It's about...us."

"There's nothing to say."

"I have a few things to explain," he said.

"No explanation needed." Or wanted.

"I need to say a few things. Where can we meet?"

Could she refuse? It wasn't a work request from a senior officer. It was a request to meet her father. Her biological father.

"Please," he said. "It's just a conversation."

She exhaled. "It has to be where no one will see us."

"I know a place in Scarborough."

"That's far. I have to transit there," she said.

"How about an outdoor café in Little Italy? College and Bathurst."

"Fine."

"Tomorrow at noon?" he asked and gave her the name.

He must know she had the week off. He seemed to know every-thing about her. "Yes," she responded, then hung up.

He was already sitting at a patio table, which was covered in white linen and adorned with a vase of red carnations. He was farther back from College Street at a table discreetly in the back.

He must have come from work; he wore a light gray summer suit. He looked like a businessman from Forest Hill as he sipped his coffee, his pedigree evident in his posture and the cut of his clothes.

Christine looked down at her linen pants, loafers and cotton top. She looked nice, but not done up. This morning, she had taken extra care with her hair, a touch more makeup, a bit more jewelry, but it wasn't for him. She wasn't in John Darlow's social class. She didn't want to be.

She hadn't told her mom about this meeting with Darlow. What was the point of discussing her father with Phyllis? She knew her mom used some of Darlow's money for gambling or alcohol. And that she had kept her father's identity secret. What did it matter when Christine had no interest in knowing him?

She sat down at the table, uncertain whether to call him sir or some other name. Certainly not Dad.

"Coffee or tea?" he asked.

"Coffee," she responded.

He waved at an aproned waiter, who came over and filled her cup.

"Would you care to look at the menu?" Darlow asked, proffering it to her.

"I won't be here long enough to eat."

He raised his eyebrows but didn't say anything, merely placed the menu on the table between them. A slice of sun warmed Christine's shoulders as she waited for him to start.

"The Operation Niagara team has a commendation coming," he said.

She waited.

"Excellent work," he continued. "You and PC Fillingham make a good team."

"He won't be on Island patrol much longer," she said, then chided herself for revealing anything about her life to her father.

"Is he transferring or doing more undercover?"

"He wants to join the Harbor Police."

"That's an elite group."

"He is a nationally competitive sailor on track to making the Olympic team and a commended police officer." Why was she defending Fillingham?

"Good for him," Darlow responded. "And you?"

She frowned. He must know what she was doing. "I'm going back to Toronto Island."

"That's where you want to be?" he queried. "You can have your pick of transfers after the Grizzly arrests."

"Yes," she said decisively. She took a gulp of coffee, half draining the cup, then set it down. "Anything else?"

He put both palms in front of him as if to stop her from leaving. "Foremost, thank you."

She regarded his almond-brown eyes, his straight nose and cheekbones. Did she look like him? Were her eyes as compelling as his?

He continued, "For all you did for Kelly. I know she can be difficult, not only because she's an addict, but also because she's so emotional. But you found her. And you saved her."

Christine tilted her head. "*She* found *me*. To blackmail you."

"You got her out of a burning building." He sipped his coffee. "She's in rehab now."

"I'm glad to hear that," she managed. All addicts should have a chance of redemption, even one as manipulative as her stepsister.

"She's not always like that. The blackmail. The jealousy. The meanness. She used to horseback ride and volunteer with seniors and play piano."

She didn't want to spend her afternoon hearing about the endearing characteristics of John Darlow's legitimate daughter.

"If that's all," she said, reaching for her purse.

"No, it's not."

She waited.

"My main reason for meeting you today," he said, "is to tell you how sorry I am about the way you've been treated."

She stared at him.

"The way you have been treated by me," he elaborated.

She didn't say anything.

He inhaled and exhaled. "I don't know what Kelly told you, the truth or misinformation. I need to tell you what happened myself."

Christine sat stone-faced. She would hear him out, let him say his piece so that everything was on the table. And then she could walk away, forever.

"I know I haven't been a model father. I didn't tell you who I was when I asked you to look for Kelly. That is reprehensible."

"Because I wouldn't have done it," she interrupted. John and Kelly Darlow were master manipulators, massaging situations to get their way.

He nodded. "Yes, I understand that." His long fingers tapped the table. "Phyllis and I—we had a deal. She would have the baby, and I would support it—you—financially."

She frowned, thinking of the times their fridge was empty or they had to leave their apartment in the middle of the night because they owed three months rent. How she never had new clothes or money to go out with friends.

"I don't remember horseback riding lessons or piano teachers," she said.

He nodded. "Again, my fault. I sent you money, once a month, but I..." he looked away, staring at the car traffic on College Street. "I didn't check. I didn't make sure that the money went for you, for your food and education and clothes. I assumed Phyllis was taking care of you."

"She took care of me," Christine responded angrily. "Every day. Working shift work to put food on the table."

He waved both hands in the air in surrender. "I'm not blaming your mother. All I'm saying is that I didn't check closely enough. When you were younger, I saw you, in the park, in your stroller. You had clean clothes. You looked well fed. Phyllis sent me photos. Some of your artwork. School tests. But I think that changed when your mom met Eddie Williams."

"It was fine," she responded, wanting to leave.

"Your stepfather was an alcoholic and made your mom into one, too. And then there was the gambling."

"What's the point of this?" she said with a frisson of anger. "I know what happened. I was there. And you know what? I took care of things. And in the end, I took care of Eddie. When he left, Mom got better. She got the job at Records. She only drinks on her days off." Christine shook her head. "No more gambling—just bingo with friends. We didn't need you, anyway."

"I know you handled things," Darlow said, gesturing with open hands. "When I realized what was happening, that you moved apartments a lot, that you were the one taking your siblings to school, I knew something was going on. And when I saw Phyllis one day with a black eye, I knew Eddie had to go."

"What do you mean?" It was Christine who had gotten Eddie to leave. After years of his drunken ranting, his abuse, the throwing of chairs, the breaking of furniture, the pushing of her mom. On the day she graduated from police college, she told her stepfather that if he ever touched her mom again, raised a hand, broke something in the house or did anything to Donna and Wayne, she would arrest him. He left the next day.

"I saw him at your graduation," he said. "He was having a cigarette outside while you were taking pictures with your mom and siblings. I introduced myself and told him to find another place to live. Preferably a different city."

Christine's jaw dropped. All this time she had thought it was her threats to her stepfather that sent him packing. That she had saved her family and turned things around. And now Darlow was telling her it was him.

"I paid for your mom to go away for a month to get sober," he added.

Christine thought back. Her mom had gone away to Quebec to see her sister. She remembered that because Christine had been left to take care of her siblings right when she started at the Women's Bureau.

"But once I found her a job in Records," Darlow continued, "and you got on the force, I knew your family was on a stable path." He sat back in his chair, looking vindicated.

Christine had had enough. It was one thing to feel rejected and that her father had never paid attention to her or acknowledged her existence. But to have him say he had helped her family, like a hero saving the day. She wasn't having any of it.

She wouldn't say thank-you. She hadn't needed him then, and certainly didn't need him now.

"Don't call me again," Christine said, standing up. "I want nothing to do with you, nor does Phyllis. Talk to me only about police business or I'll tell the entire force I'm your illegitimate daughter that you let live in poverty. I don't think you, your wife or Kelly want that fact publicized widely."

Without waiting for his response, Christine turned on her heel and left the café.

Chapter 35

"We need to find a log. A slice of tree trunk," Christine said to Fillingham. They were in the backyard of the Centre Island police station on their first shift back on Toronto Island. Christine had broken the wooden target the last time they played each other in an ax-throwing competition. The other half of the circular target was still nailed to the tree.

Fillingham shook his head. "Ax throwing is more of a winter thing." He looked around at the leafy trees and the overgrown grass tinged yellow from the July heat.

Last summer, Christine and Fillingham had raced each other on their bikes back to the station. Fillingham had given her swimming and boating lessons. Christine paid him back with wrestling coaching. Now, who knew how long he would remain on Island patrol with her? If he got through the Harbor Police interviews and a spot came up, he would jump at it.

"I'll make coffee." He headed into the police station.

Christine nodded. When she met Fillingham on the ferry over, his cool behavior had been a screwdriver to her heart. He was polite. When he spotted her, he waved, then got lost in the crowd of families heading for the amusement park.

As Christine leaned over the ferry's railing, the wind ruffling her hair in its chignon, she realized how much she had missed this: the chugging ride over to Centre Island; giving report to the officers waiting by the ferry dock; patrolling the Island by foot and bike; and chatting with residents and tourists.

Back at the station, it looked like the yard needed mowing and the dandelions weeding. The garage door needed hosing down, the station windows washed with vinegar and newspaper. That was okay. In between checking empty houses, patrolling the communities, monitoring the beach crowds and answering calls and tourist requests, there was downtime, especially on evening and overnight shifts. She would do outdoor work then. She and Fillingham were similar that way—they liked to keep busy. And since they were hardly talking, Christine knew she needed to keep occupied or that screwdriver in her heart would dig deeper.

She went inside the station, letting the screen door bang behind her, the chime ringing. The aroma of dark roasted coffee greeted her.

"Smells great!" she said, her tone perky, as if they were strangers, as if this was their first shift together.

Fillingham stood in the office, checking the logbook. He looked up briefly, smiled slightly at her remark, then returned his attention to the book.

After she filled her mug, she wandered back into the office. "Anything we need to deal with right away?" she asked.

He shook his head. "Not really."

"I thought I'd head over to Mrs. Polotov after I check the beach," she said, "see if she's good for a tea and a scone." Fillingham had a sweet tooth, like Christine. "Want to come?"

He shook his head. "You go. I'll head over to Hanlan's Point. There was a group earlier who made a bonfire. I'll confirm it's extinguished."

"Oh, okay." Most of the time, they patrolled on their bikes together, taking breaks on picnic tables or at the beach. They only separated at shift end to usher straggling tourists onto the ferries. Was he going to patrol on his own all day?

She awaited further conversation, but his attention returned to the log. Ambling over to a desk, she regarded the work schedule posted above.

Her sergeant told her she and Fillingham were on afternoons this week, but the new schedule for August hadn't been finalized. It was up now.

She was off for a couple of days after this week, then on nights for five days, then off for four days.

Wait. She scanned the names of the officers on shift. After this week, she and Fillingham were not on the same shift. She was working with a rotating list of officers from 52 Division brought in for the summer.

"Fillingham," she said.

He looked up at her.

"What's with the schedule? After this week, we're on different shifts."

He paused for a second, but his expression was neutral when he said, "I asked to be switched."

"Switched away from me?" she asked, pointing to herself. "From working with me?"

Again, he paused. "Yes," he said, his tone definitive.

She could feel the tears surfacing as they stared at each other.

"I'm sorry," she said, her voice quavering.

"For what?" He gave a derisive laugh. "Being you?"

For being her: small, cowardly, afraid and untrusting. Full of secrets.

"I'm heading out," he said. "I'll check Manitou Beach on the way to Hanlan's Point. Say hi to Mrs. P for me."

He placed his police hat on his head, his gait as jaunty as ever as he exited the station.

Her lower lip quivered. She knew things between her and Fillingham were bad, but she didn't think she would lose him as a partner. If he joined the Harbor Police, that was one thing. It was his life's dream to patrol the waterways. But to have him excise her out of his life, like a heavy burden he no longer wanted to carry, was devastating.

She sat down at the table, allowing a few tears to drip down as she sipped her coffee. In some ways, she deserved his rejection. She was too private, too insular, too afraid of being vulnerable. Yet the pressure from Julie and Darlow to keep mum had been immense. Fillingham should realize she had been between a rock and a hard place.

She wiped her face, some of her eyeliner coming off. She wore a bit more makeup now and more colorful clothes on her days off. It was like keeping her character from Operation Niagara alive, the part that she liked.

She gave a last sniff and finished her coffee.

Exhaling, she thought about who she had left in her life. Her mom, Donna and Wayne. And Gail, Sarah and Julie. Of course, there was Mrs. Polotov, who would listen to her story about Fillingham leaving their partnership and tell her he would come around.

And there was Hawk. He was married; she knew that. She still cared for him. He was one of the few people who really knew her, who liked the person she was. Who had wanted to be with her. And just like with Fillingham, she had messed that up. Again, for reasons outside her control.

Hawk was a good person, a good husband and a good father. She would drop by Centreville today to see if he was working. Not just to check in with him, but to see if she could help him. Adoption papers were under lock and key, but there must be other ways to identify a foster or adoption family. After listening to John Darlow defend his twenty-five years of absenteeism in her life, Christine wanted to support Hawk, a father trying to take care of a daughter.

As she stepped down the front stairs of the police station, she assessed the garden. The spring crocus and daffodils were long gone. The hostas were overgrown, and it looked like insects were chewing its leaves. The daisies were drooping, in need of water. And the lumpy soil was evidence of squirrels rooting for bulbs.

She remembered a line from a *Wonder Woman* comic: *You are stronger than you believe. You have greater powers than you know.*

Things were messed up right now...at the police station...in her life. She would tend the garden and help Hawk with his search for Layla. Somehow, she would just find a way to live with Phyllis without anger. And she would get Fillingham to see reason, no matter what it took.

Book 2: *Missing*

A missing student. A dead-end investigation. Can a police officer uncover the truth before the child is lost forever?

Policewoman Christine Lane feels guilty about the absent boy. Why hadn't she sensed a problem when she visited his class? After breaking up a fight between students, Christine had sent the children on their way. The next day, one boy vanishes.

Searching Toronto Island for the ten-year-old, Christine is shocked when investigators eventually conclude the child ran away. How did he get off the island? Why hasn't he surfaced anywhere? And why did he leave the field trip in the first place?

When Christine probes further, she receives pushback from her boss, the school board and the classmates' families. Then the threats begin. Can Christine figure out what happened the night the boy disappeared, before she is shut down for good?

Go to diannescottauthor.com/books to order *Final Look* and *Missing* from your favorite bookseller.

FREE SHORT STORY!

Receive a free short story featuring Christine Lane and her friends when you sign up for my monthly newsletter at diannescottauthor.com/newsletter

LEAVE A REVIEW

If you enjoyed *Lost and Found,* I invite you to leave a review at your favorite bookseller site. Reviews guide readers to my books and help me reach a new audience, so they are much appreciated.

Acknowledgments

I have many people to acknowledge for their part in the creation of *Lost and Found*. I am lucky to have ongoing conversations with women who were police officers in the 1960s and 1970s. A deep gratitude to Donna Brown, Phil Barringer and Kay Wilson for giving me insight into their policing jobs with their stories and recollections, always laced with humor and honesty. And a thank you to Bill Genova for sharing his knowledge of Toronto's history.

I thank my writers' group for their feedback on *Lost and Found*. Thanks to Leanne Lieberman and Elise Sze for their encouraging and constructive comments.

I thank my family, Michael, Claire and Matthew, and extended family for their ongoing support.

And lastly, to my readers. Your emails, reviews and interest make writing the Christine Lane Mystery series a deeply worthwhile endeavor.

About Author

Dianne Scott lives in Toronto, Canada, a short ferry ride away from Toronto Island, which is the setting of many of her mystery novels. She is the award-winning author of the Christine Lane Mystery series, including *Final Look*, *Missing* and *Lost and Found*.

When Dianne is not writing, she is walking Toronto's neighborhoods, reaching unsuccessfully for her toes in yoga and testing her Sudoku speed (slow!). She also teaches literacy skills and hangs out with her young adult children, playing board games, table tennis and pickleball.

Dianne loves connecting with readers and book clubs. For more information about Dianne, visit diannescottauthor.com.